W9-BUO-949

The Grace
That Keeps
This World

The Grace That Keeps This World

a novel

Tom Bailey

Shaye Areheart Books
NEW YORK

F

Published in the United States by Shaye Areheart Books, an imprint of the Crown Publishing Group, a division of Random House, Inc., New York.
www.crownpublishing.com

Shaye Areheart Books and colophon are trademarks of
Random House, Inc.

Library of Congress Cataloging-in-Publication Data
Bailey, Tom, 1961–
The grace that keeps this world : a novel / Tom Bailey.—1st ed.
1. Parent and adult child—Fiction. 2. New York (State)—Fiction.
3. Fathers and sons—Fiction. 4. Rural families—Fiction. 5. Outdoor life—Fiction.
6. Brothers—Fiction. 7. Secrecy—Fiction. I. Title.

PS3552.A3742G7 2005
813'.6—dc22   2005002700

ISBN 0-307-23801-6

Printed in the United States of America

Design by Lynne Amft

10   9   8   7   6   5   4   3   2   1

First Edition

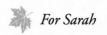 *For Sarah*

Hamilton County is the least-populated county in the Adirondack Park, and the largest. It has one million acres of unbroken wilderness. Two hundred and sixty-two lakes and ponds. Five hundred miles of groomed cross-country trails.

You don't end up in Hamilton County by accident. Directly in the middle of the Adirondack Park, the largest park in the continental U.S.—bigger than Yellowstone and Yosemite combined—Hamilton County represents a different way of life. There are no Gap outlets here. No long lift lines at the downhill ski centers. You can roar through the 750 miles of groomed snowmobile trails all day without hitting a town. It is one of the wildest areas in the country. Its residents—less than three per square mile—are here because they're drawn here. Maybe for the same reason you're drawn here: because it's one of the last places in America where the wild still rules.

—HAMILTON COUNTY CHAMBER OF COMMERCE

Into the darkness they go, the wise and the lovely. Crowned
With lilies and with laurel they go . . .

—EDNA ST. VINCENT MILLAY,
"DIRGE WITHOUT MUSIC"

Do not think me gentle
because I speak in praise
of gentleness, or elegant
because I honor the grace
that keeps this world. I am
a man crude as any,
gross of speech, intolerant,
stubborn, angry, full
of fits and furies. That I
may have spoken well
at times, is not natural.
A wonder is what it is.

—WENDELL BERRY,
"A WARNING TO MY READERS"

Acknowledgments

FIRST AND FOREMOST, my thanks to Chris Thompson of Long Lake, New York, who freely offered me his colorful stories and detailed advice about hunting and forestry in Hamilton County, the part of the Adirondack Park where he lives, the place that in my imagination became the working world of this book. Without Chris's help this novel could not have been written the way it came to be, and I owe him a debt of appreciation that I can only hope to repay with the recognition here of my gratitude.

Many books afforded me the detail and background necessary to create believable characters and to map out a fictional world for them to inhabit. Of the good ones I immersed myself in, the most significant proved to be *Seasonal Drift: Adirondack Hunts & Wilderness Tales,* by Peter R. Schoonmaker; *Living the Good Life,* by Helen and Scott Nearing; *Growing Up Strong: Four North Country Women Recall Their Lives,* by Sadie Cantin, Melba Wrisley, Marilyn Cross, and Sonja Aubin, edited by Joan Potter; *Woodswoman,* by Anne LaBastille; *Adirondack Canoe Waters: North Flow,* by Paul Jamieson and Donald Morris; *AMC Guide to Winter Camping,* by Stephen Gorman; *Winter,* by Rick Bass; and Andre Dubus's wonderful collection of essays *Meditations from a Movable Chair,* about (among other

Acknowledgments

things) the Marine Corps, Catholicism, faith, salvation, and the trials of the human spirit.

The short story "Snow Dreams" was originally published in *Double-Take* magazine and reprinted in *The Pushcart Prize XXIV*. I would like to thank both publications for planting and further nurturing the seed from which this novel was grown.

Additional Thanks

MY FATHER, Carl Bailey, Geraldine and Peter Herbert, Liz and Gary Fincke, Win and Arnold Talentino, Janet and Leo Bronson, Jack Vernon, Marsha Lemons, and Susan Bowers all generously agreed to read one or more drafts of this novel. Their enthusiastic responses and encouragement helped fuel this project from beginning to end. I thank my mother, Elizabeth Bailey, for always listening, and Jerome LeWine for his continued advice. Thanks once again to Kathy Dalton, research librarian at Susquehanna University. The joy with which Kathy does her job is a gift to all those fortunate enough to work with her. Thanks to Jeff Schreffler, who works in Facilities Management at Susquehanna, for helping me keep my facts straight; to Crystal Vanhorn, the secretary for the Department of English and Creative Writing; and to Dana Kemberling, Mailing Services manager. Thanks to Warren Funk, former vice provost at Susquehanna, for supporting my research trips to the Adirondacks. Years ago, Jane Gelfman of Gelfman and Schneider Literary Agency saved my collection of short stories, *Crow Man*, from the slush pile. It was Jane who brought my work to Shaye Areheart. I could not ask for a keener or more supportive editor than Shaye. It pleases me to think of her as a friend. I'd also like to thank Jenny Frost for backing this book. Thanks, too, to copy editor Laurie McGee and to the members of Shaye's "team," all of whom I have enjoyed working with: Tina Constable, Darlene Faster, Jacqui Lebow, Kira Stevens, Jill Flaxman, and Sibylle Kazeroid. I would especially like to thank Shaye's assistant, Julie Will, for the terrific job she does.

Most of all I am grateful to my wife, Sarah, who penciled over this manuscript more times than I can comfortably count, and to whom, with love and devotion, this book is dedicated.

prologue

Susan Hazen

Lying in our bed that morning long before dawn, I heard the geese go. *How do they know?* I thought. Their cries flung loudly down, sounding traffic-jammed impatient to get out of our North Country as they honked freely south over the house. They went, all of them together and at once, in the dark that morning—decided it was time to go, flocked up, and took off. Their leaving was yet another sign of the season that would soon howl down upon us, of the real cold and deep snows to come. The geese were a natural sign we were born to recognize, as much so as this man-made one: the day, that morning, October 18, which was the first day of deer season, gun season.

I lay in our bed and I counted geese, wishing they were woolly sheep, forty-seven, forty-eight . . . They came over in a long-wavering flight, which I could, with my eyes closed, imagine pasted in perfect silhouette, necks stretched, wings in an up-pointed flap, Halloween hat witch-on-her-broomstick-like against the orange pumpkin of harvest moon. The first killing frost had done its work in my garden. I saved what ripening tomatoes I could. The greens I managed to get covered with a tarp. The peas picked. The Cortlands bagged. When I rose after my husband and two sons left, I would begin again the boiling and the straining, canning and jarring and labeling the day away, as I had each day since the summer's fruit turned and fell. My husband had worked as hard to get enough firewood stored, and was primed now to fulfill our tags toward filling our three freezers to get us through another winter. I worried myself awake just so every year, without fail. I would not rest easy until the three of them returned home from their hunt safe to me again.

Gary was already up. He'd jackknifed straight from the waist in bed like he did each morning, suddenly and without warning, unflung like some sort of jack-in-the-box, without aid of or use for an alarm. His white T-shirt glowed faintly in the dark as he threw off the covers and turned and set his bare feet on the plank floor, fumbling along the bedside dresser for his glasses. And I'd wanted to reach out and touch him then—I remember that now, too clearly—to lay the flat of my hand on the width of his back, gently, not in an effort to tempt him to return to the warmth of our bed and the promise of his wife's nakedness beside him, but to send him off with the care of that gesture, the love I would have meant by it, though I didn't do it. I held my hands in abeyance, locked beneath my breasts, hugging onto myself, where I lay burrowed deep under the snowflake-patterned down quilt my mother made for us the summer we married.

My husband liked to believe this first morning of deer season was as special for me as it was for him and that he was letting me sleep in. And I let him believe it because the morning meant so much to him—my care for his care, which I'll call love. I had never once in all the years of his hunting gone to sleep; I had never once slept a wink the night before that first day. Gary snored and snored, flat on his back, until the moment when he sprung awake. We made it our point to need to eat what we took from the world. And so red-eyed with the worry and the care at the danger inherent in our dependence, I watched him stand and stagger off down the hall to do his part for us, his *duty,* with our two sons. He waited until he was in the bathroom with the door clicked quietly closed behind him to switch on the light, a yellow strip underneath the jamb. Thoughtful, he thought. He meant it, Gary really did mean it like that, for me, thinking of us—though, of course, it was not the act of thoughtfulness I would have chosen from him given my choice. But I had come to believe that this offered care was as much as a woman can hope for from her man. It is not that men don't love, but that their love contains within it a concern for and consideration of themselves—what they love and so think we'll care for—and not the sacrifice which is an imagining of others that is a woman's love, a motherly love born out of our bearing others.

The spoon rang the batter round and round the bowl as Gary made up his specialty, pancakes, which he always made for the three of them on opening day. I'd heard him creak downstairs to wake our eldest, tall, black-haired, curly-headed Gary David. Gary David's younger brother, our nineteen-year-old, blond Kevin, still hadn't come home. I glanced at the green glow of the clock, the slow ticking dial: eleven after two.

I lay there listening, waiting, wide-awake, the bowl singing the song of the beaten batter, the stoked woodsmoke smell rising up the steep dark stairs close-holed as a chimney flue . . . and then I heard the mudroom door mouse open, and boots step out silently—*thoughtfully*—and so I knew it must be Gary David going outside for an armload of wood, as considerate as he always was, thinking of me trying to sleep upstairs. And as I lay there a single goose honked fast over the house, racing low to catch up with the trailing V, so close by the window it sounded as though he were fat-flying right through my room. Just as that honking passed and faded, I heard the missing, miserable tick of Kevin's rusted-out Dodge pulling to get up to us. His beamed headlights flashed bright across the curtains as he turned into the drive, bumped suddenly up, shooting high, and dove sharply, then came steadily on, shining straight down the drive, the beams flickering light between the line of pines.

My younger son parked his truck behind his father's, and the projected picture that had been playing out before my eyes on the bright ceiling blanked when the engine coughed and died. The truck door popped and Kevin shoved out and stepped down, crunching snow. I heard the jingle of dropped keys. He grunted over, and I heard him sniff, then the jingle again as he picked up the keys and pocketed them. He slammed the truck's door. Then Kevin turned and with a last deep breath took that first resolute step toward the porch. Purpose stomped his path across the snowy drive. His march seemed to say he'd had it; *enough,* he'd tell his father today, now, he had something to say. But two man-strides from the mudroom door, he slowed. I caught the hesitation in the next half-step he took onto the porch, and then whatever momentum he'd worked up went suddenly out of him—he hadn't even made the second stair. He stood before the door, the lathered sweat he was in to get here and have it out with his father gone freezing on him, stopping him cold. He stood there in that icy moon-bright not wanting to go in, and I imagine something else, too. Afterward, I would find out. Now I know for sure. He'd held the news hot in him; he had given his sworn word to her. It wasn't just that he and his father had had a falling-out the weekend before about his not wanting to go on this hunt and because he'd been late again helping his father and his older brother get in the last of the wood. Kevin stood there on the porch. He took another deep breath. He turned the handle and . . .

The Grace That Keeps This World

I did not hear one word from Kevin that morning, the sounds spoken in the kitchen muffled, whispered. He never said it in my hearing what I know now he had to say. I only caught the blink of silence as Gary stopped to look at him—glanced back no doubt expecting tall, dark, curly-headed Gary David with that armload of wood for the stove—and saw our youngest, blond Kevin standing sheepishly in the kitchen alone. The glowing dial on the clock beside me read 2:33, already three minutes past their usual time to have left in order to get set in their stands before dawn.

On the mud porch, my husband and two sons bumped and stomped into their boots, scuffled into their coats, grabbed up their guns, and eased out the door. I lay in bed with the quilt pulled up to my chin and I listened as they crunched across the crust of snow to Gary's truck. The engine roared, and they drove off—and that was the last I heard from the three of them all together ever again.

NOW, IT IS in the spring, when the scratch of hills bud-bloom red and the black day brightens blue before the dawn, the robins singing and crows cawing, when I wake to it in the same house, the same yard, the same bed, wake to the same yet different work of my soon-to-be again gardening days and the smaller and smaller tubs of laundry that have been spinning out before me, the one-pot meals, and the boot-clomp echoing of gone-still, trying-to-be silence in the morning halls—the same dully remembered and then suddenly, too sharply recalled days, spearing, the crowning thorns of memory that I wear to bed and take off and twist about and stick into the same day again the moment I wake . . . making the cross at my heart, fingering the air in an endless rosary of ways that grants me the will to throw the covers back and put my feet on the floor and dress and step out into the now of days.

The truck keys are in the coat pocket. I start off the slope toward the barn. Mount Seward peaks off in the distance, gone dream blue as the glimmered fingerings of Lost Lake itself.

At Saint Pius's, Father Anthony plants the wafer that leavens hope in my palm, His offered salvation that is our beyond, and I taste His flesh, tip the cup, and, greedily, drink His blood. I touch the back of my wrist to my lips, and squeeze my lids black and then red zagging, believing with all my might. No way to bring the three of them back to me again together on this earth, pray as I may for the dull, humdrum day-to-day of laundry and picking up boots; I pray and pray. Hands clasped, eyes closed. He rose! Who knows a husband better than his wife, the sons better than their mother? Six months now this Easter Day. My life has become again just such an expectation of waiting—as it was when I was eighteen, just married, and didn't know, to twenty-eight when I suspected and was told. And then *unsuspecting* I found myself blessed, not once, but twice! Beyond the age of bearing now, I feel I've been left doubly as barren as I am bereft. At fifty-three I feel I am an old woman, at heart at least, though in other ways I feel far too young not to be a wife in naked ways. In thinking of the first summer-real, June heat to come, the huge, bright-pulling fierceness of a new moon, the earth unfrozen and given over to the prospects of growing, the sting of the black flies taking back a bite of blood for their own, I too will give birth. In this conception I can rise, reborn into the day, each day, given reason through faith: God's gift for going on when there seems no earthly reason . . .

. . . *I believe. In God. Believe in God. I believe.* . . .

The black veil is lifted from my face; the days grow cold, colder, and then crisp-clear: The snow crunches underneath my husband's boots. Gary turns to face our sons, his breath white, the metal arms of his glasses striking like brightwork across his temples: "If you boys don't quit lollygagging, we'll never get a deer."

part one

Gary Hazen

The dark green Jeep Cherokee with the yellow-and-gold D.E.C. police seal on its door turns off the log road, bumping the rut, and powers up into the cut's landing. It's my younger son, I expect, nineteen-year-old, blond Kevin, who promised me he'd be here by noon, home from school for the weekend to help us get in the last of this wood. But it's that new lady environmental conservation officer, Josephine Roy, always busy scouting around our North Country, who's somehow managed to find us at work out here on this tiny twenty-four-acre private parcel inside of Hamilton County's blue-lined million-acre part of the park.

It's past lunch, after 1:00, and when I see who it is, who it *isn't*, the Stihl 034 in my hands grumbles, and I return to my work. Rocking the blade of the chain saw back, I give it the juice, slice forward, the honed sharpness singing into the wood. Chips spit past the goggles that mask my glasses. *You can't be too careful.*

Kevin's brother, my older son, dark, curly-headed Gary David, stands behind me steadying the trunk of the tree-sized limb, but hustles around to the front at the end of my cut to ease the log's falling, helping not to let it pinch the blade. Forced to work the jobs of two men, he catches the log as it falls, before it can drop, lopped off into the snow, and turns and tosses it on top of the mounding pile sinking the springs of our rusted old, red and white, half-ton F250 Ford. He then steps quickly back around me again to steady the limb for the next cut—right where I need him, when I need him, no waiting around. And there's no time to wait. We've got wood to get in— *always* I can hear Kevin say, being smart, now that he's a college man, he's always being *smart*—there's always work to be done.

Trouble is, this morning we woke to another two-inch dusting of snow, and gun season starts next Saturday. We're hot in a race against the coming North Country cold, caught between a rock and a hard place of the dual necessities of getting in this waste of good wood before the big snows begin and bagging our limit of deer to help us make it through one of these no-fooling winters again. Both Kevin and Gary David know the importance of these two needs because I brought up both my boys to know them. The way we choose to live we have no choice. We have to work when the working's good, not when we *want* to. If we want to be warm and eat, that is.

For us deer season's not a matter of mounting a staring head or congratulating ourselves over a rack of horns. For us hunting's as crucial as surrounding every inch of spare space under our extrawide porch and eaves with carefully cut, split, and cured wood—never imagining, not even able to imagine nor capable of comprehending in the blistering chain-saw heat of summer, that we could ever in twelve straight hard winters use all we've stacked, and then and again be stumped equally as incredulous every May when we have to scrabble up the last skinny sticks and shavings of bark to heat up the freezing kitchen at 5:00 A.M. This one single and unforgiving truth, out of which the responsibility I'm speaking of was born: that it's already time to start the dragging and sawing and splitting again that very same afternoon if we're going to be ready for the first freeze come September. It's all about living up here—*surviving*—and so far as I'm concerned there's no difference between the two, but it's a huge *difference* between us Hazens and other folks who don't know or have any idea at all about the cold.

Officer Roy parks in the clearing and climbs out of her shiny-new Jeep. The vehicle is fully equipped with red bar lights and two silver spotlights above each sideview, antenna for the radio, and a shotgun resting on the rack against the Plexiglas that cages off the tan leather back seats. She starts up the slope toward us, carefully picking her way through the maze of sheared stumps and left limbs. Before this block of trees got singled out to be felled, their reaching limbs held up a cathedral-like, beamed canopy, a forest ceiling of hallowed hemlock. Now the clear-cut, crowded with the aftermath ugliness of stumps, the forest floor churned by the turning treads of the skidders that dragged out the logs, looks like a hot spot where we might have got ourselves dropped, a war zone—the blasted jungles where I served my hitch in Vietnam—a hell of a place, for sure.

The massacre happened right here at our feet, the bodies of hundreds of hemlocks hacked up, every single limb lopped. The valuable trunks were carted off on the flatbeds of the heavy logging trucks with the name *Pollon Enterprises* slanted in red, white, and blue down the doors. Pollon Enterprises is owned by Armound Pollon. His crew of Upper Lake Frenchmen came in here to do the job I refused to. They simply left behind the remains, the scraps they couldn't make "real money" on, thousands of limbs toppled over each other, in every twisted position, unlikely as they fell. The only good news in the wake of this slaughter is that these left limbs won't go to waste, not if I have anything to say about it. *Waste not, want not* was my father's motto.

I bump the safety bar against my hip, and the sudden silence rings out even louder than the high whining of the saw. Gary David looks up at me and then follows my gaze down the slope. Into that ringing silence, I stand, arching against the growing stiffness in my lower back. I've reached the age I can remember my father reaching when he needed me, the son he'd raised. I take the blade guard Gary David is waiting to hand me and slide it on, leave the heft of the saw between my feet. I rest my goggles on top of my head and swipe the sweat off my face with the sleeve of my mackinaw.

"Officer Roy."

"Mr. Hazen," she says, looking up at me as she crests the knoll, a touch out of breath. It's a steep climb. She's wearing mirrored aviator sunglasses, and she flashes past me to silver her eyes at my son.

"Gary David."

Josephine Roy acts years older than she looks. I'd read in the *Lost Lake Gazette* that she graduated from college the spring before last before spending a summer at the Academy learning to become an ECO. Now she's been here almost a year, the rookie officer in our woods. She and my Gary David must be about the same age, twenty-four or so, though Officer Roy appears more mature. It's not her face, smooth and girlish milk-white skin, untouched as yet like my Gary David's by years of summer-fall-winter-spring winds and rains and snow and sun, by the experience of caring for things she feels she must protect and sometimes can't—though looking around this clearing might start to etch a line or two on her. It's her uniform, I guess.

Officer Roy's got on her usual getup, a dark green shirt and standard-issue, pressed pants, with black stripes down the legs, her earned Eagle Scout–like Adirondack Park patch, the brass belt buckle, buffed shiny, and a 9-mm Glock pistol strapped to her waist, clean mud boots, and her Smokey-the-Bear hat with the tight chin strap that she wears angled down just right, sporting her authority. Her dark hair is cut short. Sunglasses hide her baby blue eyes from us, but she can't powder over the mess of freckles bridging her nose that make her look like a kid who ought to have her picture on the back of a cereal box. Though she's petite, the last two giant strides she takes before she sets her hands on her holster in front of us make her seem bigger, a mighty mite—sure, her mouth set stretched straight across, determined. There's never been any doubt about how seriously Officer Roy takes her job, all business about the weight of being an armed ECO in our woods. But I made sergeant during my tour, and a good rule of thumb I learned for myself is to be wary of all badged or ranked authority, whether they act friendly or not. Officer Roy puts me in mind of that sort of eager, fresh-faced, young officer, first lieutenant type on whom I often had to stake my life and the lives of my men. She *appears* to be in charge.

One thing's for sure, the new ECOs like Roy are a different breed than the old game wardens like Brad Pfeiffer used to be. Brad was first and foremost a woodsman, an avid hunter himself. ECOs, as they're officially called these days, are trained ready to act more like troopers—they go through shotgun, rifle, and stick certification as well as evasive driving, DWI, and drug detection. Similar to the sorts of officers who get hired and specially trained to work for the State Highway Patrol, who pull you over to give you a ticket and never even smile at the tough luck of having gotten caught speeding, no talking to them about how fast you were going or why, the law to an ECO like Roy is something written down as a straight ordinance or code and not subject to compromise or one lick of common sense.

One day this past spring I emerged empty-handed from a twelve-hour day hunting turkey deep in the woods only to find Officer Roy had left me her calling card of an orange traffic violation tucked under my windshield wiper, even though I was parked on the incline of a logging switchback miles from a paved public road. My inspection sticker had lapsed one month!

Brad Pfeiffer was a game warden up here for thirty-seven years, and when Brad passed by the truck of a hunter he knew, he kept going. A hunter's reputation mattered back when. Not anymore. Officer Roy couldn't care less about anyone's hard-won reputation of being a conscientious hunter in these woods. She'd as soon give me a citation as she would Lamey Pierson, who is a convicted poacher. Officer Roy does the busywork of checking up on everyone's licenses and inked tags, including our own, though in my estimation we'd all be better served up here if she saved that sort of thing for when the weekend blasters from downstate come carpooling up to our North Country to turn the first day of gun season into a shooting gallery, the carnival for the killing they think of as fun.

"I won't keep you," she says right off. "I know how busy you are. I just have a few questions I'd like to ask."

"Go ahead," I say.

"Are you all set for the opening of gun season next Saturday? Do you have your licenses?"

"Of course." I shrug. "We've *had* ours. Since *March.*"

I'm joking. We bought our licenses last Saturday like most everyone else, the year's hunting license good from October 1. You have to buy them direct from Mabel Dix at Town Hall, and she doesn't sell licenses early and never has. With Officer Roy's rule-book mind, these are facts I know she's more than well aware of, but Officer Roy acts as if I'm playing it straight, as if she's taken me at my word and what I say can and will be used against me. And then without even looking at Gary David, she asks me, "Are both of your sons going?"

"Unless you know something I don't!"

At this line of questioning, I can't help but grin over my shoulder at my older son, but Gary David's gone busy craning his neck around, looking everywhere he can, at the mash of snow and leaves under our feet, the close, graying sky, the trees. He coughs into his fist. He's acting so antsy, he makes me glance around, feeling itchy myself.

Officer Roy hasn't looked away. She crosses her arms, still focused on me. And then she points the question of it straight at my chest and pulls the trigger, point-blank: "And your wife, Susan?"

I nod. "Sure," I say.

"She took the hunter safety course and bought a license last year?"

"Yes."

"And the year before that?"

"No. That's why she took the safety course last year. It was her first year out."

"Her first hunt, and she took a buck?"

"Not bad, huh? A hundred-and-sixty-pound eight-point."

"Not bad at all." It's Officer Roy's turn to nod now, her bottom lip pushed out, and then she says, a series of statements disguised as questions, her thinking out loud to herself, trying to pin me down: "But last year was her first year? She never took a license to tag a buck when Brad Pfeiffer was game warden? Now, I wonder why that is?"

I thumb back at tall, gangly Gary David. "Well, Officer Roy, another buck in the freezer makes a big difference when you have grown sons like this one still living at home to feed."

Officer Roy uncrosses her arms and hooks her thumbs through her belt loops, listening down at her boots. When she looks up, she says, "I just wanted to make sure I had the number of licenses right. Before Brad retired as warden you only bought three licenses and filled three tags, but since I started last season, you've purchased four licenses and filled four buck tags."

She goes silent, thinking, and then she says: "You all were good friends, weren't you, you and Brad?"

And that's when Gary David clears his throat and pipes up out of nowhere, surprising all of us, most of all, I imagine, himself: "You know we take our hunting pretty seriously, Officer Roy."

She lights her eyes on him then, and a ray of sun catches the mirrored lenses and bulbs brightly as if she's flashed a photograph to book us, me and my older son left standing in the wreck of shoved snow and mud surrounded by the aftermath stumped devastation of the clear-cut.

"I know you do," she says. "I respect that. But as serious hunters I know you know the law as well as I do: one buck per person, one person per tag, and you can't fill in someone else's tag. That's the law." She sets her hands on her holster again. "I guess I wasn't aware that Susan hunted. I thought she had a reputation around Lost Lake as more of a gardener."

"Well," I say and shrug, try a grin. "Susan is a *Hazen,* Officer Roy."

Officer Roy stretches her lips back at me without managing to actually smile. "I know," she says. "I was just at the house talking to her. She's the one who told me where to find you out here." She holds my gaze, and then she touches the brim of her hat. "I'll let you get back to work, Mr. Hazen," she says. She flickers her eyes at Gary David before she turns and starts winding her way back down through the labyrinth of limbs to her truck.

I slide the guard off and hand it back to Gary David, who stows it. I turn to the log, reseat my goggles, flick off the stop, and pull the cord. Still hot though the afternoon is turning cool—the air already freezing in blue shadows beneath the pines, our breath huffing white—the engine sputters, then revs high. Gary David takes his place behind me, and I pulse the gas a few times, sending the sharp chain spinning, and then bend again and touch the blade to the wood, wondering again where Kevin is, *no excuses,* because he knows full well who he is and what he should be doing.

Kevin

Kevin sped down a slope and swooped through the blow-down of the bogs, racing the clock, though he knew he'd already lost. He drove with both hands gripping the wheel, leaning far forward, his nose close against the glass, scooting his butt on the bench front seat to help the old truck go, hurrying the whipped Dodge as fast as he could along the skinny two-lane road. It was nearly 4:00, and he'd said he would meet his father and his older brother, Gary David, at the cut they were working by noon. The needle of the speedometer pulsed back and forth between 65 and 70, the engine ticking as if it were going to explode. The last of the day's sunshine flashed, going past fast, glittering gold across the snow as it set, black swooping in silhouette the sky-pointing pines.

He veered off onto Hatteras Road, slowing only long enough to bump up and down over the abandoned railroad crossing so that he wouldn't flatten his oil pan taking the jump, and then sped onto the gravel of Country Road Number 4. He glanced at the dial of his watch gone glowing blue in the now black cab, gone dark in the coming winter afternoon shortening's deep of woods, fumbled the dash with his left hand and pulled the lights. The log road shone white before him.

Kevin couldn't help but rehearse what was getting ready to happen to him for being late. He'd bump into the landing and climb out into the cut. His father would be working, his brother shadowing his every step. His father would stop whatever he was doing, kill the saw, the silence echoing. *Where've you been?* he'd ask, though he knew they both knew—and so no reason to ask, but he'd ask. And when Kevin told him what they both knew, blaming *school,* his father would fold his arms, chin on his chest. *What's the difference between a good excuse and a bad excuse?* he'd ask and look up, waiting for the answer he'd taught them to respect, his eyes a deeply disappointed dark lake-blue behind his square-rimmed glasses. And it would be Gary David, of course, who would provide their father with what he wanted, the pat answer, on cue, by rote, without meanness, not even trying to backstab his brother, simply doing what it was he did, being who he was, the purveyor of his father's bidding, practicing what his father preached, doing the damage. This hurt, nonetheless; their father's words spouting out of his brother's mouth as if he'd set him on his knee and yanked a cord from his brother's back, his brother's jaws moving, mouthing his father's words: "*Nothing.* They're both excuses."

At the very least, he guessed he should've called, Kevin thought. But he hadn't bothered to call; what was the point? How could he have called? Who could he have called? Another excuse, sure. But his father didn't allow a radio in the woods, much less something as irredeemably at right angles to his strict code of living in the North Country as a tower-beamed, everywhere-you-go trilling connection to a cell phone. And his mother, back home, couldn't have gotten word to them way out where they were anyway. In any case, what would Kevin have said? What would have been the point? So, he hadn't called. He'd known what he was doing, naked, in bed with Jeanie, at least he guessed he had—at the time he had.

The argument with Jeanie had started small—worse, ridiculous—but then it had snowballed. He and Jeanie were sitting side by side in one of the pink plastic booths in the school cafeteria after class that morning when she told him her parents were coming up from the city the following weekend to visit.

"They want to take us out to dinner Saturday night. Isn't that sweet?"

Kevin dipped a french fry in the squirt of ketchup on his plate. He'd met Jeanie's parents. They owned a summer camp on Lake Serene, which is how Jeanie had grown up knowing about North Shore Junior College and why she'd chosen to come there to boost her grade point average before transferring to Hamilton, where her father had gone to school. Kevin liked Jeanie's parents—he hadn't seen them since the summer—and he would've been more than glad to go, but there was no way. Not a chance.

"Not next weekend. Next weekend's the opening of gun season."

He should have paid more attention to Jeanie's silence then. He wished he hadn't scoffed. He could have been more sensitive. But it had seemed to him a pretty good joke, asking his father if he could miss the first day of deer season to go to dinner at a restaurant. It was nice, her parents offering to take them out to dinner; it wasn't about that that he was thinking.

Kevin turned to smile at Jeanie, who he found frowning back at him.

"I don't want you to go," she said. "I don't believe in hunting."

Kevin looked at her. It was true, Kevin knew. He had known this about her from those long, into-the-night conversations they'd had when they first met: Jeanie was all about life, living things. The very idea of killing anything—to eat or otherwise—went against her nature. She was a vegetarian. She grew spider plants in the sunlit windows of her dorm room. She loved horses and dogs. On her wall was a color photograph of the stallion she'd learned to ride on, King, and on her bedside table she kept a silver-framed picture of her gray-muzzled golden retriever, Taylor, back home. She didn't like guns. Not only did she think hunting not right, more to the point, she felt very strongly that hunting was wrong.

Kevin had known these things about Jeanie all along, but it hadn't come between them before. They'd met the previous winter after buck season had closed.

"How can you go hunting?" she asked. "Do really want to go? Is that it?"

Kevin looked at her. He didn't want to say the wrong thing. He shrugged. "No," he said. "I don't know."

"You don't know?"

"I don't care," Kevin said. "But I don't have any choice."

"You don't care! You have to care!"

"I mean it's not my choice."

"You're nineteen years old, Kevin. Of course it's your choice! You mean to tell me that you've never said no to your parents before?"

"No is not something you say to my dad, Jeanie."

"It's not something you say. You've got to stick up for yourself, Kevin. You've got to care! You can't let your father run your life for you. You act like a twelve-year-old boy."

At that moment, still looking at him like that, Jeanie seemed to come to a decision about him.

"Okay. Go hunting then," she shrugged. "I don't care what you do."

"Jeanie," Kevin groaned, feeling her slipping away. The conversation had spun out of control.

She pushed her shining hair away from her face and stood up

with her tray. "You do what you have to do, Kevin." She left him sitting there alone.

When he'd finished eating, Kevin followed her back to her dorm room. He knocked on the door, but she didn't answer. He knew she was in there. He knocked again. He should have left right then. If he had left right then, he'd have made it to the cut by 12:30, only a half hour late, which would have been bad, but not *inexcusable*. He would not have been so late, and he would not have promised her what he should never have promised her. But Jeanie opened the door. She couldn't control the radiator heat, and the room was sweltering. She'd changed into shorts and a thin-strapped tank top. She wasn't wearing a bra.

Standing in the hallway looking at her, Kevin felt something give and his stomach slide inside him.

He held up both hands. "It isn't really about hunting," he tried.

"Do you shoot animals? Do they die? Does your father kill them? If you go with him, are you expected to kill them?"

Kevin suddenly saw the futility of his argument. "You don't know what you're asking." He shook his head. "Okay," he said.

"Okay what?"

"I'll tell my father I won't go on the hunt."

Jeanie shifted her weight to her other leg, jutting her hip. She set her left hand on it, regarding him. "Promise?"

"Promise," Kevin said. "Cross my heart." He smiled.

Jeanie left the door open for him. He watched her walk into her room toward the single twin bed set alongside the wall under a framed poster of pink ballerina slippers pointed in that pose where they wobbled along on their tiptoes. Kevin looked up and down the hallway, and then he followed her inside, clicking the door closed behind them.

Jeanie and Kevin had been sleeping together since the spring before. Over the upcoming Thanksgiving break, Jeanie had an appointment at her gynecologist back in the city to be fitted with a diaphragm. Jeanie absolutely refused to go on the pill; she didn't care what the reports they'd read for Health said about it actually being good for women in reducing the risk of ovarian cancer. "I'm not putting those chemicals in my body. You take a pill." Kevin had been raised Catholic. He'd served for years as an altar boy and even now that his altar boy days were past, he attended the 10:00 A.M. mass every Sunday with his mother and brother. He genuinely liked their priest, Father Anthony, and with him behind the curtain he didn't dread going to confession. Because he attended mass and confessed, Kevin considered himself a good Catholic. But good Catholic or not, Kevin wasn't crazy. No matter what the Church said, he felt he could think for himself. They used the LifeStyles condoms Kevin had bought—*Don't Worry! Hook Up!* When they ran out, Kevin was supposed to have the wherewithal to pull out of her, and sometimes he actually did.

They made love and dozed and woke again, skin to skin. It had been nearly 3:00 by the time he'd roused himself from her warm bed. He pushed up on his elbows to go face his father, but Jeanie hugged onto him from behind, her long hair tickling down over his chest.

"But I won't see you all weekend."

Oh, Lord, Kevin thought again.

And then, speeding fast-tracked toward the cut where his father and brother were waiting for him to help them get in more wood, with the conflict of these thoughts and feelings driving him, it hit Kevin. *What was he in such a goddamn hurry for?*

"Fuck this," he said out loud in the cab, feeling his arms pump tight. What the fuck did he care if he was late? To hell with his father anyway! Kevin couldn't wait until he transferred with Jeanie to Hamilton next fall. He was going whether his father said he could or not. Then he'd be too far away to have to come home every single, goddamned Friday. He couldn't wait to go to a real college; he'd get a four-year degree. He was leaning toward a major in communications. Maybe he'd go into a field like advertising to pay back his loans. A high-paying city job seemed the way to go. Though, truth be told, the only class he really enjoyed was Survey of Literature with Mr. Weeser on Monday, Wednesday, and Friday mornings from 8:00 to 9:05. Mr. Weeser was different from any teacher Kevin had ever had. Sometimes he recited poetry to them in class, and he didn't even look at a book. Some of the other guys in the class rolled their eyes and tugged the bills of their baseball caps even farther down over their eyes when Mr. Weeser tipped his head back and went into his "act," closed his eyes and crooned the words of some poem like Robert Frost's "Directive":

Back out of all this now too much for us,
Back in a time made simple by the loss
Of detail, burned, dissolved, and broken off
Like graveyard marble sculpture in the weather,
There is a house that is no more a house
Upon a farm that is no more a farm
And in a town that is no more a town. . . .

They looked at their watches, yawned, scratched themselves. They carved things like *I'm dying* into the tops of the old desks or *I'm dead*.

At first, Kevin had been a little embarrassed that he'd been so fascinated by Weeser. "What a fag," he heard some guy say as they left Weeser's class, and Kevin felt himself bristle. He'd wanted to grab the guy by the back of his neck. Jeanie understood. She wrote poetry herself. They read the assignments in his anthology together. Kevin didn't always understand what was going on in the poems, but he found he loved the words, just the words, the way they were arranged and sounded.

In class now, they were finishing up *The Odyssey*, and the assignment Mr. Weeser had given to them the week before to be completed over the weekend was to memorize a "substantial passage"—"Not an entire book," he'd joked before the class, but had not gotten a laugh—and "in the spirit of the Homeric tradition" to stand before the other students and recite their chosen part of the epic.

Kevin's palms had begun to sweat at the first mention of the assignment. Straightaway, he'd typed out the passage that he'd picked from Book XI in The Kingdom of the Dead where Odysseus encounters the spirit of his mother, Anticleia, who he discovers died of grief, believing in her son's long absence from Ithaca that he had died.

By Monday at 8:00 A.M. Kevin had to know the passage by heart. He'd been repeating the lines over and over, mumbling them under his breath to himself whenever he had a moment, feeling a little like a first-grade reader trying silently to sound out the words. When he did dare to read it out loud before the mirror locked in the privacy of his bathroom at home, he realized he was reciting the words as Mr. Weeser would, with that sort of feeling and inflection: *"My son, my son, the unluckiest man alive!"* Already, the typed sheet of paper had been rubbed soft as a chamois cloth from taking it out and stuffing it back into his back pocket so many times. Deeply creased, it folded naturally back into its own lines.

So he was a little late, Kevin thought, slowing as he sat back, thinking of Jeanie and school. What was the great big, hairy, fucking deal anyway? He'd been late before and the world hadn't come to an end. Gary Hazen would get in his wood in time; of course he would! He didn't *need* Kevin. And he didn't have to have him with them to go hunting either. That was the truth! He'd get his bucks. He wouldn't have any trouble filling Kevin's tag. Hadn't he filled their mother's last season? And whether or not his father wanted him to, he wasn't going. Jeanie had helped him make up his mind. His mind was made up.

That was that! There was nothing else to think or talk about. He'd decided now.

And then, this shock, almost too suddenly now, he was there. There he was: in the last vestiges of light he caught, through the thinning of the pines and bluer spruce surrounding the clearing that had once been a stand of hemlock, the moon-glowing cut. Parked up the slope from the landing sat his father's red and white truck. Kevin slowed to take the turn, holding onto the wheel. He put his turn signal on—stalling—and he took the turn slowly. He bounced off the road and lurched up into the landing.

He stopped and jammed the shuddering Dodge into park, killed the engine, and stomped on the emergency brake to hold it on the slope. He glanced up at his father and brother both standing staring down at him. Kevin took a deep breath and grabbed the latch to open the door. He realized that he hadn't even brought a pair of gloves. *He hadn't even thought to wear his boots!* What had he been thinking of? Too late now. He put his head down and marched up the slope without gloves, sliding about on the slick bottoms of his loafers as if he were wearing skates. He grabbed the first log he came to and turned to throw it into the bed of his father's truck, slipped as he pushed off, and landed smack on his butt. He sat, waiting.

"Where . . . ?" his father started in on him. "What's . . . ?"

Officer Roy

The first time I saw him anywhere without his father was that summer at the Lake View Diner. I was standing before the register paying for my lunch when he strode in. When he did, Anne Marie Burke, who'd been ringing up my order, lit up, beaming over my shoulder. I had my sunglasses off, tucked in the top pocket of my uniform, and I turned around to see what socket she'd stuck her finger into, and our eyes caught, sparked, and I received the unexpected jolt.

"Officer Roy," he said shyly, and looked away, cast his glance down. Gary David had the most beautiful eyes I'd ever seen on a man. He stepped past me, tall and skinny as could be. Inside, he swiped off his baseball cap. He had black, curly wild hair. A tuft of beard sprouted on his chin. Anne Marie Burke cleared her throat to turn me back around so she could count out my change and get rid of me before the other waitress stepped over to the counter and took his order. Her big chance at him, no doubt.

"Have a nice day," she said, ringing the register drawer closed with her hip, and flounced over to him in that flap of black skirt. She had sprayed her bleached blond hair up in a huge, curling frontal wave fixed impossibly far away from breaking over her forehead and had glued on inch-long red fingernails that looked to me like bloodied claws. But you can never tell about some men. They are as bombarded as we women are by the advertisements on billboards and in the magazines, on TV. We all get sold on what we think a woman ought to look like. The most ludicrous things imaginable: silver glitter over bruised blue-shadowed eyes, miracle bras that strip away to reveal nothing spectacular at all, and toenails painted black so that they look as if they had gotten slammed all at once in a sliding glass door. Both sexes are led to believe that every woman ought to wear a D cup, achieved without silicone, and still have the sort of slim hips that slide straight into jeans.

"What can I get for you today, Gary David?" I heard her say. She set her elbows on the counter and leaned forward so she could squeeze her elbows together, ballooning her breasts for him.

I counted my change slowly, curious to see how he would take it, what he would do. He had turned to face the view she was offering him an unavoidable gawk at, giving her his order, and so I stepped out the door into the sunny parking lot, shrugging. *She can have him.*

The afternoon that I walked out of the Lake View Diner after having seen Gary David for the first time without his father was the sort of cool, blue June day that if you have ever visited Lost Lake you can never forget, the sort of weather that makes the place famous as a summer resort. I held onto the heavy glass door pretending that I didn't want it to slam to give myself an excuse to look back at him only to see he had turned all the way around to watch after me.

Zapped a second time, I snatched my hand back from the door and turned into the sun toward the Jeep. I grabbed at the mirrored sunglasses in my front pocket and fumbled them against my chest, shot my hand out to catch them, and batted them end over end into the air. They landed in the middle of the street. Two loggers passed me heading inside to eat, and one of them grinned and called back, "Nice catch, honey!" I glared at them until they wiped the smirks off their faces. When they stepped inside, I made myself look both ways before I stepped out into the street and picked up the glasses. I stuck them on and marched across the parking lot and climbed back in the Cherokee and slammed the door behind me.

"Jesus, Josephine," I said.

I never needed a ring like some of my friends who'd gotten engaged, splaying their fingers to show off the rocks their fiancés had bought for them. I graduated magna cum laude with a degree in finance, a two-time captain of the forensics team, preparing—I'd told everyone, including my parents—for a degree in law, and when I showed my suitemates my acceptance letter into the Academy to be trained as a conservation officer, they didn't even shriek in disbelief. They just stared at me as if I'd sprouted a second head. Josephine Roy—the Freak.

THE PARKING LOT of the Lake View Diner was already packed. I pulled into the gravel lot across the street, catty-corner from Saint Pius's Catholic Church. Though it was shy of 5:00 the sun had already set behind the mountains to the west, a prelude of the close early winter's dark soon to come. I hesitated with my hand on the door. The day had turned decidedly cooler since I'd climbed out in the clearing to confront Gary Hazen in my shirtsleeves early that afternoon. Some local hard cores, Gary David's father among them, stuck by their mackinaws through the worst of the cold, twenty-five, even thirty below, acting as if such weather didn't bother them at all—as if twenty-five below weren't *real* cold. I grabbed my fur-collared ECO's jacket off the passenger seat and slipped it on.

The bell above the door announced my arrival. "Officer Roy." I nodded back at the men in the booths who looked up as I passed, meeting their eyes. By now some of the men even offered me a friendly smile, not getting defensive and acting threatened by the mere sight of a woman in uniform like others I could name. My usual seat at the counter was waiting on me. I plunked down my hat and set the walkie-talkie beside my plate so that Ellie on dispatch could reach me in case of an emergency.

"Evening, Officer Roy," Val said as she flapped out of the doors that led back to the kitchen. Val and Chet Harrington owned the Lake View. With her hennaed hive of red hair and her pasty skin, the red lipstick she drew in a happy grin around her lips, Val had always reminded me of one of those made-up, professional Ronald McDonalds who dress to work the crowd, waving and shaking hands in an indirect effort to sell another billion Big Macs.

Val's brown eyes brightened when she saw I'd put on my winter coat. She reached for the coffeepot on the warmer behind her. "Thinking maybe we'll get our first big snowstorm tonight, Officer Roy?"

I turned my cup over for Val to fill, but I wasn't willing to give up my jacket just yet—no matter how much ribbing I took for wearing it. "Better safe than sorry."

Val chuckled at that. "You're learning, Officer Roy."

She set the pot down and pulled her pad out of her apron pocket. "Poached egg sandwich on toasted whole wheat with scallions, hold the mayo? You want hash browns with that?"

"Hold the hash browns, too. I'm not getting as much exercise as I'd like, Val."

"If it's exercise you want, Officer Roy," she said, quickly jotting down my order and tearing off the ticket, "try working here for a day."

She slapped my order on the sill of the little waist-high window that looked into the kitchen. "Chet!" she called back to her husband. A hairy hand groped after it. Chet bent down to the level of the window. He winked good-naturedly at me. "What is it out there, thirty-two? Thirty-three?"

"Freezing's all I can say for sure, Chet."

I settled my elbows and blew on my coffee, but before I could take a sip, I caught the pickled, putrid, old-liver smell of him slinking up behind me.

"O'cer Roy."

Lamey Pierson mumbled his gums when he spoke. I could hardly understand him, but didn't want to risk getting too close. At the very least, I wished he'd gotten hold of a bottle of Scope to swig on rather than the rotgut that was slowly decomposing him from the inside out.

"Lamey," I managed, swiveling the stool to face him. I unrolled my silverware and raised the napkin as if to wipe my mouth.

He didn't look any better than he smelled. Decades of North Country cold had wasted Lamey Pierson's face and neck ancient, and his long chin, squared off with the indentation of a pronounced cleft, hung his jaw slack, his tongue riding his lower lip as if there were too much of it to swallow all at once. The sum effect made him appear a wandering guest from White Hills Asylum that we were sometimes called upon to taxi home. But Lamey wasn't feeble. He had thick wrists, and the backs of his large hands that stuck out from the sleeves of his grimy army surplus parka that he wore no matter what the weather looked surprisingly powerful. It was his eyes that held you, though, and cautioned that he was neither simply lost nor merely crazy, but actually might be dangerous as well. Yellow as a coyote's, they had that same sort of clever, plotting glow.

I was not the least bit interested in gloating with him. No doubt it was Lamey Pierson's belief that he was employing me as the legal instrument to enforce his will. Finally, after all these years, he was making good on the revenge he'd sworn against Gary Hazen for turning him in for poaching a doe. He had taken his tip about Gary Hazen falsifying their tags directly to the easygoing captain of our barracks, Dave Tabert. When Captain Tabert had first joined the force, he'd served under the old game warden, Brad Pfeiffer. Brad Pfeiffer and Gary Hazen had been best of friends, both of them men Captain Tabert said he'd looked up to all his life. Captain Tabert had been with the two of them the day they'd arrested Lamey. While Lamey Pierson had been convicted for the stories he'd told, time and again—until now at least—Gary Hazen had proven to be as good as his word. Admitting from the start his reverence for Gary Hazen and his prejudice against Lamey, Captain Tabert had turned responsibility for the inquiry over to me, the rookie. It was my job to remain objective. He called the case my first "official investigation."

A few of the men sitting at the Lake View had lifted their faces from their food, curious to hear what Lamey Pierson and I could possibly have to say to each other.

"I told you so," Lamey said, whispering close. "The truth don't lie, do it, O'cer Roy?"

After the little talk I'd had with Gary Hazen at the cut that afternoon, I was 99 percent sure that he was guilty. I no longer doubted Lamey's story. All I lacked now was the proof. But enough was enough. Lamey had taken to calling the barracks constantly and leaving me piles of exclamation-marked "URGENT" phone messages. He haunted the Lake View to pester my progress. Certainly I didn't feel I needed to dignify Lamey with a reply.

Val backed out of the kitchen carrying my meal, and I swiveled back toward my place, turning my back on him. He pawed at the sleeve of my jacket to get my attention again. And then he said loud enough for anyone to hear: "You feeling okay today, O'cer Roy? You look a little peakish. Maybe you're not getting enough sleep. Me? Nights I can't sleep, I take a little walk through the woods. I walk all over. Puts me in the mood. You in the mood to sleep nights these days, O'cer Roy?"

Out of the corner of my eye, I caught the grin hanging crookedly on Lamey's face as if he'd just told a joke and was timing the delivery of the punch line. Then, without another word, he winked one golden eye at me.

A stool came open at the far end of the counter, and Lamey took it, leaving me sitting up straight, feeling as if one of those hairy-legged centipedes that scuttled down the drain of the bathtub in my cabin when I flipped on the light at night had slithered down my spine.

Val set my plate on the counter and plopped a bottle of Heinz next to it. "I don't know how you can stomach eggs without ketchup." From the opposite end of the counter, I could feel Lamey eyeing me for my reaction, grinning with his tongue splayed out, happily panting at my predicament. No matter what he'd seen Gary David and me doing, I was determined not to reveal anything more to him now.

"More coffee, Officer Roy?"

Val, I knew, drank from twelve to fifteen cups of coffee and smoked no more and no less than three packs of Winstons a day every day. A mug huddled warm between her elbows and a cigarette poised between the two fingers of her left hand, she sat before the TV in the corner watching the weather or the soaps when the Lake View was empty. When it got busy, she snatched back for a sip or a drag as she sailed past between orders.

"Maybe just warm it up a touch if you would, Val. I can only drink one cup. I'll have a heart attack."

"You won't have a heart attack!" Val said. She cleared plates from a place down the counter and set them in a gray plastic tub before swinging back with a fresh pot. "Studies show, a little caffeine is good for the heart, Officer Roy. Hell, I'm living proof!"

Val hacked out a laugh, sounding as if she were going to give up a lung. When she caught her breath again, she said, "Speaking of our first big snow, you sure you don't want to get your bet in this evening, Officer Roy? I still don't see your name on a date this year." Val thumbed over her shoulder at the calendar that hung above the register: HOT BUNS! "You can see for yourself there's still a few choice dates in December."

"I made a donation last winter, Val," I said and picked up my sandwich.

The calendar was a staple at the Lake View. Besides the diner's good, inexpensive food, warm atmosphere, and the swift service, the calendar was one of the main reasons locals made it a point to stop by at least once and sometimes two or even three times a day to put their heads together over who had wagered on what square. In early August, about the time we'd finally shaken off the chill of the past winter, Val and her husband, Chet, did what they always do to get the diner ready again for the winter to come: they set out the calendar beside the register for everyone to look through to see who could guess the day of the first big snow, measured at a foot or more. Anyone who wanted could ante up five dollars on a square and write their name on their personal date. If it snowed on the square you purchased, then you won whatever cash was in the jar left sitting out on the sill. The pot usually totaled three hundred dollars or more, which was serious money up here.

This year it had been Val's turn to pick the calendar. Instead of the cherry red racecars draped with bikinied babes that Chet preferred, every month from January on featured a man in skintight swim trunks posed with his rear end facing the camera. I got a kick out of watching Val make the men who stomped into the Lake View dressed in their orange hunting caps to eat Chet's scrambled eggs and sausage and sit hunched over black cups of coffee and their morning cigarettes have to ask her to see the calendar. Val played up such moments for all they were worth. She looked around with her eyebrows raised and snapped her gum. She worked up an audience before she turned, making a big show of pulling the calendar off the wall and unveiling the centerfold as she handed over the picture to the hunter or fisherman or logger who'd asked for it.

"Here you go, baby cakes!" she'd say. "Enjoy." Everyone on the stools and at the tables and nearby booths would have a good laugh before the guy could grab the calendar and fold the picture back so he could concentrate on picking a date.

But no matter how embarrassed Val made the men who flocked to the Lake View, she knew the old boys couldn't resist their chance to choose. Cold weather was always a hot topic, the lottery of living in the North Country, and everyone had to get their day down, their bet in.

Gary Hazen was not considered to be a betting man. He'd made his reputation around Lost Lake by taking the care of making good on a sure thing. But all summer long I'd listened in as the men up and down the counter huddled together keeping track of the woolly caterpillars he found in his woodpile, considering the dates in October that no one else had seemed to want to take a chance on back then. As the summer cooled toward fall, I heard word circulating around the Lake View that Gary Hazen's woollies had turned from orange and black to black with a shrinking band of orange. By the end of August the caterpillars that had not already burrowed underground had gone solid and appeared, it was said, long and tapered black as the ash off an untapped, hand-rolled cigar. On September 1 Gary Hazen strode in and put down five one-dollar bills on October 18, the opening day of gun season, starting the run to buy up the rest of the remaining dates in October into early November. By now all the early squares had already been named. A late date gamble at this point would be added in as a mere contribution to the pot—a tourist's bet. Growing up in Guilford, Connecticut, my older sister, Francine, and I prayed for a white Christmas every year, but it always felt like something of a miracle when we actually woke to one. Up here, by late December, the question would be moot, Lost Lake buried under at least five feet of snow. My first year on the force, I lost my five dollars holding tight to one of the last available dates in January. I knew better now.

I finished the egg sandwich, wishing I'd ordered the hash browns. When Val stopped by with my bill, I said, "Maybe I ought to pick a date. I suppose it is possible that Gary Hazen could be wrong this year."

Val grinned even wider than before, showing off the gap between her two front teeth. "*Anything's* possible," she said, taking my plate. "But Gary Hazen's been right more winters than *The Farmer's Almanac*. Now, that's a certifiable fact."

Just then the swinging doors split open and Anne Marie Burke popped out of the kitchen. She usually worked the morning shift. Her mother, a sweet, cloud-white-haired woman with the permanent tan of someone who regularly visited a booth, worked evenings. Though I knew Anne Marie Burke's name, I'd yet to have occasion to say it to her, and she'd never once said mine to me, though as a public servant, it was pinned above my left breast for her to read.

When she saw me, she walked past behind the counter, tying on her black apron with her chin in the air. She worked as hard as she could to never have to wait on me. When she was forced to, she asked what I wanted, squinting over my shoulder as if she were wishing as hard as she could that she could make me disappear. I knew she knew about him and me somehow, the way a woman does. For my part, I didn't think I was being especially catty wondering that her bottom didn't freeze, wearing a skirt that short. Whenever she bent over to take a plate into the dining room, the men at the adjoining tables would glance up, nudging each other. The sad part was Gary David had never so much as mentioned her.

But Anne Marie knew the place, and Val was busy taking another customer's order. She took real pride in the fact that her family had lived in Lost Lake for generations longer than Val's, maybe even as long as the Hazens' had.

"Excuse me," I began. She'd stopped across from me to put on a fresh pot of coffee, her wave of big hair curling more dangerously over the height of her forehead than usual even.

"What can I get for you?" Without looking back at me, she banged the filter and old grounds in the trash can and fit a new one.

"I was wondering if you could tell me, do Gary Hazen and his sons eat at the Lake View the morning of opening day?"

She poured a pot of water back into the huffing machine.

"I'm conducting an investigation."

She flicked the red brew button. "No. Of course not," she said and turned, drying her hands down on her apron. "They never have. Everybody who's anybody around here knows that."

I nodded, feeling my face warming, but I kept my cool. "Everybody else eats here on opening day, but they don't. Why?"

"Mr. Hazen makes pancakes for them before they go. He calls them his specialty. It's his father's batter recipe. Anyway, they leave too early. We don't open until four-thirty. They're long gone by then. They leave around two-thirty. They have to, to make it to their spot before dawn."

"And where exactly is this 'spot' of theirs?"

She kissed up her berried lips in a smug little pout, crinkling a condescending smile. "Their spot's top secret. They don't want other hunters crowding them. Only Mr. Hazen can tell you where it is. Or maybe one of his sons." She crossed her arms. "Is there anything else I can tell you about the Hazens for your *investigation,* Officer?"

"No. Thank you, miss," I said, dismissing her. "You've been very helpful." La-di-da. So what if she'd lived here all her life? As if she knew him. Like she owned some right to him simply because his father preferred her to me.

While I'd been eating, the day had shut down. Outside, it was completely dark. While Val rang me out at the register, I tilted down the brim of my hat and zipped my jacket all the way to my throat.

"Stay warm, Officer Roy!"

I took care to look both ways before I crossed the street, doing my best to ignore Lamey Pierson's face pressed against the glass, keeping a close eye on me with that coyote's conniving look, interested, ears perked, grinning with his tongue hanging out, drooling after me as I went.

Gary Hazen

"It's *irresponsible*, Kevin," I say, raising my voice to him. I've brought up both my boys like I've managed to train every dog I've ever owned—with a biscuit in one hand and a switch in the other—and I'm burning now to smack this son of mine with the lesson of what he knows is right. "If you'd have been here when you said you would, we'd already be done with this job. We'd be on our way home. I shouldn't have to remind you that it's going to snow soon. Your brother and I have been out here since dawn. I'm not a betting man, but if I were I'd be willing to wager ten to one you've been with Jeanie all day. What do you have to say for yourself?"

Kevin stops as if my voice has yanked him up short, as if he's hit the end of the length of leash that connects us. He whirls to face me at the question. Obviously, he *does* have something to say, beyond the expected excuse of school for where he's been and the reason that he had to study for being late that he's offered me, and his slipping on the slicks of those silly loafers and falling on his butt has gotten him worked up enough to just say it. His mouth opens—whatever has been bottled up in him ready to shout out, trumpet. *This'll be good,* I think. I cross my arms over my chest, standing big in front of him. Really, I can't wait.

He opens his mouth, but before he can say it, get it out, his feet shoot out from underneath him again as if his older brother has shoved him down from behind. But Gary David hasn't moved an inch.

Kevin scrambles back to his feet, red-faced, huffing. Facing me, his mouth opens as if it's going to work, and then it closes, goes open and closed like a bellied fish's working its gills on dry land, gasping after air.

"Well?" I prompt and raise my eyebrows for him, but he doesn't say anything. No words come forth. His mouth starts to open one more time, but then he shuts it. His jaw grinds so hard that I see his temples pulse. Without another word, he turns and snatches a log and storms past Gary David and slams it into the truck, following through by grabbing on to the bed to hold himself up.

It's Gary David who finally breaks the silence, saying gently, "Here you go, Kev."

Kevin lets go of the tailgate to face him, and his older brother tosses him a log to throw into the bed.

After that the three of us get down to business, working together like I know we can, like we always should and how I've worked hard to teach my boys to—like I brought them up. For the logs that are farthest away from the truck, we form a chain and throw each limb down the line. I grab up a log and throw it to Gary David, who turns and tosses it to Kevin. I hardly bother to glance back, simply bend, turn, throw. The bed fills, piling higher than the level of the cab. When we finish loading my truck, we back Kevin's up the slope.

Long after we were told we could never have them, year after year, Susan and I went on praying for our chance with kids. So we felt we'd been blessed when we discovered she was pregnant with Gary David, all we could have asked for, and then doubly so with the complete surprise five years later that we were to have Kevin. Watching my two grown sons working side by side tossing what's left of the six face cords we've cut into Kevin's truck, rounding the load, I have to wonder if folks didn't get the idea that Susan finally was able to have one or the other of them by visiting long, lazy afternoons with the postman—summer day to winter night different as these two boys are. Kevin's more simply the spitting image of who I used to be before I suddenly, at the age of nineteen, while serving my time in Nam, split out of my issue with a last thirty-seven-pound, three-and-a-quarter-inch growing spurt, when I still had all of my own straw-blond, thick, and wavy hair, before I rolled over fifty-five and my own bright blue eyes dimmed, and I got fixed with these squarish, silver-rimmed bifocals. Standing next to him, Gary David—both in looks and in his shyness and care—mirrors his grandfather, Susan's black-headed, part-Onondaga daddy, as if he'd sat up in the grave and lurched back out into the world for one more tall, stiff try at things.

The other, bigger, difference between them is that my youngest, Kevin, is the first in either family to go on to school past the twelfth grade, taking classes now up at North Shore Junior College in Lake Serene. Next year, though, he wants to transfer full-time to Hamilton College when this young lady he's been seeing, Jeanie, does. He's brought Jeanie around once or twice, and I guess she's blond-haired and green-eyed cute enough for dating. But she's from *New York City* of all places, just going to school up here in our North Country so she can ski six months of the year, and she isn't remotely of our kind. Ever since they began "dating," all Kevin talks about is Jeanie this and Hamilton that. His plan is to live nearly three hours away and pay more for tuition and board than we make in a year to earn himself a *real* degree. I can't imagine what he thinks. His going away to school every day already leaves us constantly shorthanded—at five dollars an hour or more he knows I can't afford to hire on another hand—and he still lives at home, the room and board he's entitled to whether he shows up to work or not, and so he's already costing us in more ways than one. He wouldn't let it go, though. He even went so far as to bring home slick brochures about *financial aid* to help us with our "decision." The good news? *He* could take out *loans*! All we had to do was cosign the debt.

The first two times Kevin brought up these schemes to us I felt the pressured dollar sign of it ticking-bomb-big behind my left eye. The third time I exploded, yelling out before Susan could grab my knee and squeeze, *You just want to be on the parental dole your whole life! You don't want to have to ever work for a living!* Gary David, who's more sensible about these things, is going to be a forester and handy-man carpenter after me. He'll find himself a pretty, practical girl like that Anne Marie Burke who waitresses down at the Lake View Diner and whose family's lived here in Lost Lake near long as we Hazens have. They'll marry and name their first boy together Gary. But what I find most curious in my sons' natures is that while Gary David was born with the heart and desire, born with the *belief* in the building and the work we find to do in the woods, his brother, Kevin, has the better hands, a sharper eye for the truths of wood grains, and the absolute honesty of plumb lines. Though perhaps even more strange still is that my two boys—these two men—aged a good five years apart and night and day opposite as they are, can be such good friends.

The three of us keep at the wood steady without a break until we've loaded the bed in Kevin's truck with as many logs as it will take. I peek back my sleeve to see that it's almost 7:00.

"That's a day," I say to my sons.

Without a word, my youngest turns away and cuts through the

headlight beams and climbs in the driver's side of his truck—acting as if he's the one who has the right to be angry. He slams his door. Gary David and I stand looking after him. Kevin screeches the starter. The tired Dodge *thu-dumps,* and rolls over, and then catches. Kevin races the engine, roaring like a lion now that he's safe behind glass, threatening to throw a rod.

I touch Gary David's shoulder. "Tell your little brother to go easy over that rut at the bottom of the hill, else he'll leave his drivetrain behind him on the rocks."

Gary David climbs in, and I see him turn to tell Kevin what I told him to tell him. In response, Kevin stomps the gas, sending the RPMs spinning. "*Kevin!*" I feel my arms pump with anger, and then fall away from my chest, my hands going out, grabbing after them as he pops the clutch. The truck jumps, rocketing forward, and Kevin kamikazes off the slope, headlights jouncing, and rams head-on into the rut. The front wheels go down and then leap up and the truck, bowed down with the weight of wood, bottoms out as it scrapes to get over the lip, the steel undercarriage sparking on the rocks underneath. Logs leap off in every direction, bailing out as if they were trying to save themselves.

The truck comes to a halt like that, hung up on the edge of the rut, the load of wood weighing it back. Kevin gears down and gives it the gas. That '77 Dodge doesn't have four-wheel drive, and the rear wheels spin on the iced slick, polishing snow. Then, caught at that unlikely angle, with the full weight of the wood pressing heavy against it, the tailgate gives, goes just like that, bursts like a dam, and the logs piled in the bed pour out, roaring as loudly as a waterfall, and the wood we only just finished loading floods back out into the landing. The truck rocks into place, stuck in the ditch, straddling the rut. The brake lights flash.

I go storming down off the slope, and I yank open the driver's side door. I haul Kevin out of the truck by the shirt, and he stumbles as he drops into the ditch. "What in the hell do you think you're doing?" I yell, shaking him hard with both hands. "You could have been killed!" And then I've hit him.

"Dad!" Gary David yells. He hugs my arms to my sides from behind and pulls me away from Kevin.

The three of us stand there like that, puffing. No one says a word. Kevin touches his lip and looks at the blood. He swipes his sleeve across his face and staggers up, holding onto the door of the truck. I'm breathing hard, my hand pulsing with the pounding of my heart. It's dark and my sweat's gone cold. Suddenly, I feel the chill. Control is part of being careful, and I lost control of myself.

I break free from my older son, turn away from both of them, and start up the slope. I snatch the hot Stihl off of the forest floor, open the passenger door of my Ford, and set it on the floorboard. As I walk around the back of the truck, I yank the tailgate to make sure it's good and shut and jam a few of the top logs into the dark spaces around the bed, rounding off the pile.

There's just enough landing left for me to drive by. I make a point of taking the hump slowly, letting the treads and the weight of the wood work for me, *careful,* and my tires don't even spin. I make a point of not looking at Kevin as I pass, rolling down my window to ask Gary David if he wants a ride, though knowing him and how he is with his brother I know he won't take it.

"I guess not," he says.

I've got chains, and I could easily pull him out, but I won't do it. I *refuse* to. Kevin's got a come-along in his truck—unless he's forgotten that too—but it will take some doing. They might just be lucky enough to get that truck unstuck and loaded again before I wake them at 5:00 A.M. to be back here again by first light to finish this job.

The Grace That Keeps This World

I roll up my window as I brake a bit to take the dip, sagging over the embankment, and turn left onto the log road toward home.

SIX MILES OF log road lead me out of the deep woods away from the cut. I look past my bloodied knuckles gripping the steering wheel to the crossroads point where gravel and dirt meet asphalt and curl off to the right onto a single lane that cuts a corridor through the pines. The first sign I see reads HAMLET OF LOST LAKE 11 MILES, below the words a profile picture of a mother bear leading her cub, a sight I've witnessed for myself countless times up here.

Before me glows a coal-bed of stars, the sparks of them streaking the sky. A three-quarter moon sits on the tree line. Just off the edge of pines, the eyes of a coyote wink like reflectors in my lights. It's huddled back, waiting to cross. Coyotes are smart. A deer might very well bolt in front of the truck. I've totaled one truck like that and dented a few. Deer often jump out, no warning, no sense in such matters of men, but not coyotes. Coyotes look both ways, in more ways than one. I have always been amazed at the way they can sense death. One season when I was hunting with Brad and we were taking turns at the tumpline dragging his buck out of the woods, a coyote trailed behind us for over three miles. We could hear it yipping behind us, circling closer the whole while, just out of sight. In my right sideview, I watch the one waiting to cross lope across the road after I've safely passed, its coat flowing silver in the moon's flooding light.

If it were daytime, I'd be driving straight into a view of blue majesty, the High Peaks country to the northeast filling in the picture-framed gap cut by the road. On a clear afternoon we're able to see the shadowy-distinct panoramic picture of the four-thousand-foot-plus peaks of Mounts Seward, Seymour, Street, and Santanoni. The tallest of them all, the highest peak in the state, 5,344-foot Mount Marcy, darkens the sky farther east while Allen Mountain, at a mere 4,350 feet, seems to offer a stair-step down beside it.

Closer to home, our mountains aren't quite so tall. There's the knobbed 2,324-foot lookout above our own Cat Mountain Pond and the pointy, teepee-shaped 3,360-foot peak of Kempshall Mountain to the north, 3,136-foot Mount Morris and a couple of other two thousand footers, Long Tom Mountain and Arab Mountain, off to the northwest. If you were on the peak of any one of them, looking off to the south, back over across the immense stretches of pine, you'd be able to see the great shaggy brown bear humps of the hills and low mountains that bunch up to make the Five Ponds Wilderness Area. Filling in and between and flowing around these more modestly sized, forested peaks is water.

Our North Country is a land of such peaks and forests and water—lakes and ponds and bogs and brooks, seasonal runoffs and the since-time-began flow of rivers—boulders the size of houses and gouged-out gorges that the slow-going glaciers left behind, miles and miles of white pine, brush and spruce, hemlock and yellow birch, ash, and hardwoods like maple, some of it valuable bird's-eye.

I think how, if I were pressed, I could probably name a hundred of the 262 clear creeks and lily-padded ponds, blue lakes and frothing rapid running rivers, and the low bogs and seasonal brooks that make the country that surrounds Lost Lake what it always was before we agreed on our maps to say what it is. I tick the names off as I go, using my fingers to keep track, like an abacus, counting off in groups of ten, letting my mind range far and wide over this North Country that I've covered in one way or another, either on foot, cruising timber or hunting, or coursed through in a canoe. "Loon Pond," I say, my words silvering the cold air inside the close cab of the truck, "Bettner Pond, Burn Pond, Clear Pond, Lake Marian, Black Pond, Sucker Brook, Six-mile Creek, Glasby Creek, Cold River." That's ten, and I tick off my first finger. The glass is icing up, and I reach for the defrost.

"Lost Lake and Upper, the Little Upper, Serene, Cranberry, Stillwater Reservoir, Heavens Lake, Wolf Pond, Brandy Brook Flow, Jocks Pond." I tick off my second finger. "Mink Brook, Slim Pond, Sand Pond, Doctors Pond, Lake Lila. There's McRorie Lake and Mud Pond, Mosquito Pond, Grampus Lake, Moonshine Pond." Thirty. "Mohegan Lake, Sperry Pond, Antediluvian Pond, Sly Pond, Charley Pond, East Charley, Little Charley, Lower Pond, Middle Pond, Upper Pond." Forty. "Pine Creek, Crystal Lake, Salmon River, Otter Pond, Deer Pond, Grassy Pond, Little Grassy Pond, Rich Lake, Bog Stream, Boulder Bay."

With five fingers counted off, I start on my right hand.

"Boulder Brook, Sister Pond, Stillman Brook, Blueberry Pond, the Marion River, Paradise Pond, Bradley Lake, Plumley Bay, New Pond, Bear Brook." With six fingers up, I start counting down. "Peer Pond, Hamilton Pond, Pollywog Pond, Cat Pond, Pilgrim Pond, Rock Pond, Stony Pond, Partridge Pond, Little Antler Pond, Turtle Pond." Thirty to go. "Lonesome Bay, Robinson Pond, Round Lake, Trout Pond, Moose Creek, Goose Pond, Duck Lake, Fly Pond, Fishing Brook, Tangly Brook." Twenty. "End Pond, Corner Pond, Calkins Brook, Seward Pond, Beaver Brook, Sugar Pond Outlet. . . ."

Eighty-six down, and I give a pause. I don't want to repeat myself.

I go ahead and reel off the last fourteen: "Owl's Head Outlet, Pickwick Pond, Lily Pad Pond, Midden Cove, Catlin Bog, Minnow Pond, Cascade Pond, Little Forked Lake, Hedgehog Pond, Trapper's Pond, Bog River, Brandeth Lake Outlet, Buttermilk Lake, Devil's Hole Bay.

"One hundred," I say and fold my right thumb down.

I *know* this place. But I can't help wonder if between them my boys could name thirty.

The truth I can say about it is I work hard not to kid myself about the little I do to feel natural in this world, else I'd give up my chain saw and my truck, the electric lights we see by, the flow of water that runs the plumbing in the house. But I feel strongly, too, that there's something gone past that we can't afford to leave behind. Call it my care of the world or simply doing a job right, not because it pays to but simply because that's the way a job *ought* to be done if I'm to face myself and who I am in the mirror each morning. If I can't face myself, who can I face? How could I be a father to my sons?

The weight of wood in the bed of the truck glides me down off the hill toward the body of Lost Lake that in the dark stretches both ways as far as I can see from the greened-iron bridge that spans the bottled neck between banks. I rattle over and when my wheels touch the opposite side I'm officially "in town," and speed along under the flickering rows of streetlights that line the beach, the Adirondack Lodge—called the Lodge around here—overlooking it from the other side of the road, and the green swinging sign out front. In the window of Rick's Place—the bar at the Lodge—a red and orange Budweiser sign neons bright alongside a green and blue glowing advertisement for Genny Light.

For the length of a skinny half-block along the lakeside of the bank stretches the North Way Market, the only grocery between here and Upper Lake—so it's the North Way or no way is what we joke. I look at it again for what must be the millionth time as I curve by, climbing past the Lost Lake Apartments and the sprawl of Stanton's Boatyard. On top of the rise looking toward the north end of the lake sits our brick high school, where both our boys went and from which Susan and I graduated one day and got married the next at Saint Pius's, which is practically next door, huddled just back in the woods at the edge of the lake with its graveyard that slopes down the bank. My father is buried there in our family's plot and, more recently, Susan's mother, who lived with us until her end. In the little white rectory set quaintly beside the road, I see that Father Anthony's lights are still on; he's up reading, no doubt. I beep as I pass, like I always do. Sometimes I stop to say hello.

For my money, Father Anthony is just the sort of priest we need up here. When he first arrived in Lost Lake, he wore his once-upon-a-time black hair slicked straight back and black-rimmed glasses and dressed in a solid black frock, serious-looking from head to toe about being our priest. Years ago, he gave up his long black frock for jeans and a black shirt with a collar. He's mostly bald now, and he smokes up a stack, the fingertips and nails on his right hand stained yellow.

Brad's packing up and moving away to Florida made me recognize that Father Anthony's been here for twenty-two years. The two of them are my best friends, and I grow worried that he'll retire and move away as well, though he assures me that's nonsense and that he's here in Lost Lake to stay. "You'll bury me here, Gary," he says. "I've got my resting place all picked out under that big crooked wood pine beside the lake." Still, I worry about it. In exchange for Brad Pfeiffer as game warden we got saddled with Josephine Roy as environmental conservation officer.

In the little swale behind Saint Pius's lies the baseball field, the only flat ground around here that's been completely cleared of trees—the open grassy place fronting the lake that's favored by the good-sized flock of Canada geese that veer away from the usual flyway to nest summers in Lost Lake. You can sit in the bleachers on a summer Saturday and watch a pop fly rise above the army-green stand of hemlock and brighter pine fencing off the lake, stop for that second, speck-white above the distant blue of the high peaks, caught like that for that instant before it falls into someone's outstretched mitt.

Whenever there's a medical emergency in town, this is the flat, cleared spot where Billy Hirsch lands his copter—the rotor blades blowing back the spray of needles, dust or snow flying, depending on the season—to get anyone out to Mercy, the little hospital in Lake Serene, or farther away to a full-scale medical center like the one way down in Syracuse.

In the blowdown of '95 Billy landed on the ball field in seventy-mile-an-hour winds to pick up a young lady who had been whacked on the head by a limb—nearly as big as a tree itself—that fell at the Silent Pines Campground overlooking Slippery Rock Falls south of town. There were so many trees and limbs down along the road that led through the bogs that Brad Pfeiffer called on everyone who could wield a saw to come quick and swing one. She'd sustained a severe head trauma and so no matter how much work we'd done to get in to rush her out it wouldn't matter unless they could fly her to the hospital, and fast. Billy said he'd try. He landed on a dime with the tips of the already crooked pines beside the field bent all the way over near doubled to dip in the lake. She survived, and Billy earned a ribbon for that one and got his hand shook by the governor even. His picture was in all the papers, too, a local celebrity.

Opposite the baseball field sits a row of houses; three of them are the sort of long-planked houses that are original to the loggers who settled these woods, at least since the English and French worked their way in here. The fact is there hasn't been any major construction in Lost Lake since the high school was built in the early fifties.

The Lake View Diner looks out over the south end of the lake. The aroma of pancakes and eggs and Canadian bacon drifts up the opposite hill to our house—a good enough reason to get myself out of bed if I wasn't up already, which I always am.

At one time, our house, perched on the high ground at the

southern edge of town, commanded an uninterrupted view of the lake and pines and spruce and the mountains beyond. Now there's a Mobil station a hundred yards up Route 28N. And directly across the road from us, Big Moose grins with his tongue slurped out of the side of his mouth selling ice cream to summer passersby. From our back corner bedroom we still have a clear view both ways up and down the length of the lake, and we can also see the green roof of the Lodge and the high school and the Lake View Diner and Saint Pius's and all the boats in dry dock stacked about the boatyard.

As I say, the house wasn't always so bordered and bound in. The seven sisters and brothers of my father each got a slice of the greater pie. Over the years they continued to parcel it out themselves. My father's younger brother sold off his share and left for California, never to be heard from again. He owened that good chunk across the street, which has been sold and resold and subdivided again and again in the past seventy years so that by now our last name is a distant one down on the deed. The land the gas station and ice cream stand are on now used to be his. In the past two hundred or so years since the direct descendants of our line arrived here from Norway, tough times, and sometimes just plain greed, have taken a toll on the related strains of who we've become as Hazens and where we've ended up, by hook and by crook, marriage and divorce, births and deaths, branched out into distant cousin connections. Though there's still a remnant of kinship among these factions of family, the feuds that began over this land have ended up keeping us mostly separate. Strangely enough, given the influence of all we once owned, Hazen is not one of the names commonly shingled on everything around here from Stanton's Boat-yard to Percy's Plumbing Service to Steele's Hardware to LeFevre's Beauty Boutique.

I turn right onto Route 28N going south and then take the first right again onto our long gravel drive. The house is set a good ways back from the road, at the far edge of the three acres that surround it, at the steep end, built to overlook the lake, our big, red barn, and Susan's fenced garden placed off to the left. In the winter, we hear the occasional rev and vroom of a logging truck gearing by. In the summer after the hatch of black flies dies, the steady stream of tourists pours in. From late June through Labor Day, cars mob the ice cream stand and get in line at all four gas pumps. Even set far back from the road, our blue-painted front porch grows dull under the coats of dust laid on by all the cars that drive by. Inevitably, there's the crunch of metal and tinkling glass, the blue flash of the sheriff's lights as he writes someone a ticket for rear-ending.

In the summers, we turn our backs on the road. We eat our meals in the kitchen with the windows wide open and afterward sit outside in chairs angled to watch the sun splay orange and pink as it sets over the lake. Summer nights Susan and I walk the wooden steps that wind crookedly back and forth down the fifty feet of cliff-steep slope to the lake and sit on the dock in the dark. From there, we can hear the quiet of water lapping against the wood.

I'll admit I've thought more than once about selling the house and all the land and lakefront property we own and buying something tucked away deep in the woods, especially during those hard times when we're living month to month. A Realtor from Upper Lake who handles some properties down here came poking around, trying to make a commission on lakefront property, and he promised me a good price. But I could never bring myself to sell. I've lived here my whole life.

I pull the truck past the barn, and then throw my arm over the seat to back up to the shed we built to store our split wood. I pull on my gloves to unload the wood and hit the horn quick with the heel of my hand to let Susan know I'm safely home.

The Grace That Keeps This World

By the time I'm done unloading, I'm sweating again. I leave my gloves on the dash wedged against the glass where I know I'll find them first thing in the morning and start across the rolling expanse for the backdoor light that she's left on for us, my boots crackling the crust of snow as if I were walking across shattered glass. The snow smells old, like cold earth, not clean crystallized as it would if we were going to get more tonight. Tomorrow will be a clear, sunny, seasonally mild day.

I find Susan standing in the kitchen windows before the sink. Underneath the bright lights I see her clear as day—it's as if she were standing on a stage and I was watching, standing back in shadowed wings behind the dark audience. She's facing toward me, bowed a bit as she works washing at the sink, as if she is saying some silent prayer. My wife, I think, standing there, watching, could have been anything she wanted to be—she graduated first in our high school class of twenty-three, was editor of the school paper, president of our student body, Lost Lake's fall parade Maple Syrup Queen.

There is something in her face that has always drawn people to her. Strangers will turn and talk to Susan wherever we are. Standing in line at the North Way, they turn to ask her the time or complain to her about the rising price of heating oil. Looking at my wife, it's easy to see why. Susan has always been beautiful, though she hardly makes a fuss about it. Most of the day, she wears her shoulder-length brown hair pulled back away from her face, no-nonsense-like. Not five feet from where I stand facing her, seeing her looking out, I can see her green eyes, which I know are flecked gold, the irises rimmed by a thin band of blue. She doesn't need any drugstore-bought lipstick to make her lips pink. Her cheeks are flushed from her work over the stove.

We're no longer the young sweethearts we were, but when I catch sight of my Susan like this, it's like meeting her again for the first time, though that incident never took place. I've known Susan Steele my whole life.

And then she raises her chin. If she heard the gate slam and my boots in the snow, she would've expected me to clomp onto the porch and yank the mudroom door. I wait, too, for what I'm not sure, some sign from her. I don't move. She cocks her head slightly, listening. She turns her head, waiting, and then she faces forward again, looking out blindly into the blacked glass past her own reflection—seeing herself and the slow frown of worry that passes over her face. But she must know that I'm out here somewhere; she must guess I'm watching her. She smiles questioningly, and I smile back at her, though I know she can't see me. For that moment I have the eerie feeling that I'm too far away to communicate with her, on the other side of something. I'm in the dark where she can't see me, though I can see her clearly in the light, and I cannot wave to her it's all right. Suddenly I have the urge to let her know we're fine. Everything's going to be okay—even if I did lose control of myself and lay hands on our son. Tomorrow, with the three of us working together like we ought to again, I'll make it up to him. But I can't tell her out here standing separated. I clomp loudly up onto the porch and pull the door and am greeted by the warmth of the Upland.

"It's me," I say, peeling out of my coat. I hang it on a peg by the door and then, before she can ask, I say, "The boys will be awhile yet. We should go ahead and eat."

Rolling up the sleeves of my shirt to wash my son's blood off my hands, I step into the kitchen to find my wife holding on to a ladle, facing me again. She looks at me, reading my day.

"What happened this time?" she asks.

My cold glasses have steamed blank in the blast of heat, ghosting the scene before me, and I snatch them off, circling them clear with the tail of my old mackinaw, squinting one-eyed up at the blur of my wife. I slip my glasses back on so I can see her true. I step to the sink and turn on the water. The lye soap slides round and around in my hands, stinging my cut knuckles, and rinses smelling hard-clean. The dish towel waits neatly draped over the rack.

"Kevin didn't bother to show up until dark. His excuse was that he was at school. He was wearing loafers and he didn't even bother to bring a pair of gloves. Then he got in another one of his huffs and got the truck stuck. The gate fell open and all the wood poured out in the rut. I got mad and lost control. I hit him and left them to clean up Kevin's mess. When they get the truck unstuck and the wood loaded again, they'll be home. Let's eat."

Susan stands her ground, and I have to step around her to take my seat. Wren fierce, she will not back down. "You *hit* him?"

"He's just got a little bit of a fat lip."

"God, Gary." She shakes her head and turns away. She stands like that with her back to me, looking back at me in that blackened glass. "I don't know what you've got against him going to school."

"I'm not against *school,* Susan," I say. Then I stop myself from going further, before I say something I'll regret, something that'll come between my wife and me about our younger son and the sloppy, selfish ways in which he behaves, the promises he makes but doesn't keep.

My wife looks straight back at me, her green eyes shining a challenge I refuse to take up. She ladles out two bowls of rabbit stew and walks our supper to the table. With Susan standing beside the table and me sitting down, she's taller than I am. Susan is still holding our bowls, waiting for an answer. I reach up to take mine from her, but she pulls it away, just out of reach.

"They're good boys, Gary," she says. "Both of them."

I usually have the manners to wait until Susan takes her seat before I eat, but tonight as soon as she bangs my bowl down I go ahead and take a big bite, make myself savor it, a tasty chunk of rabbit and tomato, onion, and wild mushroom. Chewing helps me keep my mouth shut.

Susan reaches behind her and pulls the tie of the bow at the small of her back, slips out of her apron, and drapes it over her chair. Her face softens then, and she turns the curves of her body toward me rather than offering me the block of her back, pulls out her chair, and takes her seat beside me at our round kitchen table.

"Officer Roy stopped by today," she begins, changing the tack of our conversation safely away from the boys.

I wait.

"She wanted to know if I had my license for this season and if I was going to fill my tag."

"And?"

"I told you. I'm not going to lie for you about this, Gary."

"Susan," I say, wiping my mouth.

"I told her," Susan says, "that I hoped to. I told her we needed for me to, but that I wasn't much of a hunter."

"And what did she say to that?"

"She said that it looked like I was a very good hunter. The record showed we were the best hunters around. All four of us filled our tags last season and my first buck was one most experienced hunters would be proud of. She said that as a family we were pretty unusual in this regard. 'Remarkable,' I think was the word she used."

Though I may well be as quick to anger as my youngest, Kevin, only a few things make me truly mad. I don't like rules and regulations any more than the next guy, but I abide by them when they make sense. I don't mean to say I'm in the right legally. Brad was my best friend, and if I'd shot a fourth buck and used Susan's tag to bring him in and Brad had found out and had to arrest me for it, I would have felt horrible for him, even though I would have still believed I was within the bounds of the laws the state prescribes for the good of the deer population. Most hunters never get a buck, but I'm a better hunter than most, and unlike most, we strive to live off the meat we hunt—venison, rabbit, turkey, squirrel, duck—and the legal-sized bass or trout we take, and so I refuse to feel guilty about it. Since Brad retired and fulfilled his promise to his wife, Lucy, and moved them from a life in our North Country to a retirement condo in Florida and Officer Roy took his place, I've felt no compunction to abide by the state's way of counting our kills. And so I'm no saint, and though my filling Susan's tag is a crime that might very well land me in jail if Officer Roy catches me at it out in the woods, it's not a sin I feel is worth considering having to confess to Father Anthony. Certainly I'm no Lamey Pierson.

The time I turned Lamey in it was July, months before hunting season, and I was out cruising timber. I had no idea and sat down to rest a bit from the steepness of the hike, mopping my face with a bandana I carry stuffed in my back pocket, and looked down and there she was—a young doe staring straight back up at me from inside the hollow of the log. My heart missed a beat, and then took off, racing. Her skin and legs were in there, too. It was a fresh kill, only hours old. He'd skinned out the carcass and taken the meat. Hot as it was the hide hadn't started to smell and draw the flies. I marked the spot, tying the red flag of the bandana on a limb, and hiked off the mountain to fetch Brad.

Brad followed me back with Dave Tabert, captain of this barracks now, though back then he was the rookie. That dog of Dave's dragged us through the hills, straining against the leash, all the way back to Lamey Pierson's camp of tar-papered shacks, with two rusted-out cars up on blocks, and a refrigerator and other trash strewn about the yard, a smoldering barrel, his own mutt beagles in a pen, doing

flips against the fence yapping at us. The shepherd ignored them and
nosed into the open shed, whining with excitement himself, and there
on the floor was a mess of deer hair and bright-dripped blood. The
meat still on the butchered rib cage hung from the rafter by a wire.
Then we spotted Lamey, caught in his bare feet, halfway between the
cabin and the shed, toting back a bucket of water, the bloody knife
still in his hand. Dave let his shepherd off the leash to chase him before
Lamey could make his break, and Dave's dog held him, snarling to
keep Lamey at bay, while Brad stepped forward and disarmed him,
pulled his arms behind his back, and clicked on the cuffs. Lamey just
stood there, ignoring Brad while he read him his rights, and looking
mean at me all the while—yellow-eyed, with bad teeth, a squat, powerful man with hairy wrists big enough around to snap a watchband,
the bald patches of his crew cut obviously self-inflicted. I looked right
back at him, my arms crossed across my chest.

That was eight years ago, and he's hated me with a vengeance
ever since. Poaching is bad enough, but killing a doe at any time of the
year up here is a serious crime for sure. You can't even buy a doe tag.
That episode cost Lamey $2,036—an end-of-the-rainbow pot of gold
fortune for a fellow like him; he could very well still be paying on it—
and his old .30-30, not to mention his hunting license for five years.
Somehow still, not surprisingly, Lamey always has meat enough. And
he takes his getting punished for poaching personal, as if the law had
declared war on him alone.

I have absolutely no qualms about being a "tattletale" about such
things. I knew Lamey's kind in Nam, and I could tell some stories of
things that men like him are capable of that would make most
people's hair stick up straight. I've run across others of his kind here at
home, too, worked beside them doing carpentry, say, on a government
job like HUD. Those same people might just go ahead and tear out

their already straightened hair to see the work these men do, screwing everyone but themselves. When I have nightmares of evil in this world, it always comes to me in this man-shape of sloppiness and a too-easy, unearned return. And it's this evil that I'm constantly on guard against—my mission, I guess. In passing on an honest way of living this life I hope to give the strength of such conviction to my two sons, a strength which they'll have to call upon to fight against it long after I'm gone.

I wash and Susan dries, standing side by side at the sink. The boys still aren't back when we're ready to turn in.

"You're sure they're all right?" Susan asks as she sets aside two bowls of stew for them.

"They'll be fine," I assure her. I leave the back porch light on and the door to the mudroom unlocked.

Hands behind my head, I lie in bed, waiting for my wife. The water hums in the pipes, squeaks, and then creaks off tight.

Susan walks into our bedroom barefooted wearing her white cotton nightgown. Her hair gleams, shining deep, dark red in the lamp's glow, just brushed. The gray hairs she doesn't bother to pluck out offer her natural highlights. She looks at me, and I sit up and fold the covers back for her.

"Don't get any ideas, Gary Hazen," she says.

"Ideas?" I say, hearing my throat in my voice. "Susan, I haven't got a thought in my head."

"*Shhhhhhh,*" my wife says and presses a finger against my lips. Before she climbs in, she turns and flicks off the light. She peels her nightgown off over her head, then smoothes in close beside me under the covers in the dark.

Often, nights like this one, tired together from our day of work and chores, of trying to live in this changing world, caught betwixt and between the differences we share about our expectations for our sons, we come together like this, so slow and comfortable with each other. Certainly, there's not the frantic heat and hot hurry there once was in high school, say, when we didn't understand anything more about love than the burning desire that drove our bodies together on the front seat of my father's truck. These days, this is our comfortable love—the rest of our relationship—and, I feel safe to say after being married for thirty-five years, one of the principal joys of our life together as man and wife.

Kevin

"Fuck you!" Kevin yelled after his father, running out into the log road after him to give the finger at the receding glow of his taillights. "Asshole!" The red lights winked around the bend, and the darkness curtained down behind their father's leaving them.

Kevin stooped to grab up a handful of snow and pressed it against his mouth. He spat blood. "Why are you looking at *me* like that? Hell, I'm the one who got punched." Kevin scrambled into the bed and creaked open the big toolbox, buried himself inside it, digging to come up with the come-along. He stood, holding the cable and hand wench up for his older brother to see.

Gary David wrapped the cable fast around the sturdy trunk of a white pine growing directly across the log road from where they were stuck. Kevin took the hook end and crawled underneath the front of the Dodge to fix it to the tow bar. "You should have at least brought gloves," his brother said, winding the handle of the wench. The truck inched up the slope. When he was out of breath, he turned the crank—and his gloves—over to Kevin. Kevin's hands wouldn't work right trying to fit them on, and his brother had to hold the gloves for him while he jammed his fingers in.

Kevin grinned. "Next thing you know you'll want to massage my toes."

It was an old story between them. They'd been out playing in the snow as kids when Kevin had started to cry his feet had gotten so cold. Their dad had warned them about the dangers of frostbite. Kevin hadn't had anything nearly as serious as frostbite, he'd just been numbed with cold, but it hurt enough to make him cry. He couldn't walk another step, he said, and plopped down in the snow. Gary David had taken the situation seriously, doing what their father had instructed them to do if such a case were to ever occur in the woods. He'd pulled off Kevin's boots and wet socks and cradled his bare feet in his lap, stuck them inside his coat under his shirt, pressing them against the heat of his bare stomach, and rubbed and kneaded them until they glowed red again, circulating warmth.

"You should be rubbing my feet," Gary David said. "I've been out here since six A.M."

Kevin felt that. "I'm sorry," he said. "I really am. But I just can't stand him. It's that big bastard I can't stand."

The weight of the truck creaked the cable. The two of them settled into a steady rhythm, passing the crank and gloves back and forth. They had to work the back tires over the rut. They had a good three feet to go.

When they'd worked the rear wheels over the edge, Gary David said, "Okay," and Kevin slid in behind the wheel.

"Go easy this time, will you?"

Kevin waved back at him in the sideview mirror. He waited until he felt the treads of the rear wheels bite. The truck lurched onto the log road and ran up fast on the slack in the cable.

"Whoa!"

The truck flashed and rocked to a stop. Kevin threw the gearshift into park. He stepped out, grinning. "See there? I'm more careful than you think."

Kevin unhooked the come-along and took the cable from his brother to stow it. Standing tall in the bed of the truck, he could look down at the mess of the wood they still had to pick up.

"Fuck," he said. "Fucking. Fuck it."

Gary David dumped a log into the bed at Kevin's feet. "An impressive conjugation of the verb. Is that what you've been spending so much time learning up at school?"

Kevin raised his finger. "You want to hear what I've been learning?" He put his left foot up on the tailgate and spread his arms. He coughed into his fist and then he began to recite, speaking first for Odysseus's mother, Anticleia:

> No sharp-eyed Huntress showering arrows through the halls
> Approached and brought me down with painless shafts,
> Nor did some hateful illness strike me, that so often
> Devastates the body, drains our limbs of power.
> No, it was my longing for you, my shining Odysseus—
> You and your quickness, you and your gentle ways—
> That tore away my life that had been sweet.

Kevin paused. "What do you think?"

"Not bad. So far. Do you know any more?"

Kevin took his left foot down and put his right foot up, answering for Odysseus:

> And I, my mind in turmoil, how I longed
> To embrace my mother's spirit, dead as she was!

Three times I rushed toward her, desperate to hold her,
Three times she fluttered through my fingers, sifting away
Like a shadow, dissolving like a dream, and each time
The grief cut to the heart, sharper, yes, and I,
I cried out to her, words winging into the darkness:
"Mother—why not wait for me? How I long to hold you!—
so even here, in the House of Death, we can fling
our loving arms around each other, take some joy
in the tears that numb the heart. Or is this just
some wraith that great Persephone sends my way
to make me ache with sorrow all the more?"

My noble mother answered me at once:
"My son, my son, the unluckiest man alive!
This is no deception sent by Queen Persephone,
This is just the way of mortals when we die.
Sinews no longer bind the flesh and bones together—
The fire in all its fury burns the body down to ashes
Once life slips from the white bones, and the spirit,
Rustling, flitters away . . . flown like a dream.
But you must long for the daylight. Go, quickly.
Remember all these things
So one day you can tell them to your wife."

Kevin dropped his arms and Gary David applauded.

He took a bow. "What I'm *learning* up at school is to think for myself. Let me ask you something, Gary David. Why are we picking this wood up tonight? There's no good reason that this has got to be done tonight. These logs aren't going anywhere," Kevin said. "We could leave them until tomorrow. We've gotten the truck unstuck.

Let's go home and get something to eat. We'll take care of this tomorrow first thing."

Gary David rested his hand on the tailgate. "It's your decision," he said, swiping down his hat. He wiped sweat off his face. "I'll do whatever you think we ought to do." Gary David looked up at him until Kevin looked away.

"*Fucked*," Kevin said.

It took the better part of an hour for the two of them to reload the wood. When Kevin tossed in the last log, Gary David yanked hard at the tailgate to make sure it wouldn't flap open on them again.

The engine turned over on the third try.

"You ever think about buying a new battery?" His brother's breath blew white in the cab. Kevin rolled down the window so he wouldn't frost the glass.

"Right," Kevin said. "Now you're forgetting: I work for Mr. Gary Hazen. I get paid five dollars an hour plus room and board. I can hardly afford the gas of running back and forth to school."

"I imagine what Dad might say to that is you don't have to go back." Gary David scratched at the tuft on his chin.

Kevin put the truck in gear. "You know, there is a difference between an excuse and a reason. They're separate words. They mean two different things. That's what I'm going to explain to him next time."

"What was your reason for being late today again?"

That gave Kevin pause. He didn't answer and then he shrugged, giving up the answer.

"So," Gary David said. "It was that Jeanie Prescott? Again? Dad was right?"

"I fell asleep."

"Ah. Now I see the difference. Well, at least you've got a good *reason*."

"I was tired. We were in bed. You know."

"I do know. I'm tired," Gary David said. "I'd like to be in bed." They were idling on the log road. "Let's go home and eat."

Before them in the path of the headlight beams they could see the tread of their father's tire tracks left in the snow, and they followed along fixed inside them as if they were rails. They shone around the bend and caught a doe just as she emerged from the woods on the right side of the road, eyes aglow.

Gary David put his hand out to slow him, but Kevin had already braked. She stumbled at the edge, caught blinded by the brights, and then bounded straight across the road in front of them, snow exploding from the brush as she crashed down the slope on the other side of the road. Kevin flicked the beams to low. Another doe burst across, then another, their white tails flagging as they leapt away. It was early yet for the rut, but still they sat, waiting.

Gary David whispered, "There he is."

And there he was, had been, standing just back from the road, though even with the headlights on him he'd remained hidden, gone perfectly still, blending in with the snow and brush, the buck: a big, strong twelve-point. He stood staring straight into the lights, chin up, challenging them, and then, with a loud snort, *Hrumpf!* he surged forward in one motion, his big shoulders and hocks flowing with strength, and vaulted the width of the log road and disappeared over the edge after the does.

That's when Kevin heard himself say out loud to his brother: "I've made up my mind. I've decided not to go hunting this year."

His older brother didn't answer him immediately and the words hung in the cab between them. They came to the end of the log road and turned onto the plowed strip of asphalt that led to Lost Lake. They drove for a long time between the rows of pines before Kevin cut his eyes at Gary David staring straight ahead. Maybe he hadn't heard him. Kevin wondered then if he'd actually spoken.

And then Gary David said, "Is that right?" And then he said, "Officer Roy was out checking on us today about our tags. She's onto him about filling Mom's last season. Dad told her he's already paid for yours this year. He told her both of us were going to go."

They rattled across the bridge in silence. Above the lake the moon hung haloed about by a ring of white light. It reminded Kevin of eyeing down the swabbed-bright of a rifle barrel that he'd somehow managed to get fumbled around and aimed awkwardly back at himself.

Officer Roy

"Evening, Jo."

It was after 8:00 when I got back to the barracks at the end of my shift. I walked in, stomping snow off my boots on the black rubber welcome mat cut out in the shape of a loon, to find Captain Tabert leaning his elbows against the tall dispatch desk behind which Ellie Holmberg sat, the silver bars on his shoulders winking in the overhead lights as he tilted back a sip of coffee from a supersized New York Rangers travel mug. Captain Tabert was a rangy-looking guy of forty-five with gray in his long sideburns and a snow-white handlebar mustache that drooped below his chin. He'd always seemed to me to act more like a misplaced cowpoke from someplace like Montana or Wyoming than an upstate ECO. He cultivated that sort of slow drawl and deliberate manner. The Winchester belt buckle he wore low down on his hips underlined a slight paunch.

"Dave."

While Captain Tabert didn't insist on many rules, the one he was adamant about was that we use first names on the job. I forced myself to call him Dave to his face though I still thought of him as Captain Tabert. In the same way he had assumed I could easily call him by his first name, he'd simply addressed me as "Jo." From my first day of Little Miss Muffett's Nursery School on I'd been as particular as my parents had about me being called *Josephine,* and I'd been surprised myself that I hadn't set him straight immediately. Now when I wasn't on duty as Officer Roy, I was known as Jo, the two halves of the whole person I'd become in Lost Lake.

Trapper III, Captain Tabert's K-9 three-year-old shepherd, lay sprawled on the gleaming linoleum floor of the barracks. His ears had perked when I walked in, but he didn't raise his head up off his paws. His tail swished on the floor behind him as I bent to scratch him behind the ears.

"How are you feeling, Ellie?" I asked, straightening.

"Better maybe, I guess. The books all say the first three months are the worst."

"Ellie's been a trooper all right." Captain Tabert beamed.

Ellie smiled shyly from behind the counter that fronted her desk. She had the prettiest face, with doll blue eyes and bobbed white-blond hair. She and Captain Tabert often spent evenings together flirting, though I was pretty sure that was as far as it went between them. Captain Tabert invoked his wife, Debbie, in almost every sentence he spoke. "Well, Debbie says . . ." They'd been married for eighteen years, and they had two girls, Samantha and Savannah, two grades apart in high school, both of whom he absolutely adored. The smiling faces of his family beamed back as the screensaver on Captain Tabert's computer and also in frames aimed to be seen from the chair at his console desk no matter where he rolled his lumbar chair or how far he leaned back in it. Ellie had just gotten married herself the fall before, to a young, pink-cheeked musicology professor at the local junior college in Lake Serene. Underneath the red and black snowflake-patterned sweater and black stirrup pants she wore, the swell of her belly was just beginning to show.

"Jared already out on patrol? I didn't see the other Cherokee out back." Jared Acres had seniority on me by a year and four months, a fact that he somehow managed to weasel in to every discussion we'd ever had. He shaved his head completely bald, and at five feet eight inches and 235 pounds, he looked built to bowl things down. He'd played fullback at Cortland State and had graduated with a degree in elementary physical education. Jared would have been the first to admit he wasn't the brightest bulb, but he was a nice enough guy once you got to know him. The fourth ECO, Paul Stauffer, just a year from retirement, had served the bulk of his career as an old-time game warden under the command of Gary Hazen's buddy, Brad Pfeiffer.

"I sent Jared down to the Lodge. Little Nancy's been trying to get into the Dumpster again. This time Rick said she'd got on top of it somehow and was jumping up and down on the lid, making enough racket to beat the band. I swear, there's nothing that old bear won't try for french fries. That's been about the extent of the day's excitement in Lost Lake. What about you?"

"I stopped by the house and talked to Susan. Then I tracked Gary Hazen down at the cut he was working to question him," I said. "For a start."

Captain Tabert nodded, impressed. "And?"

"And I ran into Lamey Pierson again at the Lake View."

Ellie wrinkled her little nose. "Why, that'd ruin anybody's supper."

Captain Tabert sipped his coffee, his lips curling up around the edge of his cup. But he said seriously to me, "Good work, Jo."

"Thank you. And now if you'll excuse me I'm going to go home and put my feet up. Tomorrow's my day off."

I stepped into the hallway leading back past the restrooms. I took my card from its slot and punched the time clock.

"Best rest up," Captain Tabert said as I passed by on my way out. "You know how rough next week's going to be. No fooling around."

"I know," I said. And I did. Last gun season, I'd worked over a hundred hours of overtime. I suddenly felt the weariness of the long, cold hours setting up roadblocks to check licenses and tags, scouting for violations, or scouring the woods for the occasional lost hunter. The opening of gun season was our busiest season by far. Not even camping and hiking during the height of the summer came close.

My 1984 rust-red Volkswagen Rabbit was parked around the side of the barracks, 178,000 miles and going strong. The car had served me since my sophomore year, driving back and forth from Syracuse, where I'd gone to school, to Guilford. The Rabbit throttled up on the first try, but the black, rubber-vinyl insides left me stone cold after the warmth of the Cherokee. I hunched deeper into my coat and mashed the nearly stripped gears in search of reverse. On the way home, I pulled into the Texaco gas station and convenience store and hopped out, leaving the car running in the hope that the heater would actually start to work. It usually kicked in just about the time I got home.

The Texaco Stop and Shop was the only place from here to Upper Lake that you could buy beer or bread after the North Way closed at 5:00. The smiling, mustached faces of stock-car drivers plastered the fronts of the Coke and 7-Up machines outside. The long-haired boy behind the register who, if it were humanly possible, seemed to work even more hours than Val at the Lake View looked away from the blare of the TV. "Officer Roy!" he said as if he were the outpost at some remote station and hadn't seen another person in years, though in fact I stopped in here nearly every night on the way home. I picked up a carton of eggs and some cheese, a head of lettuce, an apple, yellow celery, and a day-behind *New York Times*. I could not twist the rabbit ears of the antenna to pick up even one TV station at the cabin and reading old papers had become the only way I could keep up with what was happening in the outside world—that and the articles my mother sent me clipped from magazines like *U.S. News and World Report,* the *Economist,* and *Yankee.* I set everything on the counter and then walked back for a six-pack of longneck Rolling Rock.

Two miles past the Texaco, I turned right off 28N. The Rabbit dug in as I geared down, jarring over the snowplowed dirt road that circled around the west side of the lake. It took me another fifteen to twenty minutes to negotiate the long way around to my place, skirting the shore though it was less than one straight mile away from the bridge that passed through the center of Lost Lake. I pulled in beside the rented cottage that had been advertised for three hundred dollars a month plus utilities. The two-room winterized cabin had a good-sized screen porch that overlooked the water and was set with its own dock adjacent to the last state access put-in for this end of the lake. For a winter rate, three hundred dollars a month was high, but it became a sweet deal during the summer when the price of available lakefront rentals skyrocketed.

My older sister, Francine, lived with her ob-gyn husband and my three nieces in Cambridge, Massachusetts, and when she'd visited, she couldn't believe I dared to live way out here all alone. I couldn't help myself: I told her about the time a Kodiak-sized male black bear woke me raking at the log walls trying to get at the smell of trout I'd left in the trash can in my kitchen. I'd stepped out into the night in my hot pink nightshirt, gripping a frying pan, and yelled and banged an alarm for him to beat it, which he did. You learn. And I tell her anytime she wants to compare statistics on rapes and murders, we can. Though I had to admit that was before I became aware of Lamey's concern for my night's sleep.

Inside, before I turned on the lamplight, I pulled down all the shades and yanked the curtains tight. I preferred to leave the curtains open and the windows up, protected only by screens. It was one of the principal reasons I'd chosen to live out here with no neighbors. From the very beginning Gary David and I had treated our isolation as a sort of Eden-like paradise, forget the fig leafs.

With the windows covered, I yanked the switch and fit the beer and groceries into the minirefrigerator. I checked the thermostat and unlatched the doors of the woodstove. Once I'd kindled a fire, I took off my coat and pulled off my boots. I unbuckled my holster and left my weapon hanging on the straight-back chair beside the front door, unbuttoned the shirt of my uniform, and stood on one leg to stork out of my pants. My dad was a businessman who always wore a suit to make the rounds of the chain of Kinko's copy shops he owned and he'd given me his old suit press. I was teased about it in my family the same way that we teased my father about calling himself a "sort of modern-day Ben Franklin." I would admit that using a suit press way out here seemed a little incongruous—that I did tickled my sister to no end—but I used it every night. Dry cleaning was an extravagance on an ECO's salary, and I had to drive all the way up to Lake Serene to have it done.

I let the water steam up before stepping under the drizzle of the shower, a little tub with a clear wraparound curtain. One plus was that the cottage had a mammoth one-hundred-gallon hot-water boiler. I could stay under as long as I liked. The well water smelled of iron and had stained the porcelain orange.

The steaming water pinked my skin. I washed my hair and rinsed it and then kneaded in what felt like half the bottle of conditioner. Using the bar of Ivory, I foamed my legs and shaved them carefully, thinking of him. I twisted the water out of my hair and stepped out of the shower and wrapped myself in my extrawarm terrycloth robe. Even after all the conditioner I'd used, the comb grabbed, making me grimace at myself in the oval mirror at the pull of the snags.

Back out in the main room of the cabin, I popped the top off a bottle of beer. My feet ached, the arches feeling bruised from the steel shank insole support in my Swampwalker boots—and I used to complain about having to wear high heels. I sat back in the rocking chair and put my feet up on the old wrought-iron bed. I picked up my book. When I arrived in town, one of the first things I'd done after I found a place to live and had my electricity and phone connected was to sign up for a book group at the junior college, which I saw advertised in the *Lost Lake Gazette*. We met once a month, a mixed group of stay-at-home mothers and secretaries from the college, a retired logger, a volunteer fireman with eight kids, a local woman poet, and another woman with dyed maroon hair, mystically named Raven, who owned the only jewelry store around, Elegant Emotions in Lake Serene. We were reading *Don Quixote* for our next scheduled meeting at the end of the month. I was embarrassed that I'd graduated from a respectable university without ever having been required to read the book.

Nights alone, reading, waiting up for him, or lying in bed naked, anticipating his being with me, I would hear the raccoons' fiddling or a possum's fussing with its young. You couldn't tell the difference unless you knew, and I'd learned to, taught so much about the woods in such a short time: the soft *chock* of his paddle against the gunwale, my own heartbeat in anticipation of his arrival. He paddled the mile from their end of the lake in the dark. He left me asleep before his father rose to wake him again in his bed downstairs in their house. None the wiser.

That first night I'd been in bed, still up reading by the one lamp, when I thought I heard something strange. That was the week of the afternoon I had first seen him alone anywhere without his father, and I'd been carrying that electrified feeling inside me ever since, a gnawing hollowness in the pit of my stomach, a quickening anticipation that could have almost been mistaken for nervousness. *Where did he park his truck?* had been my first thought. I could say that I almost expected him and had been wondering what I would really do if he really did show up beyond the fantasy of imagining it. But he had not driven up. I was familiar with the unmistakable crunch of truck tires on gravel, the sound of a fisherman backing his boat down to the launch or a happy family with their canoe at the put-in at the state access.

Moths batted against the screen to get at my light, and I listened carefully to the mating calls of the bullfrogs, groaning lonely in the dark. A loon echoed zanily out over the lake. My cabin had no air-conditioning. I didn't even own a fan, and I had left the three windows and the door open, the screen secured only by a hook latch. I reached beside me and flicked off the lamp, giving myself the cloak of darkness. Thinking the big Kodiak fellow I'd chased off before had returned, I folded the sheet back. I stood silently, barefooted against the rough plank floor, my nightshirt brushing the tops of my thighs, waiting for my eyes to adjust.

Then I heard footsteps creak the bottom stair to the porch—no raccoon, no possum, not a bear, but in that care I knew it was a man. I stepped silently forward toward the chair and flicked off the snap of my holster and eased the cold, powerful weight of the pistol out. I pressed myself against the wall beside the screen with the barrel down, and I pulled the action of the 9 mm back and let it ring forward, warning that a bullet had been loaded into the chamber.

The footsteps stopped. He cleared his throat and said calmly, "Officer Roy? It's me, Gary David Hazen."

I closed my eyes at the sound of his voice. I was not afraid, though I certainly felt the charge in the moment. I recognized the danger of clichés—but Gary David's showing up really was best described as a *dream come true*: what I would have wanted him to do if I could have had my wish. I probably never would have. But he had done it. He had come to me.

I eased my weapon down and stepped up to the screen so that he could see me. Gary David Hazen was standing on the bottom step. He was wearing jeans and a T-shirt. He smiled. "Hi," he said. He swiped his baseball hat down, holding it against his chest, his dark curly hair matted against his forehead, as boyish and disarming a gesture as I have ever seen from a man. His eyelashes were twice as long as mine.

"It's so hot," he said, fanning himself with the hat. "I thought I'd stop by and see if you wanted to go for a swim."

"A swim?" I said. I pushed at my own hair. I had to laugh. "Why in the world not?" I shucked the bullet out of the chamber and stuck the pistol in its holster. I reached down and unlatched the screen for him.

"Can you give me a minute?"

I stepped into the bathroom and pulled on my navy blue one-piece suit. It was still clammy from the laps I'd swum in the lake that morning before work. I looked at my face quickly in the mirror. *What you see is what you get,* I thought, grabbing two towels.

"Let me help," Gary David said. He took the beer that I offered him from the fridge and both towels. "After you."

We stepped carefully down the path to the lake. On the dock, he turned to set down his beer, and I quickly shed the suit, bold as could be—my turn to be brave. But before he could turn and see me, I dove. I rose and smoothed my hair back.

"Is it cold?" he asked.

"You better believe it's cold."

He was looking down at the suit I'd left. From the safety of the water, I watched him strip his T-shirt off over his head and loosen his belt. Almost before the buckle hit the dock, he splashed a shallow dive and swam strongly out to me. Together we stroked farther out into the black water, the lake as full as the sky with the reflections of the constellations that I could still recall from the astronomy class I'd been tested in—the Summer Triangle of the stars Altair, Vega and Deneb, and Draco the Dragon, Virgo the Virgin and Ophiuchus the Serpent Bearer, and Polaris, better known up here as the North Star. We touched mud on the opposite bank of the cove and swam lazily back across to the sandy shore of the beach close beside the dock, Gary David lounging back, gazing up. Once you were in, it didn't seem all that cold. He looked at me, and we both laughed, embarrassed now.

"I've seen you without your father once. Make that twice."

"I had to find some way to see you alone. You know how Dad can be."

"Be about me, you mean? Why does he hate me so much, Gary David? What have I ever done to him? I'm just trying to do my job."

"He doesn't hate you. He doesn't know you. It's change he hates. He's scared, I think."

"What could Gary Hazen possibly be scared of? He's scary is what he is."

Gary David smiled. "I was scared you wouldn't want to see me."

"I can't believe you just showed up. I've been thinking about you ever since that day at the Lake View."

"I would've come sooner. I came as soon as I could."

"I'm no good at waiting."

He put out his hand, and I stood and walked through the water to him as nakedly as that. We kissed standing waist-deep in the water, pressing against each other, and then he sat back, weightless, pulling me onto his lap. I took his face between my hands. I ran my fingers through his hair.

On the sandy beach before the cove, he laid down the towels for us, soft underneath me as I lay down with him. I could smell the heavy scent of pine needles in the air.

"You look so beautiful."

"You look beautiful yourself, Gary David Hazen."

He kissed my lips, my neck, my breasts. I pressed closer, and then closer still, opening my legs for him. He pushed back and I gasped. He rose on his elbows, breathing hard, and I put my hands on his hips, slowing him, the way I like it, and moved my own hips faster and faster now. In the frenzy, I was lost to him. I felt myself go away for a long time before I came back to him on the towel in the sand. "My God!" I said and my body jumped, making the connection I'd been fantasizing about all week. I heard the force from my body carrying back to me from across the lake with the power of his name in it, and when he came, goose bumps sprung to his flesh, and he arched for a long moment while I watched his face and then he collapsed back against me with his lips in my wet hair. "Josephine," he said. I wrapped him with my arms and legs and hugged him with all my might, smiling straight up into the stars, the night.

The next morning I woke alone naked in bed as if it actually had been that sort of steamy dream that leaves you shocked at yourself and wondering. He'd left while I was sleeping. I showered and dressed again in my pressed uniform, trying not to let myself think anymore about my charged body underneath every time the stiff cloth rubbed against me.

I looked up from my reading then. I'd stalled on the first sentence. My robe had fallen open, and I closed it. Some nights he couldn't make it. He couldn't call and I wouldn't know why until he showed up again. I'd be left with a hollow feeling of disappointment. Other nights I would start awake from a deep and dreamless sleep to see him standing naked over me, smiling down. I took another sip of the beer, and forced my eyes back to the page, absently stroking the skin at my throat as I read on about Don Quixote's sad, sweet travails.

Gary David

I was five when he was born and Mom and Dad brought him home. The three of us stood looking down at him in the bassinet, wondering, I'd guessed, what we were going to do with him now. He had reddish hair and he'd gotten beaten up some getting born. Breached in the womb I'd been told, thinking of him gone longways jammed like a log in a chute. His nose had gotten squashed and he had the pinch of bruises on either side of his forehead from the forceps and already a yellowing mouse under his left eye from where the doctor had had to drag him out kicking and screaming. "A fighter," Dad grinned and put his hand on my head, proud of him already.

He'd been born three weeks premature. Whether or not he was a miracle, he felt like one—to me, too: I'd watched my mother grow, and grow. And then he popped out. Mom and Dad left in the middle of the night to go to the hospital in Lake Serene. I woke to find Father Anthony seated in our kitchen drinking tea. He was dressed all in black and had his back to me, and I remember the flutter that took fright in my heart that he was there to minister the comfort of bad news.

Kevin came home long as the dickens but only weighed five pounds—a runt. When Lucy Pfeiffer stopped by to see him, she patted Mom's arm. "Don't you fret, Susan," she said. "Some of the ugliest babies grow up to be the most beautiful children."

When we were kids I taught him to flap out snow angels. I lay down and made mine first, showing him, on my back, facing up into the snow coming down, waving wide with my arms and legs. I stood up to show him, and he laughed, delighted. He lay down to try it on his own, his arms and legs flurrying fast as a windup toy's. I lay down beside him and waved and flapped again, and then he stood and ran to the other side and lay down beside me. We alternated big and little angels like that all the way around the house, touching together wing to wing like those paper cutouts Mom helped us ring around our Christmas tree. We were soaking wet by the time we'd finished circling the house and ran together to get Mom to see for herself.

"They're beautiful!"

By the time Dad got home from work that night it had begun to blizzard. He was later than usual because in those days of early dark before Kevin or I was old enough to go with him he managed his logging jobs with our horses, Joe and Ray, and he not only had to get in the wood, but when he was through for the day he had to take care of them, too—feeding and currying, keeping constant check on their hooves. Water in the winter was the problem; it froze. He'd have to go out all hours and in every sort of weather to swing the maul to break it free for them to drink. As soon as he stumbled into the kitchen, looking, Mom used to joke, like Nanook of the North, the snow and ice plastering the full beard he wore back then, we scrambled to lead him back down, Kevin grabbing on to his right hand and me to his left. Soaking wet and chilled through from falling down again and again after the hitched lurch of horses in the snow since 6:00 A.M. as I know now he must have been, he let us lead him. We stood outside to show him, us in our steaming hot jackets and boots and wool caps, which had hung before the wood stove all afternoon to dry. Mom followed, too, arms hugged across her coat, and the four of us stood in the yard, in the dark, the sky sifting down on us like the meteor sparks of falling stars, the yard glowing blue, but they were gone. The angels we'd flapped out around the house had been snowed over as if they'd never really been there, and Kevin started to bawl like he always did.

"That's just the way angels are," Mom assured him, touching the back of his neck. "But they're still here even when they seem to have disappeared." Which made my little brother go silent, finger at his mouth, spooked, looking around.

"IS THAT RIGHT?" I said the night he told me he was going to skip our hunt as we drove home from the cut. With his lip jutting out like that, he looked determined enough to go through with it. I rode along in the expectant silence that followed, staring straight ahead for a time, thinking of all the things I might say, the advice as his big brother I ought to give him about how to better deal with our father. I opted instead to let Kevin know the facts about our tags so that he could come to his own decision about what to do for himself. As I'd come to mine.

"Gary David," she'd said, miffed because I didn't completely agree with her point of view. She pressed back against the pillows and crossed her arms, huffing up her breasts.

I traced her thigh. She swiped my hand away, forcing the issue, and so I tried again to explain. Somehow or other almost every night we were together we managed to find our way back around to the same topic—the point of her investigation. "It's just that I still don't think you understand yet about Dad."

"Don't understand your dad yet?" she interrupted. "What's not to understand about Gary Hazen, Gary David? He either filled an extra tag or he didn't."

I held up my hand. "It has to do with respect."

"Respect!" she said. "How can you respect a man who breaks the law with impunity, Gary David? In that regard he's no different than Lamey Pierson."

"Josephine," I said patiently, not mad at all, even though it seemed to me we were beginning to probe awfully close to the heart of the matter. "Lamey Pierson's a criminal. He does what he wants without regard for anyone or anything else. Whatever Lamey does is all about him. Dad's doing what he believes is right for us as a family. That's what I mean to say: he isn't selfish."

"I don't know what you're talking about, Gary David. Gary Hazen is the most selfish man I've ever met. No, don't smile at me like that. There's nothing funny about this. It's no joke. The fact that I'm trying my best to do my job doesn't seem to matter to him. So what does it matter if we tell him about us before the hunt or after? Or whether I arrest him or not?"

"I'm happy to wake Dad up and tell him about us tonight if that's what you want. Then next Saturday you'll haul my father out of the woods with handcuffs on. One big happy family for the rest of our lives, right?"

She was a warden of the game law, and it was her duty to enforce it. That was her job. I didn't want to argue about that. She was right, so far as the law went. But I knew, too, that my father would not shrink from the rule of his own convictions.

I kept telling her. I told her again. "After this hunt. We'll announce our engagement. We'll have a fresh start."

"After this hunt," she sighed.

She let me touch her thigh then. I traced the tops of her breasts. She uncrossed her arms and tangled her fingers in my hair. I rose up on my elbow to kiss her. She parted her legs.

Is that right?

My brother's telling me that he'd *decided* he wasn't going on the hunt this year, which was really his way of asking me what I thought he should do, brought to mind the question that had become his search for the shell bag that we'd ended up buying for Dad the Christmas before. Kevin had first seen the shell bag, which he'd convinced me would be the perfect Christmas gift from the two of us for our father, in a handsome, notebook-sized catalogue from a company way off in the Boundary Waters country of Minnesota called Duluth Tent and Awning. The watercolor painting on page 16 of the catalogue showed the shell bag to be a handsome, olive drab satchel with a leather bottom and an adjustable, leather strap that looped over the shoulder. The bag was sewn from heavy eighteen-ounce canvas, just like the heavy-duty camping packs the company sold. Made to carry shotgun shells, it would work as well for bullets, which made it doubly versatile, Kevin pointed out.

We were agreed that Dad was the worst person in the world to have to buy a gift for. He didn't want for anything, it was true, and if you bought him something he didn't need, something for which he couldn't immediately see some utilitarian purpose, a practical use, he'd simply hold the present, the gift, up in front of him (as if he were dangling a barn mouse by the tail, Kevin had always joked with me, or I joked back, a stinking-black banana peel out of the garbage) and frown. "What am I supposed to do with this?" he'd say. He'd say it out loud! Then he'd look around at the three of us—Kevin, me, and Mom—who sat gathered around him expectantly. He expected an answer.

This sort of behavior by our father had always appalled Kevin. But every year, no matter how many times he told me that he wasn't going to worry about Dad's present this Christmas, that he didn't care, he'd be the one out searching for the one present that would please him.

He showed me the picture of the bag in the catalogue one evening after supper. It was still early, just after 8:00, but I had to be up by 4:00 to be at work with Dad deep in the woods by dawn, and I was already getting ready for bed. Kevin didn't have class until mid-morning. He could afford to stay up reading, wake late, and still make the hour drive to North Shore Junior College. He followed me into the bathroom where I was brushing my teeth and set the catalogue, folded over to page 16, down on the counter in front of me.

"What do you think?" he asked, so seriously.

I stopped brushing my teeth. "About what?"

"Dad's Christmas present."

I leaned close. "What is it?"

Kevin flushed. "It's a shell bag. Haven't you ever seen a shell bag before?"

"No."

Kevin took back the catalogue. "You come up with something then. I don't care what we give him. I can't worry about it anymore."

I shrugged and went back to brushing my teeth.

Kevin stopped in the hallway and stood looking down at the picture again. "It's thirty-five dollars and seventy-five cents apiece. That includes shipping."

The next morning my brother purchased a money order at the Lost Lake Post Office and filled out the order form. He put all of our money on the big one: the #400, 13Hx16Wx4D, QTY. 1, CAT. NUMBER B-114, DESCRIPTION Deluxe Shell Bag in the olive drab. For the address he checked for pickup at the post office. He worried Dad might pull open our mailbox and see that we'd ordered something from a catalogue.

Ten days later when the package arrived, Christmas was closing in with the smell of the snow and shriek of ice deepening down across Lost Lake through the past two weeks of subzero-degree deep nights. I can imagine Kevin walking the present home, tucked up under his coat to sneak it past our mother, who was folding laundry on the mud porch. In his room, with the door shut and locked behind him, he took it out of the package and wrapped the bag again himself. He wrapped it in a box—to fool our father, though the idea of Gary Hazen getting down on his hands and knees to crawl around under the candlelit tree to squeeze a present to try to make out what it was would have made even Kevin laugh out loud at himself. There was a precedent for my little brother taking such care. When he was eleven, Kevin had saved all on his own to buy Dad a red and black mackinaw from L.L. Bean, a gift that had actually won him a smile from our father. Kevin had glowed over that success. Dad still owned that shirt; it was a good shirt, even though by now, eight long-wearing falls and winters later, Mom had had to sew leather patches on the elbows, and the cuffs were frayed to a buckskinlike fringe at the ends. Kevin, I'm sure, would gladly have bought our father another shirt like that to recapture that easy smile from him, but he could too clearly imagine the pronouncement in Dad's voice: Why do I *need* two shirts? In wrapping it as he had, Kevin wanted Dad to think it was a shirt, and then to discover, to his pleasure, that it was a shell bag—something else that he could use.

Of course, we both knew our father didn't think about such things. He probably didn't even remember that it was Kevin who had given him the mackinaw he wore nearly every day from September through May, but Kevin himself couldn't seem to forget it somehow, and so he kept trying. He did his best. When Christmas morning finally arrived, I'd felt myself holding my breath for him as Dad peeled back the paper and lifted the bag off his lap. He held it in the air before him by the strap, the bag twirling a bit, first left and then all the way back right. Time ticked on the kitchen clock. I turned and raised an eyebrow at Kevin. Mom, with her hair down long, still in her quilted robe, sat with her hands in her lap, worrying a frown herself.

"Boys!" she tried, her voice beaming delight and surprise.

Finally Dad said: "I think there's been some mistake. I must've gotten your mother's gift. Is it a purse?"

"It's a shell bag, Dad," I said. "It's to keep our shells in when we go hunting."

Our father looked at the bag again, still holding it in front of him. "It looks like a purse," he answered. We watched him watch the bag turn slowly back the other way. "Thanks, boys," he said and set it beside his chair. "Is that all?" He stood. "We should get the porch shoveled."

Mom touched Kevin's hand, our father already gone down the hall toward the mudroom to put on his boots and coat. And I grabbed Kevin by the back of the neck. "Don't sweat it, Kev. We'll use it if he won't."

What I suppose I could have told my brother driving out from the cut that night when he told me he'd decided not to go hunting with us that season was that working with wood is no worse or better than you think it is; it's all in how you keep it in your head, or maybe hold it in your heart. I loved being outside at work surrounded by snow, breathing in the cold, and so didn't have to worry or need to chafe against the lead of that. For me living with Dad really was nearly as simple as that or I'd made it that simple—easy for myself. I was doing what I loved to do. His care made good sense to me. I could have said these things to my brother, an explanation in part of my relationship with our father, which was easier than his in this way because I had chosen to do his bidding and maybe harder in other ways he would never have to know about: living up to the expectations of a firstborn. Dad and I had struck a working bargain. Maybe that would have helped Kevin. Though perhaps it's that some things simply can't be said. Only in the silence of our living can they be known, shown, our beliefs made manifest in the day-to-day workings of our lives. I simply tried to work mine out in a way that would keep me happy keeping him content, showing respect for the way we chose to live.

I wish I could have told Kevin more. I would have liked to explain. But Josephine Roy was not mine to share; not yet she wasn't. I'd already picked out a ring at the jewelry store up in Lake Serene. All I had to do now was find a way to pay for it.

Mom had left two bowls of rabbit stew out on the counter. My brother and I ate them silently, standing. "You might want to ice that lip." When Kevin closed his door, I stepped into my own bedroom and switched off the light. I yanked the covers up over the pillows and raised the sill. I left the window open a crack behind me. I kept close under the icicled eave of the house so I wouldn't leave tracks until I stepped onto the path worn by footprints going back and forth to the pile of wood back by the barn. The moon bolded bright. I had come to know the lake better in the dark than in the day.

"A rock there to your right," I called out to Dad from the stern. We'd been caught paddling home in a fog one long, wet fishing trip, and then the boulder loomed suddenly up, a bow breaker, and glided silently past, hulking in the cloudlike air as if it were flying by and we were the ones set immovable, still. The sort of hiding fog this lake was named for. He stared back at where the boulder had gone, and I said, "Strainer down from the bank." And when it appeared, he turned all the way around from where he was kneeling against the bow seat, rocking the boat to look back at me as if he'd suddenly discovered himself in the canoe with someone he didn't recognize and even after taking a long look at still wasn't sure he knew. I stared past him, calmly navigating us around the rocky points we couldn't see, cutting across the wide mouths of coves he may not have even known were there.

I glanced back at our dark house looming on the rise.

I unhitched the painter and pushed off, kneeling amidships. I leaned my hip against the gunwale and settled into the silence of an Indian stroke, the water lapping lightly underneath our old blue wood and canvas canoe as I paddled the length of the lake to be with her.

part two

Lucy Pfeiffer

Folks around town could not believe that we would actually sell out and move to Florida—to the Comfortable Years, a retirement community. Are you kidding? they asked while standing on line at the North Way, half-grinning, eyebrows raised, waiting on me to deliver the punch line. No, I answered straight back, straight-faced, while Brad sort of stood hanging his head, peeking around from behind me to see how people would take it, embarrassed for me. He needn't be.

Did he want to go? And was I being selfish? You could see the questions in their eyes, glancing from me to him—sorry for *him* always. They were not questions I hesitated to answer for one more second after thirty-seven years of living up there. I'd served my time. My sentence was up, done: worrying about him out there all hours in every kind of weather, frozen cold—anything could happen and very often did. Did anyone ever ask me then if I thought Brad was being selfish, all those years, winter after winter after winter? Keeping me, his wife, frozen at home like a side of beef on a hook? I saw the accusation in their eyes: she's just bitter. Well, *duh,* I would have said, hands on my hips, if any of them had had the courage to say it to my face. No secret, and I didn't try to keep it one. I was not North Country born. My family was from Brooklyn; my father owned a drugstore, a Rexall. He was a university-trained pharmacist with hands permanently pinked from soap, fingernails trimmed and scrubbed bright. He never shot a gun in his life! So I hadn't fully realized what I was getting myself into when I said, "Yes." I kept four, count them, four down quilts on my bed, shivering my bones from September through May, the fire stoked to blazing as if our bedroom were a forge.

"You got to put a little meat on you, Luce," was my husband's answer, coming in nights from patrolling in the snow—out searching for another lost hunter or tracking after a poacher. It works for whales and seals. So I got busy eating. And for a while Brad tried to keep up eating all I cooked. We packed it on like there was no tomorrow. You should've seen the two of us riding around in the cab of the truck, two strained faces stuffed in a jar.

But it didn't help at all. The doctors up in Lake Serene warned me about my heart, the strain of carrying around 203 pounds on my little frame. Now I take care. We eat a salad or fish most every night, and Brad and I have both become as rail skinny as we were that summer afternoon I first caught a glimpse of him in his army uniform standing on the sidewalk out in front of my father's store. "Hel-lo there!" he mouthed at me on the other side of the glass. I was setting up a display for Valentine's Day. He performed a crisp turn on his heels and rang the door to ask my name, just like that! He'd been one of those who'd made the D-day landing at Normandy and had a chestful of medals to prove it. Talk about dashing! And you should have seen the envy in my girlfriends' faces when we took a stroll that evening. I held his arm. I was seventeen. My older sister, Irene, had been a WAC overseas.

Now Brad and I walk together every morning and again each evening at 6:00. Brad can't stand the heat and runs back to the air-conditioning in our condominium as soon as we're done. Not me! I take my book and One Calorie No Caffeine Diet Pepsi and I go to the pool. I like to sit in the sun and soak it up, right there beside the Gulf. Feels like I'll never be warm enough. "Like a lizard," Brad sulks, coming down in a camouflage T-shirt and khaki shorts I finally got him to wear, and his bright-orange baseball cap. "Cold-blooded," I snap right back.

As the days begin to shorten toward fall, he starts to get that wistful, long-jowled, and brown-sad, puppy dog look in his eye, pleading. Oh, I know! When I was a young bride he tried to bring those things home for me to butcher and clean, and I pointed him right back down the road to one of those fellows with a "DEER PRO-CESSING" sign hung in his front yard. He mopes around the pool reading *White Tail* or *Deer Hunter's News*. Thirty-seven years! I slather on more Hawaiian Tropic, lean back in my chair, sip my Pepsi, and pick up my *Star* or the latest John Grisham.

"You're killing yourself, honey," I used to say to Susan, over a cigarette and coffee in her kitchen after she'd had both boys and had gotten herself busier still, if that was possible, slaving to raise them, the little one running screaming like a hooligan through the house and the other one, too tall and silent for his age, with a girl's soft brown doe's eyes. I used to spend a bunch of time over there during gun season when Brad and Gary would go off hunting together every day until they'd filled in their tags.

"It just doesn't pay to work like you do," I'd say. "Aren't you exhausted?"

And what would I get for showing my concern for her laboring so hard, doing double time as a wife and mother, housecleaner and cook, a farmer, for Pete's sake? A smile! Happy humoring me! But, unlike them, Brad and I never could have children and maybe that's a difference I'll never know. Back in the days when we were both in the same boat, when we shared the same affliction and a closer friendship born of it no doubt, that and the fact that our husbands were best friends, I used to try to make light of it, saying that maybe it was the cold that had left its mark on the two of us and then suddenly, some-how—*snap!* just like that—she became pregnant and the joke was on me alone by myself.

I had thought more than once after she had the wonder of her second that the cold I felt was the thinness in my stomach; no matter how much I ate, I never could get big that way. We never had the warmth of a family to insulate us—unless you count all our dogs, which we did for years. You know how it is, Labradors. For years I traipsed around to dog shows; I sold and made my own money on champion puppies. The Hazens could say. Over the years they received the gifts of a few of the best for pets, though Gary put them straight to work hunting ducks. All in all, I enjoyed the dogs. But that didn't change the facts: thirty-seven frozen years! And the morning after he got his plaque for thirty-seven years of service I had our cabin already on the market, priced to move, and had fifteen boxes packed with our dishes and things wrapped in the crumpled newspaper I'd been saving in the shed for years awaiting the occasion. Brad came back from breakfast with Gary Hazen at the Lake View and both of them just stood looking down at me go—a regular whiz once I set my mind to it. Dormant all those years. Locusts go seventeen and wake well rested, red eyes blazing. Double that sort of revving finally to get going and you'll feel what I mean.

At the Comfortable Years I have many new friends. We play a mean game of bingo, and a bunch of us gather after supper in the common room to watch *Wheel of Fortune* or *Jeopardy!* I don't know how they know all those things! Sometimes I pick up my cell phone and call Susan. I tell her at least she ought to come visit and see for herself what she's missing. It's seventy-two degrees in December! The water and sky are light blue year-round. The sand is white as snow, if that would be a reassurance to her. Another plus is all our meals are prepared! They come perfectly portioned on sterilized-shiny trays. I never wash a dish or lift a hand to vacuum. There's a Mr. Quick Convenience Store right around the corner that has anything else you'd ever think to need—from microwave popcorn to razorblades, shoestrings, and magazines. I signed up for America Online and got myself computerized. We opted for the 162-channel cable TV offer. There's no end, it seems, to the number of bass-fishing shows Brad can watch. I tell Susan she ought to get a computer and get an e-mail address herself. Then we could communicate back and forth. I ask if they have cable TV up there yet. Maybe she ought to get a satellite dish and get connected. We've entered into the new millennium; she can't hang back any longer. People are going to do all of their grocery shopping online! They'll never leave their homes to buy books or clothes!

"The world's become a wonder."

"I'm glad you're happy, Lucy," she says.

"Well, go on and freeze," I tell her, trying hard to kid.

Anne Marie Burke

The bell over the front door jerked, jangling, and I glanced up to see the three of them surface into the light. Mr. Hazen held the door wide for his boys. The blond one ducked under his arm, quick to get past, and then Gary David stepped inside. All three of them were dressed in their winter work clothes, mackinaws and Carhartt coats, gloves and insulated mud boots. It was 6:00 A.M. on the nose, which is always when they came in if they did come in Saturdays. Or most Sundays when he would return at 7:00 after early church with that smoking priest, Father Anthony, from next door. But the Hazens wouldn't come in the next Saturday, not on opening day, no way. I knew. But she didn't, that freckle-faced girl who dressed in wool pants and a trooper's hat like a man. Call it soap operaish if you like. I've always had an intuition about such beckonings of the heart. A flick of the eye or a sudden start tells me all I need to know about love. What I could not imagine was his attraction to her.

"Good morning, Mr. Hazen. Where would you all like to sit this morning?" I held three menus pressed against my chest, smiling brightly. I dipped my chin and raised my eyebrows, risking a glance at him again. His dreamy eyes were shot red as the eyes of truckers who stumble in after driving through the night against the death-defying onrush of headlights. The younger one hadn't even bothered to stick on a baseball cap. His blond hair stood roostered up in a coxcomb across the top of his head from sleeping funny on it. Though there wasn't nothing funny at all about the way he had his hands jammed deep in his pockets, shoulders slouched. He was pouting for sure, his bottom lip stuck out so far it looked as if he might trip over it. Unhappy as could be about being up to go to work on the weekend would be my guess. Only Mr. Hazen appeared clean-shaven, pink-cheeked from the cold outside, smelling of a slap of Old Spice, and looking like he felt squared away and right with the world.

We opened at 5:30. The Lake View hadn't gotten crazy yet. The next Saturday on opening day we'd start serving at 4:00, and by 4:30 there wouldn't be a seat to be had. It was our busiest morning of the year. By the time we normally opened most of the hunters would have already climbed down off their stools, standing in line to pay, hurrying to be set in their stands by first light. Val was in the back helping Chet get set for the regular Saturday morning rush that would begin around 7:30 and last until 9:00. The Hazens would be long gone by then, out in the woods, at work.

"Morning, Anne Marie," Mr. Hazen said. "You waiting the counter?"

"I got the whole place," I said and swept my palm over all the available seats in the diner as if I was the Vanna White of the Lake View.

"What do you think, boys? Why don't we sit at the counter."

"Right this way!" Of course, he didn't need a hostess to seat him at the counter, but I always tried to be bright with him, and he smiled kindly back at me. He carried a torch for me and his oldest son. If it were up to me or him, Gary David and I would've been married already and Jeremy would've had a brother or a sister to keep him company. My family has lived around here almost as long as theirs.

Mr. Hazen straddled the center stool. Gary David sat to the left of him and Kevin, with a seat between them, to his father's right. When I picked the coffeepot up off the warmer behind me, the Braun heaved a steamy sigh over the calendar picture of Mr. October in his Day-Glo orange Speedo. "Pumpkin Butt," Val called him. My pet name for our hottie-of-the-month was "Basketball Buns." I filled their cups and set the pot down, pulled my notepad out of my apron pocket. I clicked my pen.

"So, what can I get for you gents this morning?"

"Kevin?" Mr. Hazen asked. "What would you like?"

The blond one turned to look out the window, elbow on the counter and his chin in his hand, and that's when I saw the cut on his lip that was making it stick out like that. He'd gotten popped all right.

"Why don't you pick for us, Dad?" Gary David said. "You always order best."

"How about three Logger's Specials then? Two eggs sunny side up on a short stack of pancakes, sausage, and hash browns."

"Coming right up." I gathered the menus that only Mr. Hazen had bothered to look at and took their order straight back through the flapping doors into the kitchen to hand it to Chet.

On my way back out, I paused before the little square of glass. He'd been nearly five years behind me in school. His blond brother five years younger than that even. Gary David was just a kid when I was cheering back when. He couldn't have had a chance at me then.

That darn Dirk. Sometimes I go stunned to realize again when I wake with another day before us that I have a son who is ten. Me! I didn't want to scare him off. He hardly ever spoke a word and seemed much too shy to be teased about a crush. They are Catholics, and I didn't know the rules, but it wasn't like Dirk and me were ever married or anything, so I am not exactly a divorcée. That was one thing going for me.

The three of them sat without talking. I checked myself out in the glass, making sure I didn't have lipstick smeared on my teeth or raccoon eyes from my mascara smudging in the heat of the kitchen, before pushing back through the doors into the dining room. I hurried smiling and brought him coffee and filled his cup again and again. I fetched his pancakes and eggs and sausage and set them down before him. He looked like one of those Frenchmen. *Anne Marie!* they call black-eyed from the red leather stools at the bar in the backroom watching me go from the kitchen into the dining room and back. But after Dirk Pollon I will not mess with one of them again. Let them hoot and whistle. I'll wear what I want. They say I'm trying to catch a man, and maybe I am. So what? But not one of them.

He was a Hazen, but not so stern looking as his father; he didn't look at all like his father, though the younger one did, sort of, though a littler version, who bends and blows the steam from his coffee, like fog clearing off the view of Lost Lake I see out these picture windows so many mornings. The lake isn't there—lost—and then it is, found. The tourists who come in like that sort of thing when I tell them.

Her and her big investigation.

Being a young mother in this town can get lonely, I'll tell you. People that come to visit Lost Lake say how beautiful it is, say how lucky we are to live here, which can get old. But they are tourists is all and no one up here takes them seriously. Jeremy stays all day with my mother, who works the evening shift. I have become my mother! We have three rooms in the Lost Lake Apartments. From the front room, we can see over the green and white sign of the North Way Market across the street to a view of the lake and the pale mountains beyond. In the summer the beach is full of the scrapping cries of children, bright as gulls. Summer is the easy time, once the black flies leave. After my morning shift I pick up Jeremy and my mother goes to work. I take him to the public beach across the street from the Lodge. This past summer I ordered a red bandeau bikini out of the Victoria's Secret catalogue. In the magazines I read, the stars seem to lead such bright and shiny lives, like that Blaze Farley who *People* named one of the "50 Most Beautiful People in the World" for the third straight year in a row. But I've seen her in here in the empty afternoon in her black cat's-eye sunglasses, with her hair piled up and no makeup, not even lipstick, smoking like a chimney while she goes over her scripts. She reminds me of Big Bird, she's so tall. Instead of yellow feathers she wears all that orange hair. But I guess it's for others to say what beautiful is.

"Y'all come back now, hear," I said in my best *Dukes of Hazzard* southern drawl. I watch a lot of reruns. That Catherine Bach's got nothing on me. I'm saucy by nature, which is why I do well on the morning shift. The boys walked out, but after he paid, Mr. Hazen paused to fish for a toothpick, staring after them. Gary David and Kevin were standing on the shoveled pile of snow that lined the side-walk waiting to cross the street to where their truck sat parked on the other side.

Mr. Hazen looked after them, and then he turned back to me. I thought for a moment that he looked sort of tired or sad or something, not cleaned up right and ready to face the world as he'd appeared to me at first to be. Everyone says how tough he was on those boys, but he was always sweet to me.

"You take care now, Anne Marie," he said.

I stood behind the register with my arms crossed, watching Gary David until a customer rang his water glass with his spoon to get my attention. "Hey, doll." I turned, my smile flashing on as if he'd flicked a switch. "What can I get for you?" I make more in tips than any of the other girls. I have to.

I always thought that Gary David was my chance, a good catch. I always thought I would become someone other than I am, but I guess not.

Gary Hazen

By dawn, we're on the job at the cut. Logs and limbs loom forward in the dark. The forest surrounding us slowly masses before taking on the singular shapes of individual trees as the yellow sun rounds over the ridge. Light ladders long between the trunks of the giant, hundred-year-old spruce that bar the boundaries of this cut.

It's no secret to anyone around here that from the start I was against clear-cutting this twenty-four-acre stand of immature hemlock. In 1891, a fire wiped out this forest. That blaze is still on record as the worst in the history of Hamilton County. For years afterward, ash trees ruled this forest. Ash is a fire tree. Its seeds take to the wind like dandelions. Ash goes on the fly, seeking out such devastated places. It grows in direct sunlight, roots anchored in embers. By now the ash is all but gone, except for a stray here and there—ash is a forty-year tree, tops. It grows up to offer the shade needed to bring the seeds of other sorts of trees up, like the spruce and hemlock, the maple and beech. Once it's given the other seedlings their start, the ash dies, leaving them the sun.

This stand of hemlock had grown up in their shadowing. In another ten years they, too, would have matured, been at the height of their health, and then I would have gladly marked them with red ribbons for felling, because once they've reached their peak they start their decline. At that point it's better to cut them and clear the forest for new growth, new trees, time in the cycle to give the seedlings their full share of the sun.

This is the way a forest works. Most people see trees and that's all they see, but I imagine a wood in all its diversity, as a living, changing thing. Most folks I know live one day to the next, paycheck to paycheck, and in our day to day, we're sometimes forced to as well, but as a forester in charge of making the call of which trees to cut and when to cut them, it's my job to count off in increments of at least ten years. I look at five seedlings huddled under a spruce, glance up at the spread of limbs, imagining the reach of their crowning against the blue sky, and see through the thinning of time to a single, sixty-year-old red pine. Most of the work I do in planning the harvesting of these forests is work I'll never live to see completed. There's no doubt that that affects the way I see the world.

But I'm just the forester on this land, I don't own it, and when the price of timber soared, the advice on how to grow this timber I'd been paid to give the past twelve years proved suddenly worthless. The owner of this cut is a fellow named Phillips, who makes his living out in California as the CEO of a computer company he could not believe I'd never heard the name of. He put in a grand appearance once a year to look over his investment from the driver's side of a rented Range Rover he drove up from New York City. When I told him I flat-out refused to do the clear-cutting he insisted I do, he got furious enough to fire me and hire on Armound Pollon and his crew of Upper Lake Frenchmen. For his part, Armound was only too happy to jump on the chance of making a buck off the land I'd tended. He's got a brain like a cash register, Armound does. So it was no surprise to me when I heard he'd gotten permission and the permits for a clear-cut so that he could bring in his big machines. A clear-cut is the fastest and cheapest way to do a job. I don't mean to be unfair. Armound is a hard worker, and he's done work I respect. But I've worked the North Country with him for years, and the complex questions of what to cut, when to harvest, and how best to get the wood out with the least damage seems for Armound to be too bottom-line simple.

I make my income when a tree I've red-ribboned for harvesting is finally felled and taken to the mill. I manage over forty thousand acres for private concerns, and the selective cutting I agree to do keeps the paychecks trickling in. In a given year I walk hundreds of miles cruising the timber in my care. We didn't make one cent on any of the hemlocks Armound took from this clear-cut. As compensation for the work I'd done for him, Phillips owed me permission to take the limbs.

By 10:00 we've already cut six face cords, the three of us working in sync together, matching the entire day's worth of work Gary David and I did yesterday working on our own. Kevin keeps his head down, not talking or joking around like we usually do, obviously still brooding about last night. I'd like to find some way to make up, but I can't quite bring myself to outright apologize—though I was in the wrong, he certainly wasn't in the right. By 2:00 we've finished cutting and loading the last of the limbs and logs left in the clearing.

"That's a day," I say. I'm well pleased with the work we've done. All that's left to do is to unload the wood at the house. Splitting is a job that's never really through, but we can afford to take the rest of the afternoon off.

I take off my gloves and turn to face my sons. "I'm buying."

FROM THE PARKING LOT at Rick's, Lost Lake blues away before us for as far as we can see. The mountains have already rusted out and most of the leaves have fallen. In warmer places they would just be starting to blaze. The TV above the bar is blaring college football, and Rick Schoonmaker is leaning his heavy forearms against the polished bar. Rick makes his living serving draft beer and burgers and fries at the bar, and in the dining room fresh brook trout, salmon, even venison in season. Folks come from as far away as Toronto and New York City, farther even, to eat the wild game that Rick prepares. Above the check-in desk is the humongous head of a moose Rick shot ten years or so ago up in Maine. Occasionally, Susan and I go down to Rick's Place to eat and watch a little TV—a big night on the town for us. We can't go too often, though, because Rick won't let us pay for anything. I try my best to make it up to him by dropping by a few ducks or even a wild tom turkey, a mess of rabbits I've hunted special for him. And, of course, I won't ever accept a penny of the money he tries to palm off on me either. The truth is we like this way of being friends.

"Well, look who it is," he says, straightening as we step into the bar. Rick glances back over his shoulder at the clock. "And in the middle of the day no less. What's the occasion? Hey, Kevin, did you get accepted into Hamilton?"

I give Rick a look. The last thing we need today is any wisecracks out of him. Then, as my eyes adjust, I see that it's just our luck that Armound Pollon is sitting at one of the little round tables with a mug of beer. His son, Dirk, and two of his crew of Upper Lake Frenchmen are with him. I don't recognize them. The Frenchmen he brings down from Canada are wonders. They live to work the wood—worse than damn beavers. Dirk's the only one of the four not in clothes to cut. He's wearing creased khakis and a red wool sweater with a collared shirt underneath. He parts his hair neatly to the right side. Armound likes to think of himself as a businessman, and he sent his son out of state to school to learn how to take care of their books, thinking, no doubt, of the future of Pollon Enterprises. Dirk is older than my Gary

David. He and Anne Marie Burke were an item back in high school, and he got her pregnant. Dirk never married her or claimed the boy publicly. We all heard the rumor he started that Anne Marie had been sleeping around—so it could be anybody's kid was his claim—which is a lie anyone with eyes can see just looking at his son, who is the spitting image of his dad. Anne Marie was either too proud or too hurt to bring down the law on him. Of course, Dirk ended up marrying a French Catholic girl from Upper Lake and she and Dirk have two legitimate children, last-named Pollon. Whenever we happen to meet up, he calls me Gary instead of Mr. Hazen.

The Upper Lake Frenchmen aren't the only ones crowding Rick's Place; a group of doctor-lawyer types stand off by themselves before the windows that look out over the lake. They're still dressed in their Orvis gear from the fishing trip they're obviously here on. At our end of the room, at another of the tall round tables, huddled close, putting their heads together over glasses of white wine, sit three young women and a young man. The women are manicured and look exercised thin, probably in their late twenties or early thirties. One of them has sort of reddish-brown hair, auburn-colored, I guess. The other two wear their hair in identical bleached-blond manes. The young man, I see on second glance, is only pretending to be as young. He wears his long, graying black hair pulled back tight in a lacquered-looking ponytail. A pointed goatee tufts his chin. The four of them are dressed in black turtlenecks and perfectly blue jeans and shiny black boots, uniformed like a team. A black leather jacket drapes the back of each of their chairs. I'm surprised to recognize the language they're speaking as a different breed of French than we're used to hearing up here.

"Rick." I step up to the bar and reach for the wallet that I keep close, chained to my belt. "Armound."

"Garee," Armound says, pronouncing my name with too hard a *g* and too much *e,* like he always does, and flashes me the bite of his sharp white smile. Armound reminds me of the stuffed black bear that stands in the lobby of the Lodge. He's short like that bear—no bigger than five foot six or so—but squat, powerfully built so that you wouldn't choose to fool with him hand to hand if you didn't absolutely have to: round all over but with strong, stubby legs, and arms bunched short with muscle. He's also hairy as a bear, the black curls matting his chest, tufting up out of his bright blue flannel shirt.

"What do you think about the coming of these early snows? It is a serious topic, no?"

Without looking back, I say what I'm sure he already knows, "I put my five down at the Lake View on October eighteenth."

I raise three fingers for Rick. "Genesee's."

But Kevin steps past me to tell him, "Make mine a Saranac, Rick," which makes Armound smile even wider, sharper. His beady eyes take careful aim; Armound doesn't miss a damn thing. He uncrosses his short arms to thumb over his shoulder at my son.

"Saranac?" He elbows Dirk. "No wonder Gary Hazen can risk five whole American dollars on a bet! You must be making the big money on my cut, taking our wood, yes? You English," he laughs, "are rolling in these dollars. We poor French." He sighs. "We must drink Labatts."

He shrugs and grabs his mug, leaves foam all over his beard and mustache grown to nearly hide the pink strip of his mouth, until he smiles or laughs, which he does, broadly, then. Of course, most around here would think of Hazen as an English name, but Armound knows perfectly well that my father's side of our family is Norwegian. He doesn't care though. It's all part of his Upper Lake Frenchman shtick.

He turns to his son and his men lean in, and he talks fast to them in French, and then they laugh like they always do. They pound down their beers and stand all at once, scraping back their chairs.

"Okay, Garee, back to work, no? Always the work, you know." He gives an exaggerated cluck of his tongue and shakes his hairy head.

I hand Gary David his mug, then turn with Kevin's—a darker color than ours.

Armound tosses a ten on the bar. "For these Saranacs," he says as Rick sets down my frosted mug. "If it wasn't for you we would not have gotten this job at all."

"No, Armound," I say. "I should pay for yours. If it wasn't for you and your crews cutting down every tree in sight without regard for anything but how much money you can make, we wouldn't have all this firewood."

"Ha!" Armound says and slaps Dirk on the back. "Mr. Hazen makes a joke. Take account of that. Au revoir." He leaves his money on the bar, and they clomp out the door.

Both Gary David and Kevin have stood beside me during this exchange. There's no love lost between me and Armound, that's for sure, but we've never come to blows. I have my wallet out. "How much?" I ask Rick, who knows better than to get into this.

"It's on the house, Gary," he says.

I squint up at the chalkboard above the cash register. I'm not used to Happy Hour prices.

"Three seventy-five," I tell him and count out the singles from my wallet and fan them out for him. Rick leans his elbows against the bar again.

"Hey, don't look now," he says, whispering close, "but that goateed fellow sitting at the table back there with those three women came in asking after you yesterday. He said Miss Farley gave them your name."

Like Phillips, whose twenty-four-acre clear-cut we've just come from, Miss Farley is another one of the absentee landowners I cruise timber for. She has a six-hundred-acre tract, mostly white pine, some spruce. The land she bought had been raped off of hardwoods in the early 1900s, but in the hundred years since it has come back nicely in softwoods.

Blaze Farley is a movie star, the real thing. Though I've never seen any of the movies she's starred in for myself, I have glimpsed her face on the shiny covers of magazines as I stand in line before the register at the North Way waiting to pay. Both Gary David and Kevin have gone to see her movies at the theater in Lake Serene, and Kevin still keeps a poster of her in a bathing suit that she autographed for him on the wall of his room.

But not only is Blaze Farley a famous movie star, she is also a self-proclaimed conservationist. One Sunday Kevin brought me a *Parade* magazine out of the newspaper. It showed a black-and-white photograph of her with all her orange hair up under a baseball cap, a feat in and of itself, wearing new hiking boots and shorts, leaning against a one-hundred-year-old-sized spruce I thought I recognized. The question posed in italics asked about her commitment to the preservation of the Adirondack Park. Not only had she given a significant amount of money to lobbyists down in Albany, she was so committed, Blaze Farley was quoted as saying, that she'd renamed the old railroad baron's lodge she'd bought Forever Wild.

If that reporter had called me up, I could've vouched for the committed part at least insofar as she took a personal interest in the trees we logged off of her land. The only timber she allowed taken off of her property were trees that were so far past their prime that the wood wasn't worth much more than firewood anyway. I'd finally convinced her that by selectively logging the land she wasn't killing trees; by judiciously thinning she was actually giving the gift of life. She'd spent an entire day walking her woods with me, and though she'd never taken off her sunglasses, not even once, she'd never rested either. I would've slowed down for her—for myself—but she'd kept up and so I pushed on to stay in front of her. I don't like to think of myself as a chauvinist, especially one of the male pig kind, though I imagine there are women who would label me that or, little better, call me plain old-fashioned. Still, I have to admit it unsettled me a bit that she was nearly as tall as I was.

"They're staying here?" I ask, indicating the man and three women sitting at the round table behind us.

"They rented the entire second floor! Come all the way here from Paris, the guy said. Knows Miss Farley from somewhere in the movie business. It's got something to do with a documentary or something they're filming on the migration of Canada geese."

"The migration of Canada geese?" I ask. "Then what in the world are they doing in Lost Lake? That big flock that feeds on the baseball field leaves every year to come back here, but they're off the flyway. Now if they want to discuss mergansers or ducks, mallards, say, or blacks, maybe teals, we could talk."

"You don't have to tell *me*," Rick says, both hands up.

"So why talk to me?"

"They need someone to help them kill a few geese. Sounds like they're willing to pay."

"Have them talk to Officer Roy," I say. "There's no season on Canada geese in Hamilton County. It's as illegal as can be. Or, if they need an expert in poaching, have them go see Lamey Pierson. Why do they have to kill them anyway? I thought they were filming them?"

"They asked me if I'd get in touch with you. You mind if I tell him who you are?"

A cheer goes up from the doctors and lawyers as a runner breaks free and sprints down the sidelines for a touchdown. The player who ran it in does a wiggly dance in the end zone and throws the ball down like a child. He races around pumping his arms at the sky, holding up one finger.

"Hot damn!" a big man with a cigar yells. "Go Michigan! Rick!" he calls out across the bar. "A round of beers on me. Put these fellows here on my tab. That's my alma mater. After today, we're going to be ranked number one in the country!"

"You got it, Mr. Yancey," Rick says. He pushes back from the bar and opens the freezer and starts pulling out a host of frosty mugs. He winks at us as he does.

Before Rick serves the men who are paying for it, he fills three more mugs at the Saranac tap for us.

"Oh, hell, Gary," he says to me as I sip at the Genesee I paid for, "it's only seventy-five cents more a pint. Believe me, that fellow can afford it. He's the chairman of IT Paper. The bunch of them've drunk nothing but pints of Guinness and Harp since Billy Hirsch flew them in here for their fishing trip two days ago."

I turn to look at them again. The entire whooping bunch is exchanging money, placing wagers—and the bills facing me don't look like George Washington either. A cell phone rings and one of them goes for the pocket of his flannel shirt.

"What?" he yells, clapping his right hand over his other ear. "I can't get a decent connection up here!"

I'm looking at them when I notice the youngish man with the goatee is staring at us, whispering with the women with him. I turn back to my own business, my own life.

"Be right back," Rick says and balances up a tray loaded down with three of the syrupy-dark, slow-drafting pints. On his way, he pauses at the other table and points back at me.

"Dad?" Kevin says, quietly, but even in the commotion of goings-on in the bar there's something in his voice that catches my full attention. It's the first he's spoken to me all day, but there's something else. Something in his voice reminds me of when he was a boy. When Kevin was little he tagged after me everywhere I went. I couldn't get rid of him!

He rode beside me in the truck to jobs I did and sat waiting for me the whole while, completely absorbed in watching me work. He wore lumberjack shirts exactly like mine. I bought him his own saw so he could have at the sticks of kindling while I was busy swinging the thirteen-pound maul to do the heavy splitting. I taught him how to swing an axe, to pound a wedge, to pace off the length of the sledge, and to gauge the grain to quarter a stump, and we worked together at it all day long. He practiced and practiced. As a kid, he was driven to get it right. Gary David was less adamant about technique, but he was always there, always around—more like my shadow, while Kevin seemed to be trying to actively become me, the man who throws the shadow down.

I turn to Kevin then, giving him my full attention, and he opens his mouth to say it, whatever he has to say, but then we're interrupted.

"Excuse me. Mr. Hazen?"

The young-looking gray-haired fellow in the black turtleneck is standing behind us. Unlike Armound Pollon, when he switches to English his voice carries only the slightest trace of French in his accent. He's holding his palms pressed flat before him as if he's saying grace, bowing slightly at the interruption.

"I'd like to introduce myself. I'm Pierre Pardoe. I direct a small documentary film company, Voilà Films." He sweeps his arm toward the women at the table. "These are my associates."

"Gary Hazen," I say and take his hand. I point beside me, first to my right and then to my left. "My sons, Kevin and Gary David."

"Please call me Pierre." He shakes my sons' hands, too. "I was wondering if I might speak with you for a moment."

"This isn't a flyway for Canadas," I shrug. "I'm not illegally killing geese, if that's what you want to talk about. I don't want any part of it. No thanks. I don't care how much you're paying."

"Ah," he says as if he understands perfectly the reasonableness of what I've said. "So you see our little problem. I know it must seem

117

preposterous. But film," he shrugs, "is not like real life. We manipulate images. A goose here is a goose anywhere, or so it will seem on film. Blaze Farley's acting as the producer for this project. She's very concerned about the plight of the geese. Their regular flyways are being threatened by development. She's also been generous enough to allow us to stay in her house while we shoot this particular aspect of the film. It behooves us to shoot as much of our footage here as we can."

"I can appreciate that. But a documentary? That means it's true."

"True, yes!" Pierre smiles as if I've gotten an answer right in class. "In essence it is true."

"Honest?"

"Yes. Honest."

I grin at Kevin and take another sip of my beer. They must really think we're yokels up here.

Just then Blaze Farley sweeps in. The doctors and lawyers look up, and when they see her they grab after their hearts. I'm a happily married man, but even so she catches my eye, too—clipping into the room in her tall high-heeled boots and floor-length fake fur coat, man-made to gleam like mink. Her orange hair is down long and her emerald eyes flash. Her smile is so white it seems to have lights behind it. She sheds her coat as she bends to hug the women at the table. The tan sweater she wears reveals the roundness of her figure. A green and blue scarf drapes around her neck.

"Ah, I see you've found our estimable Gary Hazen," she says. She and Pierre exchange kisses cheek to cheek in the air. She reaches out and shakes hands firmly with Kevin and Gary David. "Wonderful to see you!" She has long hands, her nails painted red.

"Can you help?" she asks me. She tosses her coat on a stool.

"I don't see how. I was just reminding Pierre here that this isn't a flyway for Canadas. As I said, the flock that makes camp every summer on the baseball field near the Lake View is off the beaten path. They've got a free license to live up here; there's no season on them in Hamilton County."

"Domestics," she says and pulls up another stool for herself. "What are you drinking?" She looks at Kevin.

"Saranac," he manages, and she says, "Yes," to Rick to pour one for her, too.

"But I thought the film was about Canada geese."

"Mr. Hazen, film is not real life," she says, echoing Pierre. "Film gives the illusion of real life."

"And so?" I say.

"So," she says happily, "we use domestic geese."

I nod slowly as if I get it, but I don't get it.

"Domestics are bred white," I say. "They're about half again as big as Canadas. They have orange beaks with a big bump on the nose. This is a *documentary* about Canadas. I think I'm missing something."

"Paint them!" she says, delighted, as if she's come up with a brilliant idea.

"Paint them," I repeat.

"The shot will be taken from a distance. We're going to drop them from a plane to simulate flight. Size in this instance won't be so significant."

"We'll need at least three geese," Pierre adds. "Maybe more if we don't get the shot we need on the first three takes. And I'd like to shoot this week. Monday would be ideal. How much would you charge? Per goose."

I feel like busting out a laugh. I can feel Rick and my boys, the women at the table, Miss Farley and Pierre all watching me as I rub my chin, as if I'm seriously considering the proposition.

"Three hundred," I say, making a huge joke out of it, naming my outrageous fee. I know a man up past the junior college in Lake

Serene who sells domesticated geese and turkeys. Live, they go for all of about five bucks apiece. They're raised to kill to eat at will. There's no season on them. It's all as legal as can be.

Pierre smiles at Blaze Farley. He sticks out his hand. "It's a deal!" he says, and I can't help but feel like I've been taken, even though he's just offered me the sort of bounty most of us can only wish for up here.

NOW WE'VE GOT something else to drink to. Not only have we finished up the Phillips cut and gotten in all the wood we'll need before the big snows begin, but we've contracted nine hundred dollars for a job, all but fifteen dollars of which plus the cost of a few brushes and cans of black and brown paint, will be pure profit. The entire scenario's so ludicrous it's hard to feel guilty about it. I try to imagine the sort of business that allows you to throw that much money away so gladly. Blaze Farley and Pierre and his three associates left in high spirits, toasting and then draining off their wineglasses, going off to her house to fix some fine supper. They left talking excitedly about the angles of the takes they were going to make, buzzing about the light.

I'd gladly spring for a few more beers, but we can't get ahead of the rounds Mr. Yancey has already bought for the bar. With three drafts down, I try to remember the last time we took an entire afternoon off and spent it at Rick's. I'm grinning like a fool myself. Must be our lucky day. *Wait until I tell Susan,* I think. I imagine all the things a windfall of nine hundred dollars could bring. Our hot-water boiler had nearly left us cold the winter before, limiting us to three-minute showers. And one of our freezers was about to gasp its last, nearly kaput. Once this job was done we could begin to attend auctions in the bid for a newer used one. We'd even be able to afford a second Briggs & Stratton generator, since it was a given that we'd lose power at least once a winter, and I could stop praying the old one would make it one more year.

"Dad," Kevin says again, starting in where we left off before Pierre Pardoe introduced himself and this harebrained scheme into our life. "Dad," he says, head down, elbows on either side of his glass of beer, getting up steam, working up the courage—I can't imagine for what, not an apology of his own certainly, and suddenly I feel my elation drop, gone hollow in the pit of my stomach. He shakes his head, and then he just says it, meeting my eyes: "Dad," he says then, "Dad, I've decided I'm going to skip my buck this season, all right?"

I'm sitting beside him, and he looks into my gaze, and I feel the smile slide off my face, and I take a sip of my beer—while what he's said slowly sinks in, takes root.

"What do you mean you've decided to skip it?" I ask him. I set my mug down.

"I mean I'm not going hunting this year. I've made up my mind I'm not going to fill my tag. Jeanie doesn't like it."

"She doesn't like what?"

"She doesn't think hunting is right."

"Jeanie doesn't think hunting is right," I say, repeating it because I can't believe my ears. I cast a glance at Gary David to see if he's heard what I have, but he's looking down at his hands. Our lucky day flashes before me, flagging red. I drop my chin as if I'm thinking about it, as if I'm actually considering what he's asked, what Jeanie's said, but I'm not thinking about it. There's nothing to consider. I'm counting as quickly as I can— ... 8, 9, 10 ... —watching the press of black numbers against the pulsing red of my lids. I take a deep breath to try to gain control of myself as Susan's advised— ... 11 ... 12 ... 13 ... —before I burst out, louder than I'd meant to, shout: "*No.* You can't *skip* it." I throw back the last gulp of beer, clap the glass back on the bar, and stand.

"Hey, Gar," Rick calls out after me, coming back with the tray under his arm, still grinning at our good fortune, as I barge past him.

"You're wasting that fourth beer!" I hear as I step out into the parking lot and the door slaps back behind me, startling up a murder of crows from a roadkill on the other side of the street. They flap heavily up and go wheeling away, cawing blackly down the length of Lost Lake.

Armound Pollon

It is simple numbers, no? It does not take a genius, even an English could do it! Ha. 50 Mbf × 24 acres = 1,200 Mbf. This figure means 1.2 million board feet of standing timber; $90/Mbf × 1,200 Mbf = $108,000 stumpage. This I pay to the owner of his land. The sawmill pays me $400,000. I pay for the trucking, $72,000. Equipment costs ($144,000), but I own my own, and clear-cutting takes no care. My loggers go in and out of there. I pay them by the day. This is just one job we do. I have seven crews. The estimate for labor is $72,000. It includes my wage. I make my money by the tree. It took four months to do his work. The bottom line profit was $4,000, when it all was through. So you see. What's to think? This is what they say is black and white. And this is why I paid Dirk's way to accounting. To handle the books when we began this business his mother did.

You cannot be too—how do they say—*precious* about such things. Trees grow back. This is a fact. Like that Gary Hazen who used horses all those years to bring out the wood! This is no joke. You cannot make money like that! And so you don't make tractor tracks? They work too slow and take too much care and it was him alone morning until night. This was fifteen years ago. Before he had sons he could yoke and started strolling through the woods bowing colored ribbons around trees for other people like me to come quick to cut with my men and machines. Oh, he could still make me laugh.

"Garee," I would say, trying to be oh so serious. How does one explain? It's all in the math. If you can count! For the wood he brought out he could've added on his two hands!

We French are the true loggers in these woods.

Susan Hazen

The friendly enough question Lucy Pfeiffer used to always ask me is whether I grew tired of eating according to the season. She thought of us Hazens cursed to meals of cabbages, potatoes, and parsnips all winter long. I had to tell her: No. Nor have I ever grown tired of green peas and fresh corn and the crisp of lettuce during the summer or, in the autumn, turnips and squash, though I would not eat a turnip in the summer or anything but dried peas in February. Most have come to depend on grocery stores like the North Way, and some folks I know can't even say whether a carrot comes dug out of the ground or plucked off a bush.

Of course, ours isn't the life for everyone, and I'd be the first to admit that living as we choose to takes work—all our time. The list of things to do never ends; it scrolls longer and longer. There is always the next season to come, to wrap up, to get ready for. But it has seemed to me, too, that we've fallen out of sync with our world, which works in specific and particular ways, which means certain things to do and eat during each summer, fall, winter, and spring. And though it's true that my work is hard and kitchen-hot and never done, I have found a certain comfort in learning to depend on the term and turn of my own produce, a consolation of the worth of what I do that can't be bought prepackaged from a store.

It's what I'd wanted desperately to make Josephine Roy take note of when she'd stopped by the house to question me. I wanted her to grasp the why behind the need that drove the "remarkable" hunting we did, the duty my husband fulfilled by hunting with our sons, and the thanks we felt.

We sat across from each other at the kitchen table with mugs of honey-sweetened tea on the table between us. She sat bolt upright in her starched-stiff green uniform, looking around at the inside of our house, the blue and white kitchen I'd painted myself, my oiled, cast-iron skillets hanging down alongside the bouquets of purple lupines I'd left to dry. She'd never been invited into our home before. This was official business. I felt it must be that Officer Roy had a grudge against my husband, and who could blame her? Since Brad had left, Gary hadn't exactly gone out of his way to welcome her to Lost Lake. Because she didn't do her job the same way Brad had done his, he treated her as if she wasn't doing it as well. I could not blame her for resenting him for that; I could resent it myself. But I couldn't see that the situation would be helped at all by Officer Roy putting him in jail.

Officer Roy took a pad of paper and a pen out of her front pocket that she wrote in while I spoke, zeroing in on Gary about our tags. *You bought a license last year? Did you buy a license this year? Do you plan to fill your tag?*

We used every morsel we took from the world, I told her. Gary David, I said, had been out there at Armound Pollon's cut with his father all day. She looked up from her pad, and I met her eyes—a dark, deep blue. She'd stopped writing. She looked away first. She had a tissue in her pocket and she took it out and wiped her nose. She closed her pad and stood to go.

"Thank you for your time, Susan. You've been very helpful."

SATURDAY I WOKE thinking: *Applesauce.*

After a quick breakfast of toast and coffee, I started a mixture of half maple syrup and half water boiling on the stove and into the roiling liquid I dropped sixths of washed, cored, unpeeled apples. I covered and kept cooking them while I worked at my other chores until I could slide a fork into any chunk and the slices began to glaze. The less cooking the better the flavor, my mother always insisted. Most of the time it took, besides the cutting and sterilizing, was spooning the sauce into jars. After I'd sealed them, I stuck on the dated labels I'd written out. When I had a box full, two rows of eight jars, I lugged them down to the cellar and ordered them on the shelves.

By the time I finished, the day had grown almost as dark again as it had been when Gary and the boys left the house that morning. Without my realizing it the weather had turned frosty, the windows inside sweated so that I couldn't see out. I heard the Ford grumble down the drive, but I only heard one door slam, hard.

Gary, and he was by himself, again.

I turned to the back door and waited with my hands folded in my apron while he stomped off his boots on the porch. He burst in, loaded for bear as my mother used to say, his face awfully set, terribly determined. He stood fuming, framed broad-shouldered, filling the doorway, looking at me almost accusatorily, as if whatever had happened out there between them this time was at least partially my fault. His eyes had gone from their usual steel blue to an icier, slate gray. He wiped the sleeve of his mackinaw under his nose. He started to speak, and then turned away as if he were going to go back out of the door, turned back again: "Now you know what that son of yours said? Do you know what Kevin just did?" he said. Gary made to go right and then walked back left. He clapped his palm against the back of his neck. "Can you believe it? He said he's going to *skip* his buck this season! And when I asked him why he said it was because Jeanie didn't like it. *She* doesn't think hunting is *right!*"

"Gary."

"That's what he said, Susan!" He made a fist. "Oh, don't worry. I didn't *do* anything to him. I was careful. I *controlled* myself."

"What did you say?"

"What do you think I said? What could I say? I told him *no*. Absolutely not! He's not going to miss this hunt. I can't imagine what goes on in that boy's head. And with Officer Roy hot on my trail, too! He won't be happy until I'm behind bars."

Gary looked at me, frankly floored—Kevin's way of thinking so outrageously wrong to him—and when I still didn't answer, now that he'd finally given me a chance to respond, he cried out, "Oh, hell, Susan! Don't tell me you're going to defend him on this one, too? Why aren't you ever on *my* side? I just don't know," he said tiredly. "I don't get it, Susan. What am I missing? What's going on?"

"It's not that I'm on his side," I said calmly, being reasonable, trying to begin a discussion about what Kevin's decision might mean to us as a family, what we should do about it as his parents. Our younger son knew what the day meant to us. He'd never missed a hunt before. But Gary was up in arms; he wasn't listening. He'd already turned and was marching toward the back door. "Gary Hazen, don't you walk away from me while I'm talking to you!" The mudroom door banged shut behind him.

I let out a breath. I leaned over the sink and circled a porthole in the glass to watch my husband disappear into the dark beyond the cast of the kitchen light. Within minutes I heard the *thwock!* of the heavy maul and the falling dry block-tumble of wood being split. A piece shot off and cracked as violently against the barn wall as if a mule had kicked it. Gary switched on the floodlights to retrieve the wood. From the window I could see his shadow, thrown monstrously huge across our yard, rising up to reap down again and again without pause.

FOR SUPPER THAT NIGHT I brought up from the cellar new potatoes and the crisp of a fresh cabbage, as well as the last four venison steaks in the freezer. By the following week the plan was to have fresh meat; this was the cycle of our seasons. There is a time for everything, I thought, glancing at the clock, 5:13, and removed the pot of boiling water to drain off the spuds. Gary had been steadily whacking the wood, and I'd only just noticed I didn't hear the maul anymore when I heard Kevin's old Dodge pull down the drive. A minute later, the front door came unstuck, and I craned back from the stove to see Gary David step into the foyer, carrying his boots down the hall. At the same moment that Gary David crossed the line of light into the bright kitchen, Gary stepped through the mudroom door. Gary stood looking at Gary David. Gary's hair was matted, swiped over wet with sweat from working out his frustration on the woodpile, and his jaw flexed with the realization of it, the knowledge and disappointment of what he must've already guessed stretching his lips, his face tight, pressured white, and said, not a question but a flat statement:

"Kevin's gone back to school."

"He said he had a lot of homework to do."

The excuse hung between us as if it had been nailed to the air.

"Dinner will be on in a few minutes," I said, speaking softly to Gary. "Why don't you two get washed up."

129

The three of us suffered through the clinking quiet. Gary David and I glanced back and forth at each other, but Gary didn't look up once. He sat shoveling his food.

When he was through, his plate cleaned, Gary wiped his mouth and folded his napkin on the table. "Thank you, Susan. Excuse me," he said. He pushed back from the table and carried his plate to the sink before creaking down the hall and up the stairs. Gary David and I measured his footsteps, looking up as he crossed the ceiling. He turned into our bedroom, and we heard him stop before the window that overlooked the south end of Lost Lake. He sank his weight into his wingback reading chair.

Gary David and I glanced at each other, and Gary David raised an eyebrow. A bite of potato bulbed his cheek.

He leaned forward. "Did Dad tell you about the deal he made to kill three geese?"

"To kill three geese? Officer Roy will have a field day."

"Domestics," Gary David said, chewing again, and told me all about Gary's conversation with Blaze Farley and Pierre Pardoe.

"For how much?"

"Three hundred."

"That's a lot of money."

"Per goose," Gary David said.

I covered my son's hand. "Oh, my lands."

WHEN I'D FINISHED cleaning the kitchen, I followed Gary upstairs to find him still sitting in the chair.

"Gary," I said. I flipped on the light.

The irony was that Gary Hazen was not a man people felt sorry for. He was not the sort that invited sympathy, and certainly not pity. He was too stubborn in his absolute belief in himself for that. I had to admit my husband grew easier to like when he showed any sort of weakness, a touch of doubt in himself, though I'm not sure that I would have loved him so if he hadn't been so resolute, sure in the rightness, even the *self-righteousness* of his life.

"Kevin's young," I offered.

"He's nineteen years old, Susan." He sat looking through himself in the glass and then he said, "When I was nineteen . . ."

I sat down on the arm of the chair "Maybe that's it," I said. "Could that be it? You didn't have time to be as young as he is. You worked full-time for your dad. We graduated from high school and got married. There was a war and you went. We so wanted to have kids and couldn't. Those are huge differences he'll never have to know."

"I wouldn't want him to," Gary said. "I'm not saying that."

"No," I said. "But he *is* young; he has time to be young. He can go to school. Make choices about his future that we never had the chance to make. Maybe that's all this is; different times, separate cir-cumstances."

"Gary David doesn't act like he does. What have I done for him that I didn't do for Kevin?"

"They're not the same person, Gary."

"But they're both my sons."

I thought how it didn't matter that another sort of man would not have felt he'd failed utterly as a father because one of his two sons had said he was not going to accompany him on a hunt. But then again that man would not have been Gary Hazen.

I combed back my husband's hair, leaned forward, and kissed him on the forehead.

AND THAT WAS how I happened to find out about them.

I woke that night to the unusual quiet of Kevin's staying out all night, not hearing the banging of the mudroom door or the unsticking of the cabinets, the opening and closing of the refrigerator, his clomping up and down the halls in his hard shoes. The clock clicked 1:37 A.M. Gary snored soundly beside me. He'd fallen fast asleep as soon as his head hit the pillow, the way he always did and it seemed I never could, especially when something was troubling me. It was the first time Kevin hadn't come home without telling us where he was. At the very least, I thought, he could have phoned. I blinked back at the dark, and then I folded back the quilt, grabbed for my quilted robe. I felt sure Kevin must be safely with Jeanie, who roomed at the school. I wasn't overly alarmed, but I remained concerned.

Downstairs, I stepped through the kitchen and walked into the mudroom to look outside. I heard the *hoo-hooing* of our resident owl, who slept all day black-shaped as a hangman's hood in the rafters of the barn, and then I saw him swoop the yard. On my way down the hall, I peeked into Kevin's room. Blaze Farley smiled brilliantly back at me from the poster on his wall. At the other end of the hall, I paused and clicked open Gary David's door. I felt a shiver. In the moonlight I saw that he'd left his window open a crack, and I looked to find the lump of him buried snuggly under the quilt and stepped closer. I softly touched the sheets, patting for his black, curly hair, and then I reached for his shoulder to turn him over, the blank white face of the pillow staring starkly back at me. My heart clogged my throat. I stripped back the covers to reveal an empty bed.

My first thought was *where*, then *who*, glancing back at the window. And then I felt it all tumble down and crash through me: beyond the fact of Kevin's telling his father that he refused to go on the hunt because Jeanie didn't think it was right, the conduct of our older son feeling forced to sneak out of the house at the age of twenty-four, as a full-grown man, struck me as a bad, squeezed thing, gone twisted, and wrong as wrong could be. How could a father who meant only good for his sons have such a pernicious effect on them?

Maybe I should have left right then, gone back to bed and remained as blissfully ignorant as my husband sleeping upstairs. Instead, I snugged my robe and propped the pillows up against the headboard. I waited, catnapping like that, until the window squeaked sharp, and his mud boot snuck in over the sill. It was exactly 5:00 A.M. He'd made it home in the nick of time. I could hear Gary, getting ready to attend early mass at Saint Pius's, stumbling blindly down the stairs to plug in the coffeepot—his father who could never have guessed in ten lifetimes that our older son who seemed to follow so pet-dog loyally after him all day every day would slip out to do anything without his knowledge. His consent.

Gary David stepped into the room and then turned, removing his jacket, and then he stopped, facing me, found out.

"Mom," he said. "Mom, I love her," he blurted. And I nodded because for the life of me at the moment that was all I could think to do.

I don't know how I knew it was her, but suddenly I did. The next afternoon I was pickling the last of the green tomatoes I'd left to ripen on the sill. Suddenly the tang of the vinegar rose to explode in my nostrils, touched off as powerfully as smelling salts behind my eyes, and I saw her dark, deep blue stare, and her name was there in the air, conjured up before me as any unbelievable thing: *Josephine Roy.*

And I had to smile for the two of them. I just had to.

Father Anthony

I lit the taper and stepped out of the sacristy, turning to click the door closed behind me. Five souls huddled together in my little church who'd braved the cold and the early morning dark to receive at the 6:00 A.M. Sunday mass. A fire blazed in the hearth. In the old days the fireplace flickered the only heat we had in this building and my parishioners had to wear their coats and scarves and gloves throughout the mass. Years ago we raised the nearly three thousand dollars we paid for a new boiler heating system. Nowadays, the fire serves more for ambience. The ancient smoke smell of charred wood, incense, and cold has long since seeped into the floorboards and cathedral rafters—traditional Adirondack pine beams forty feet long—a good smell, I think. Above the altar, a hand-carved and -painted wooden Jesus hangs nailed to the cross. In the alcove opposite the fireplace stands a life-sized statue of the Virgin Mary draped in a light blue, hooded cowl, her long hands pressed together before her in prayer. Saint Pius's is nothing fancy, for sure, but it fits Lost Lake. I'm glad to be able to leave the front doors unlocked night and day.

For the mass at matins, I wore a white robe, circled about the waist by a simple, red and gold hand-embroidered sash given to me by the children of Haiti, where I volunteer at a mission for a month each spring. Carrying the lit, silver taper across my chest, I paused to bow before the cross and stepped up to light both candles. Outside the wind buffeted the stained-glass panes, the sconces that line along the walls shining up at the shivering lead-drawn tableaus of the Stations of the Cross.

Such a good and well-lit little church notwithstanding, I'd come to this North Country with absolutely no intention of staying. I'd taken my ordination orders as a setback that I did not plan to suffer for long. I accepted Saint Pius's as a mere stepping-stone: a means to a more egotistical, self-aggrandizing end. As a young priest fresh out of seminary, I had my sights set on Rome. Albany at the very least! I was full up with ambition. But, twenty-two years later, here I remained in Lost Lake, in the exact same place where my vows had determined I'd begin, among my parishioners, my friends, where I've chosen to stay.

I turned and stepped down from the altar, smiling good morning at Gary Hazen as I snuffed the taper, and walked over to fix it back in its place against the wall. He'd once told me at one of our postmass breakfasts at the Lake View that the reason he always sat in the first pew right up front was that he liked to witness the mystery for himself. He waited for the moment when the chimes rang, the incense wafted, and the wafers and wine became Christ, His Body and Blood. Set, as he liked to say, "front and center" before the altar, he could not see anyone or anything else and so his concentration could not be disturbed. Focused forward, listening to the liturgy that at the 6:00 A.M. mass I still chanted in Latin, he said he would go away from himself into the sound of the Word, suddenly return to find his body sitting or standing, though he could not consciously remember having sat or stood. In such moments, he recognized time had passed only because we were now beginning to say the Lord's Prayer. Such moments for Gary seemed to hold out the promise that as practical as he felt himself to be, one day he might actually be able to give himself completely over to the sacrament from beginning to end and achieve true contemplation and so sublimate the list of jobs that woke him already sitting straight up in bed, cracking to get at the day each morning before the break of dawn.

I liked to kid my friend that he worshipped with the intensity of the converted, though he'd made his conversion years before I arrived. Gary Hazen had not been raised Catholic but converted from Lutheran when he married Susan Steele and agreed to raise their boys in the faith. He was confirmed thirty-six years ago by Father LeBeau, who held the fort up here until I arrived and he was finally allowed to retire at age eighty-three. Since I'd arrived Gary hadn't missed more than a handful of masses that I could count, and he'd always been as regular about attending Wednesday afternoon confession.

For Gary Hazen, the atonement granted at confession was as sensible an event as the transubstantiation of the sacrament was mysterious. If he'd done anything wrong, he joked, then give him the decades of Hail Marys to say, pile on the Our Fathers. But he wasn't trying to strike a banker's deal with God, paying up on the balance of his lifetime account so that he could glide right into heaven without having to go past Go again or wait for a Get-Out-of-Jail-Free card to hand Saint Peter at the pearly gates. Gary's notion of atonement was at once much simpler and far more complex than that. Expiation spoke to Gary, not only theologically as part of the Catholic Church's dogma, but also plainly as a man who tried his best to weigh the balance of his life by a strong set of convictions in the world. For Gary Hazen, confession made sense.

One week he'd used the Lord's name in vain twice when he bashed his thumb with a hammer. Another he said he'd felt covetous of a new Dodge Ram two-ton pickup truck Armound Pollon had bought. I meted out the penance of six Hail Marys and two Our Fathers, which he thankfully took upon himself to say. He'd told me that he liked to declare his penance out loud while cruising timber in the woods, stopping to lay his hand on a hundred-foot white pine, measuring it by eye against the blue sky. And though I had a bit of difficulty imagining Gary, *Sound of Music*–like, cavorting up hill and dale through the pines, I liked to think of him that way, out in every sort of weather, walking along, speaking his contrition into the wind and leaves.

But it was in his sensible idea of practicing repentance that Gary ran into trouble, too. Here was a man who had fought for his country without question. He'd returned home wearing his uniform to be spat upon and given the finger, screamed at, called a baby killer. People believed he must have had some bloodlust in his heart in order to sign up on his own and go to war; it couldn't be as simple and honorable as answering the call to duty. I'm afraid for him that it was, though I still feel as strongly about the good I believed I tried to do for my country by participating in sit-ins at the seminary and leading prayer vigils at the university during that tumultuous time.

Gary served for two years in the war in Vietnam and had been in combat much of his tour. And yet, outside of the confidences of the confessional I'd never heard him speak of it other than to acknowledge the fact that he'd been there, and then only if someone questioned him directly. He never bragged or boasted about his experience overseas. So far as I knew he never drank with the other veterans at the VFW outside of Lake Serene. Whatever had happened to him over there, he kept it to himself. Then one winter afternoon about five years ago he'd stopped by Saint Pius's as he did every Wednesday, but instead of confessing his covetousness over a new truck, he'd begun to talk to me quietly about his part in the war.

Though Gary began by explaining to me that he had tried everything he could to be a soldier in the most honorable sense of that word, still, he said, he felt he'd done things and witnessed things at war that he could not see how he could ever atone for, not in a hundred lifetimes paid in penance to even the score. For these, his darkest sins, Gary Hazen did not believe he could be, or that he even should be, completely forgiven. He felt that forgiveness could only extend so far before it became false, even wrong, to forgive—he did not recognize the danger of blasphemy inherent in his thinking: *There was only so much God could do.*

It was this deep doubt in his own ability to be saved that marked the outer limits of Gary's faith, if not of his seemingly boundless belief. His pain made it impossible for him to see that the two notions that he'd given voice to were inextricable—that the very creed of belief that we professed in Christ was a result of the certain confirmation of the faith that He had died for our sins—all of our sins, whatever they may have been—if we accepted Him.

He spoke, confessing his horrors: his error in having led his men into a night ambush, triggering a trip wire and the sudden lightning flash of machine-gun fire, that quick, steady thump of bullets smacking meat, the screams and whimperings, the begging he was responsible for having caused, taunting in a foreign tongue; a North Vietnamese girl, no more than eight, whose first screams he'd heard but had answered too late, afraid it might be a trick—no men around by the time he finally found her and so no one there to blame but himself—they'd left her naked, hog-tied over a fallen tree, a rock that had broken off her teeth smashed in the hole of her mouth; the hysterical old VC man he shot point-blank in the chest for raising a rifle on him, only to roll his robed body over and discover it wasn't a rifle, but a makeshift crutch. A toe-popper had blown his leg off from the knee down. He'd been gesturing for help. There seemed no end to the stories he needed to tell. He spoke, and I listened, absorbing his words, each deed, every act. And as I listened I could not help but recall the story of Jesus's taking possession of the demons and sending them into a herd of swine and then racing the mad, squealing bunch of them over the cliff, and I reached out my hand to him through the curtain—the only time I'd ever done such a thing in my work as a priest—and Gary grabbed frantically after that human gesture, as if I'd thrown him a lifeline.

IN THE DARK, early morning silence, I spoke His praises. The liturgy washed over us, and we gave ourselves to the ritual of the sacrament. After I'd served the Body and Blood and had snuffed the candles and blessed the five of them to *Go in peace to serve our Lord,* ending the service, the mystery completed, I stepped back into the sacristy to disrobe and so became again the person people can see that I am—the man who moves among them shaking hands, who smokes and jokes with them dressed in jeans and the black short-sleeve shirt I always wear no matter the season, my white collar, a priest whom I hope my parishioners will feel free to approach on a personal level.

I unwound the sash from about my waist and pulled the white robe off over my head, glanced up from underneath the curtain of it to see my friend shadowing the doorway. He often wandered back to visit after the service was through, and most Sundays we headed across the parking lot to the Lake View next door to catch a quick bite to eat together before the eight o'clock mass. Susan and the boys were still in bed. For as long as I could remember, Susan had refused to let Gary wake Gary David and Kevin on Sunday mornings and hustle them off to work in the woods with him, as he did every other day of the week that they were home. Sunday mornings were devoted to her—and to the Lord, of course. She let the boys sleep in and they attended with her at 10:00 A.M., the service that came complete with a robed choir and all the trappings of the mass: a processional and recessional, altar boys, readings by laypersons from the Gospel and the Epistles, and my prepared homily. But Gary had never been able to wait until 10:00; by then his day would be a third of the way gone, at full throttle, in full swing. He might gain the insight of a moment's contemplation at 6:00, but by 10:00 he'd be lost to the realities of his day.

"Gary," I said and strode over to greet him with a hug, which I did every time I saw him. I could imagine the sight: me, made short, and gone balding, a regular Friar Tuck, and Gary, wide-shouldered and so tall he had to double over to meet me halfway. He was not a hugger—he would have just as soon shaken hands. I clapped him on the back.

"So," I said, releasing him. "How are things going?"

I turned back to the closet to hang up my robe. Gary didn't answer. I placed the robe on a hanger and slid the door closed. The package of Marlboros crinkled in my front pocket as I fingered out a cigarette and lit up, squinting back through the first good puff of smoke.

"What's the matter?" I asked.

He shrugged. "Nothing," he said. "Except that Friday I lost my temper with Kevin for showing up late at the cut and then wrecking the truck and I hit him. Yesterday he told me he's decided to skip his buck this season because this young lady he's seeing up at school doesn't think hunting is right. And last night he didn't come home. He didn't even call to tell his mother where he was." He pocketed his hands and then he took them back out and crossed his arms over his chest.

"That doesn't sound like nothing to me. You hungry?" I stubbed out my cigarette and steered my friend by his elbow. "Actually, I believe it's your turn to buy."

Bundled against the cold, we stepped out the side stairs of the sacristy. Beyond the bonsai-like silhouettes of the stunted pines that edged the lake, the sheen of skim ice silvered back the day's first light.

"Go ahead," I coached, flipping up the collar on my coat as we started across the lot to the warmly lit Lake View. "I'm all ears." Our footsteps crunched gravel.

Gary shrugged. "I don't know what to do, Father. When he was a boy . . . I don't know how to talk to my son anymore."

I eyed him closely, waiting as we walked. Gary's face muscles were hard at work, flexing his feelings. Then suddenly it welled up in him what he'd really meant to say.

"It's that he's sloppy, Father. Some days—" he started and stopped. And then he came about as close as I imagined he ever could to voicing his disappointment in Kevin: "Some days I don't even feel like he's my son. I mean everything that matters to me he seems to hate. He doesn't care, and we can't count on him. He isn't careful. He breaks his word. What kind of man will he grow up to be?"

I watched as something that appeared to be disgust with his son passed over his features, pulling down at the corners of his mouth, but which I knew, having known Gary for so many years, was more accurately the anger at his own distress. He coughed into his fist.

Gary held the door of the Lake View for me, and I stepped gladly in under the cheerful-sounding bell. Chet and Val kept the Lake View roasting, which felt fine. My stomach growled at the strong smell of coffee and Canadian bacon. Silverware clinked and rang above the low murmuring rumble of men's voices.

Anne Marie Burke seated us against the back wall, close to where we usually sat, leaving our menus on the table for us while we hung our coats on the deer-antler pegs that stuck out of the pinewood wall paneling. We sat as Anne Marie returned with the coffeepot.

"Ready to order?"

"The question is," Gary asked, the start of their usual banter when his older son wasn't around to hear, "when are you and Gary David going to go out on a date?"

"Just as soon as he calls me!" she answered, perking right up. "I'm home most evenings. He can ask me right over the phone."

"I'll tell him," he told her, which I knew he had, numerous times. I could testify to that.

I watched Anne Marie as she took the pot of coffee and sashayed away with our orders. I tapped out a second Marlboro. "You're a bit of an unlikely matchmaker, aren't you, Gary?"

"Yeah, well," he said, shaking his head, elbows on the table, his hands clasped before him as if he were still locked in contemplation. "He needs my help. Gary David's so darn shy. I'll never get to be a grandfather."

We'd hardly had a chance to sip the first cup of coffee before Anne Marie double-timed back toward us carrying our heaping plates on a tray. I leaned away from the table, clearing back the silverware for her to leave a place for our food.

While we were eating I told Gary again how sorry I was that I wouldn't be able to go with them on opening day that season. "The bishop down in Albany has called a special meeting of the upstate parishes. Those Southern Tier priests have no idea what October eighteenth means up here. I'll stay to say the Hunters' Mass on Friday, get up early Saturday and drive."

My first fall after I arrived in Lost Lake, Gary Hazen had volunteered to take me hunting with him—the first time in my life I'd carried a gun into the woods. Gary David must have been four then, and Kevin had yet to be born, though come to think of it Susan must have been pregnant with him at the time. It didn't take a genius to figure out that the only reason I'd agreed to go with Gary when he asked was so that I could get to know my parishioner, to relate to him on his level, playing along in hopes, no doubt he guessed, of gaining his trust.

By then Gary had already filled his tag, and so he could relax and have fun with me working toward mine. He helped me obtain a license and loaned me a rifle, the old Winchester .30-30 that belongs to Kevin now. On our third morning out I shot a buck, a little spike. Gary had spotted the tracks in the dirt beside the log road when we climbed out of the truck. The edges on the track held, pressed distinct, and so he knew he was close. He set me up just so. "Stay here and don't move. That buck's going to come straight at you up the creek bed." He checked his watch. "Give him twenty minutes." That buck made a prophet of him. "Now," he whispered in my ear, and I sent that shot out into the air, eyes closed as if in prayer. The barrel shook, and I jerked at the trigger, but the Lord must have been with me, a real miracle of marksmanship is what Gary, Rick, and Brad kidded me at Rick's Place celebrating over pints of beer afterward, because I hit that buck perfectly, in the ribs of his chest, just down behind his right foreleg, dropped him without a chase.

"I was thinking of our first hunt," I said.

Gary glanced up at me. "Pretty impressive shot," he grinned. "Cleanest kill I saw all season."

"You've been telling that story for years. I wonder what kind of sin that is?"

"Flattery?"

"So it wasn't the cleanest kill you saw all season?"

"Let's call it 'praise,' Father. I'm clean on this one, right? No sin there."

"It's too close to call," I smiled back. I pushed aside my plate.

"What I could really use now is a nap," I said and lit my last cigarette of the morning. I sighed. "It'll take Lent to get me to quit again."

We rose to grab our coats, and I fished in my pockets and pitched in my part, leaving Anne Marie a two-dollar tip. I followed Gary to the register.

"Maybe he lost my number," Anne Marie said as she rang up our bill. She quickly scribbled it on a napkin and handed it to Gary with his change. She smiled like it was their joke, but I know we both saw the tightness that crinkled at the corners of her eyes.

The sun was up, beaming long across the lake, when we walked out. The early winter's dawn had a strange black light effect on our hamlet, lending everything before us, even Gary's ancient red and white pickup truck, a pearly luminescence. The sheer breathtaking beauty of the place—of the silver water and the dark green pines and the mist-blue of mountains beyond in the dawn that stretched out so magnificently before us—could have led some to mistakenly believe that this was tame country, a safe haven for tourists, but the low, long, swiftly changing sky hinted at the wild that lay just beyond the gapped inlet of Cold River. An ominous battleship-blue strip of gray dominated the horizon, backlit by a pale, dirty yellow glow. It was, those of us who lived here knew, a dangerous sky, glowering a dare, threatening the possibility of snow, and maybe, just maybe, the first big one of a foot to three feet, or more. We were always at the mercy of the weather up here. When the winter winds that swept the lake stopped, in that sudden still, the howl of utter silence could make the place seem wilder still. In the deep of winter the ice shrieked and tore, crashing as loudly as summer's thunder.

A stiff, freezing breeze swept across the lake, thrashing the tops of the pines that lined the shore. The limbs waved frantically back and forth as if they were trying to get our attention. Crooked wood, everyone called it up here—all the limbs grown sticking out in one direction, blown south—left that way even when there wasn't a ripple on Lost Lake and the skies appeared a placid blue. They'd grown to anticipate the weather they'd lived in every moment of their entire lives, from seedlings on up, holding on for their very lives, indomitable roots gripping solid rock, the trunks and limbs above frozen into permanent postures of being flailed, no two just alike, surviving as best they could, going with the gale.

Before he climbed into his truck to get on with his day, I gave my friend another hug. I held him there like that in the parking lot with his hands caught down at his sides.

"God loves you, Gary," I said, looking up at him to let him know how much I meant it, and then I said to him what I'd been waiting to say all morning without stooping to preach to him. "They're good boys, both of them."

"That's what Susan said."

Stomping off the cold inside the sacristy, I shrugged out of my coat, took down my vestments, and slipped them on over my head. I draped on my stole and looked into the vanity mirror to even its length. In the reflection, I could see through the window behind me that Gary hadn't moved. He was stuck sitting in the cab of his truck where I'd left him, staring out at the now swiftly slating lake.

It had begun to snow, a sudden squall of fat, wet flakes that stuck on the road and whited over his windshield. I turned away from that looking glass, thinking that maybe I'd been too subtle. Perhaps I should have said more. Above us, the bell in the tower began to toll, calling the eight o'clockers to the next mass.

Kevin

No sharp-eyed Huntress showering arrows through the halls... Kevin's palms were soaked and his heart was booming. He couldn't seem to catch his breath. He was deathly afraid that as soon as he stood before his peers the hard-learned lines he'd rehearsed flawlessly in the woods before his older brother would fly out of his head, and he'd be left standing there, gaping, with nothing to say. But the long passage didn't desert him. Mr. Weeser lifted his chin and said, "Hazen." It was Kevin's turn on the alphabetized roster, and he forced himself to fold the paper away and stood, pushing up on the desk, and looked out at all his classmates looking blankly back at him.

He fixed his eyes on the map of ancient Greece Mr. Weeser had tacked to the bulletin board on the back wall of the classroom to trace Odysseus's circuitous route home to his wife and son in Ithaca. He took a deep breath and began. He finished, standing there, surrounded by silence. The overhead fluorescence buzzed the room. He blinked, glancing around. It seemed he'd put everyone to sleep.

"Nicely done, Kevin," Mr. Weeser said approvingly and then he began to clap, which he hadn't done for anyone else, and one or two of the other students applauded as well. Kevin sat, and the next student listed on the roll reluctantly stood—blanched pale and willowing about as if she really was going to faint and fall out—but, inside, Kevin felt a sudden soaring elation, freed, his blood roaring in his ears. He glanced over at Mr. Weeser listening closely to the next student as she stumbled through her lines, nodding encouragement to her. Kevin wanted to be a teacher.

He rushed back to Jeanie's room in a sweat to tell her the news. He thought she'd be thrilled, too. Everything seemed to make perfect sense. It seemed he'd figured out some giant, complex cosmic riddle—his life!

But when he banged open the door to her dorm room, Kevin saw that Jeanie was still in bed. Since he'd returned to school unexpectedly on Saturday she'd been acting distant toward him. They hadn't made love immediately the way they always had when he'd come back to her before. Jeanie insisted it was because she wasn't feeling well. She thought she might have caught a stomach bug. When he'd shown her the cut on his lip, she'd actually gasped. "He *hit* you? He can't hit you. That's *abuse*," she said, touching his mouth. "You have to call the police, Kevin. You could have your father arrested for assault." Even though she hadn't been feeling well herself, she'd gotten up to swab the cut clean and had kissed it better. But she hadn't tried to hide her displeasure when Kevin told her the rest.

"So you're still going to go?" she said. "Is that it? What are you saying, Kevin? What are you trying to tell me? You promised."

"No. I mean I don't know. The point is I told him I wasn't going. I did exactly what I promised you I'd do."

Fortunately, later that night, Jeanie had begun to feel better. The trouble in her stomach eased, and she'd warmed up to him. When

Kevin made the decision to stay over for the night, he'd had the feeling he was taking a stand against his father's authority over him, but when he'd awakened Sunday morning knowing how worried his mother must have been about him because he hadn't called and told her where he was, he hadn't felt so sure.

Now, though, not only was Jeanie still in bed, she was still wearing the baggy gray sweats that she'd worn for the past two days, the outfit she usually reserved for the drudgery of doing her laundry. He could tell just how sick she felt because she hadn't even bothered to get up and brush her teeth. She hadn't even put in her contacts. She was still wearing her thick glasses, which she hated to wear. Her hair was bunched up in a clip, and she was sitting cross-legged, holding her hands in her lap, staring down. She didn't even glance up at him.

"They're both pink," she said.

Kevin set his book bag down on her desk chair. "Pink?"

"Positive."

Jeanie looked up then, her big eyes screwed small behind the pop-bottle lenses. She held out her hands so that he could take a look for himself. Kevin looked at her, and then he stepped forward. At first Kevin thought she was holding out a digital thermometer for him to read. But when he took it from her he saw there were two circles and two lines and that the lines through both circles paralleled pink. Standing there beside her, Kevin felt his own heart going even bigger than it had when he stood to recite before the class, pulsing wildly. No one could be that unlucky, he thought, no one, not even him.

"Okay," Kevin said, trying to remain calm. "How accurate can this thing be anyway? It looks cheap."

Jeanie handed him the box that advertised *Over 99% Accurate.*

"That means there's a one percent chance it's wrong, right?"

He slid the directions out of the box, unfolded them, and spread the pages between them on the bed.

Read your test result 3 minutes after you hold the absorbent wick in your urine. A positive result may be observed in as early as one minute. DO NOT interpret your result after 10 minutes. You have a positive result when you see a purple-pink line in the Reference Window and a purple-pink line in the Test Window. Even if the lines are very light, this means the pregnancy hormone (hCG) was detected in your urine. You can assume you are pregnant and should consult your doctor.

"How long ago did you take it?"

Jeanie shrugged. "Not too long, I don't think."

They sat side by side staring down at the test laid between them on the bed.

TOGETHER, WALKING SO THAT their arms touched and they bumped shoulder to shoulder, but somehow never quite holding hands, Jeanie and Kevin walked the two blocks into town and bought a second test at the CVS. Back at the dorm, Jeanie said, "I'll be right back," and let herself out through the door, taking the plastic bag with the test in it with her, and padded down the hall alone to the common bathroom with its showers and individually partitioned stalls.

Kevin stopped before the window and stared out at the other students walking reasonably to and from class. A snowball fight broke out in the middle of the quad. A hollering charge ended with everyone collapsing in the snow, laughing. Their happy cries flew out over the white campus.

What could be taking her so long?

All Kevin knew was that Jeanie had made her feelings clear—

he'd known where she stood on this issue, too—long before it had come to this, and she wasn't even the one who'd been raised Catholic.

Behind him, Jeanie stepped in and quietly closed the door behind her. She held out the second test for him. Kevin looked at her face, trying to read her eyes for signs before he took it from her. He caught his breath and looked down at the test to interpret the results for himself: two pink lines.

Kevin sank back on the bed and buried his face in his hands.

Gary Hazen

Gromley's Turkey and Fowl Farm lies north of Lake Serene. I'm slowed to stopping and starting as I catch the snag of stoplights that signal the town, which is an upscale version of Lost Lake. Lake Serene boasts several art galleries and choices of restaurants, Amato's or Chez Francois's among them, as well as a franchised Applebee's, and a Starbucks, a blue-awninged Broadway Video, a brand-new, generic-looking concrete-block CVS, and a big-chain Giant grocery store with a paved parking lot. Because of Mercy Hospital, they've got plenty of doctors. Several different national Realtors like Century 21 and AMC Villager have hung out shingles to attract a wealthier brand of patron. There's no campground to be found in Lake Serene.

I'd be happy to detour around this mess, but there's no other route to Gromley's. I press the clutch, tap the break, stop and then rev the engine to get going, lurch forward. Over coffee this morning, Susan and I agreed that the amount of money Pierre Pardoe was going to pay for this job was plain absurd, a kind of waste, but that like the left limbs and logs offered us by Armound Pollon's messy work at the clear-cut, it would be even crazier not to take advantage of such a windfall. Still, the whole thing seemed dishonest to me in some way that taking the wood hadn't.

I finally escape the weir of stoplights and am nearly up to speed before I'm forced to slow and stop again before a blinking yellow caution that signals over the crosswalk from the parking lot across the street to the stone-pillared gates of the once-upon-a-time Wiley mansion, commanding the rise to overlook the town at its feet and the expansive view of the lake, too. The great, thirty-odd-bedroom stone house now serves as the main building for North Shore Junior College, where Kevin goes to school.

I sit, drumming my fingers on the wheel, watching while the students stroll along with their book bags slung over their shoulders, yakking it up, laughing, taking their own sweet time to make it across, oblivious to the rest of us lined up in our cars and trucks on either side of the crosswalk trying to get to our jobs. And suddenly the irritation I feel begins to build, and I lean on the horn. Honks of impatience flock to mine, goosing the last of the stragglers to get going. As the traffic finally lurches forward, I've half a mind to turn in through the gates and roust Kevin out of the luxury of his girlfriend's bed and put him to work.

Still heading north, I veer away from the lake. Soon I leave the pavement for the gravel drive that takes me back to Gromley's farm, nothing more than a few Adirondack-style planked shacks and a mud-chinked smokehouse, pens in which they keep the live animals. The turkeys Gromley sells are of the domesticated variety, white with buzzardy-looking reddish heads. The Gromleys keep white ducks and the big, white domestic geese with orange beaks that I've come here after. A few of those emu, ostrich-ugly-looking things, stand in a pen, bobbing their necks to get a look at me. I see Gromley is holding deer.

The fences surrounding them stand eight foot tall so they can't leap out. The antlers have been sawn off the bucks. They herd together, nosing the fence, looking for a handout.

I park before a shack with a smokestack billowing woodsmoke and climb out into the noise of all those birds and mammals kept cooped close. Gromley meets me at the door. He hasn't shaved in a few days at least, and a stiff white stubble sticks straight out of his cheeks. He clomps out onto the porch in mud boots, duct tape bandaging what I'd guess is a hole in the left toe, pulling on his gloves. He's wearing a brown and tan camouflage Polartec sweatshirt spattered with blood and stuck with a furry white of fine down. It's unzipped, and a blunted hatchet hangs stuck at his belt. I imagine, just from the looks of him, that he's at least sixty, but from what I know of him I don't think he's fifty.

He chews a wad.

"What can I do for you?"

"I'd like to look over your geese, if you're selling them."

"You bet." He spits a brown, snaking stream off the porch into the juice-stained snow and goes heavily down the steps, heading toward the chicken-wire pens. We stop before the gate so that I can look them over. Of course, the tips of their wings have been clipped. A dog-sized gander raises his wings and charges the fence, hissing.

"That one's a dragon," I try to joke.

"He's dumber 'n hell is what he is." Gromley doesn't smile. He spits into the pen. The geese fight to pluck it up.

"I need three," I say.

Gromley reaches for the loop that holds the gate closed.

"You particular about which?"

I look them over, trying to pick out the smallest ones, but Gromley has been fattening them up. The snow's been trampled brown under the goose shit that seems to be clotted and smeared everywhere.

The trapped geese give off a moldy tang. Even muddied up, underneath I see how white they are. It'll take a bucket of paint to get them to look as black-necked and dark-brown-backed as Canadas.

"How about that one," I say, picking the smallest gander, who's squared off with the dog-big one over the juice. "And those two." I point out the two females that are about the same size as he is.

"They're five dollars apiece," he tells me, "no matter the weight. I ain't getting into your business, but we aim to please. We like to get our customers back. You sure you don't want you a plumper one?"

"Those three," I say.

"Your money." He spits again and grabs out his hatchet to take their heads off, and I put a hold on his arm.

That shadowy something wrong about this job has been tugging at me since I left the house, and now I know what it is—how to kill them.

"I need them unmarked," I tell Gromley. "Can't wring their necks either." I'm thinking out loud. "Can't crush their skulls."

Gromley squints his eyes down at me, interested now.

"What're you planning on doing with them anyhow?"

"It's a long story," I say. "Any ideas?"

"These bastards are hard to kill." He smiles for the first time. "Cut their heads off they run around for half an hour. I've crushed their skulls nearly flat with a sledgehammer and I look out later and they're walking around pecking the ground for something to eat. I finally figured it out: they don't need no brains!"

"I need the heads the way they are," I say. "And the necks unmarked."

Gromley takes his cap off and scratches at his bald spot, his longish white hair hanging down all around from the perfectly round crown. "We could gas 'em."

"Gas them?"

"Put 'em in a box I got. Hook 'em up to the tailpipe of the truck. I used to take care of some work for the county. Strays and such. Wouldn't take a second to set it up. Even the biggest, that gander there, ain't no bigger than some dogs I done. 'Course I guess I'll have to charge you an extra dollar apiece. It ain't regular by no means."

Holding onto the fence, I look back into the pen. I can't say I have a better idea.

Back by the barn he has an old crate box that he's painted black with a round hole for the tailpipe in one end and a hinged door on the other.

"Let me get my truck."

Gromley stumps off to get his truck, favoring the taped foot and leaving me back by the barn with time on my hands to reconsider. I'm not squeamish about death—death is a big part of the living we do—but I've fought not to be cruel. I begin to think of the ways in which I'm going to have to pay for this nine hundred dollars.

Gromley backs his truck, an ancient brown Suburban with the backseats yanked out and no back glass, up to the box. He puts it in park and climbs out to take a look.

"That'll about do her."

Together we pull the box up close. The tailpipe slips straight into the hole, he's left the engine idling raggedly. He's got duct tape in his back pocket, and he rips off silver strips to seal the opening so that no fumes can escape.

"Nothing to it."

He leaves me standing by the black box and strides back to the pen. He opens the gate and then, for an old-looking man, he strikes surprisingly quick. He stomps as if he's going right, sending the crowd of geese flowing to his left, but all the while he's crabbing them into a corner, and then he snakes out his hand and grabs the first goose around the neck. She flaps up unfurled near half as big as him, and he moves even faster, sweeping her stubbed wings down against her side in one quick gesture and folding her under his arm like a big football, his other hand still choked around her neck to hold her beak from nipping him. The little gander rushes him and Gromley gives him a vicious kick.

"Your turn's comin', you sonofabitch!"

He pulls the gate closed behind him again with his foot and fastens it back with the hand around the goose's neck, her beak bobbing along with his hand as if she's the one closing it.

Back at the box, I bend down and open the door.

"'Preciate it," he says and tosses the goose in, bangs back the door, and flicks the catch closed. The goose goes wild in there, thumping and banging around in what must be the total dark inside that black box. Gromley goes back and steps on the gas a few times, revving the engine hard.

"It don't take but a minute or so," he calls back. "Carbon monoxide." He's sitting on the seat with the door open and one leg out.

I stand before the box with my arms crossed. The thumping, wild flapping, and panicked start slows and then goes soft, feathering, shushing against the walls of the box. Then it stops altogether.

Gromley lets off the gas and strides back hauling at his belt and spits again. Then he bends and opens the door and hauls the limp goose out by her neck. There's goose shit everywhere and the exhaust fumes reek a deadly awfulness.

"Where you want it?" he asks.

"Back of the truck."

He drops her in the bed and steps back to the pen. I don't bother to watch him snag the next one. I go to the truck and look down. They won't get stiff for a while or decompose in the outside cold. I think how we'll have to give them a bath first. I wonder what sort of paintbrush to use.

Gromley tosses the next goose in and repeats the process. I stand by my truck while he stomps the gas. He opens the box again and snatches the goose out and drops her in the bed. He's saved the gander for last.

"See?" Gromley says, grinning. "I told you your time was comin'." He makes straight for him, but the little gander puts up a fight. He nips Gromley good on the ear and then ducks past him underneath his legs. "Motherfucker!" When he snags him by the neck, he punches him a few times for good measure.

"Hey!" I yell, remembering the command of voice I used when I was a sergeant. "That's enough. I won't take him if there's any marks."

Gromley hustles him back down to the truck. He throws the gander in the box hard and rings the door closed. He climbs in the cab and stomps the gas for thirty seconds or so, and then turns the engine off. He steps around the back and seizes the gander and drags his limp body across the snow and throws him in the back of the truck with the other two.

"That'll be eighteen dollars." He rubs at his ear. "I ought to charge you more."

I fish in my wallet and hand him two fives and eight ones. I count them out into his dirt-lined palm.

"Happy to do business with you," he says, counting the bills again before stuffing the wad of them deep into his shirt pocket. "Now don't forget we're out here. You can see for yourself we're obliging in every way. You ever eaten any emu? Tastier than any old white goose, I'd say," he grinned. "And a whole lot easier to kill."

I'M ON MY WAY home with the three dead geese in the bed when I look up to find myself stalled again before the flashing yellow caution light beside the gates of North Shore Junior College. Though it was once an impressively sized mansion, it doesn't seem all that big as a school. In a quadrangle lined out beside the original house are set two modern-looking squared-off brick buildings, and below the slope of the lawn, a flat playing field with soccer goals on it that stretches to the front of the road. A few smaller buildings, which I guess must be dormitories, ring around the back of the campus. That must be where this Jeanie lives.

Snow squalls the sky. The flakes that stick to the windshield hold for a second or two before they melt away. And then, as quickly as it came, the flurry's gone, the low sky floating blue in patches against the hanging gray. I glance at my watch. It's just past 9:00 and I've still got to buy the paint and brushes. I sit there with the engine idling—a soft feathering sound like the geese dying in that black box.

When it comes my turn to pass under the caution, I turn right and drive carefully through the stone gates of the school, wary of all the students walking about.

Of course, I have no idea what it is I think I'm going to do. I refused to visit Kevin up here before, and the only concrete clue I have as to his whereabouts is Jeanie Prescott's name. I pull into a slot beside the mansion that reads VISITOR PARKING. Students mill through the lot, heading here and there on a crisscrossed path of sidewalks that takes them past the basin of a central fountain that's been shut off for the winter. These kids don't look like loggers, that's for sure, even though everyone knows that the school supports a mostly local population. They wear sweaters and clean jackets. The girls' hair is brushed shiny, obviously just washed. I look down at myself. I'm wearing my good Carhartt coat, but even my clean clothes look stained, and suddenly my hands feel dirty, though I didn't do any of the hands-on killing myself. But I decide to take a gamble. I know he's here. I might chance upon him on his way to class.

I climb out and shut the door behind me. The meter takes a quarter and I pat my pockets. Two young ladies are walking by.

The Grace That Keeps This World

"Excuse me," I say. "Do you happen to know Kevin Hazen?"

They look at each other and then back at me. "I'm sorry," one of them says, and the other shakes her head.

They pass. I glance back in the bed at the three dead geese lying in a heap. A blue, torn tarp lies folded in the corner under a log, and, suddenly self-conscious, I flap it out to cover the bodies.

I turn back to the path. I must look a little crazy or something because as the students come toward me they river out to either side and flow quickly around me. They give me the sidewalk, preferring to tread the banks of snow piled on either side.

"Excuse me," I say and a young man keeps walking. You'd think I was a homeless man panhandling change. Me, Gary Hazen, who's never stooped to begging in my life. "Pardon me," I try and two young men and a young woman stop, but they shake their heads. I tell them he's my son. One of the boys says, "Never heard of him."

"Do you know Jeanie Prescott then?"

"I do," the young woman says. "She's in my sociology class. But I don't know where she lives. Sorry."

I turn with my hands on my hips. I'm not an idiot. I figure I could go to the administrative offices and ask where my son is. They ought to know what classes he takes. What if this was an emergency? I have a driver's license in my pocket that should be proof enough that I'm his father, that he's my son. I look around the campus, veiled soft by another flurry. It's a quiet place, even with all the young people walking about. And then, suddenly, I see myself standing beside that black box with the thumping goose inside, standing by with my arms crossed across my chest, letting Gromley stomp the gas. I recognize this abrupt visit for what it is: a last-ditch effort to make amends. I could have come to see Kevin months ago. I could have planned to visit his classes, taken an interest in what he wanted to do. But I didn't.

"Good for you, Gary."

161

A student looks back and then hurries on.

For a moment, I'm left thinking of my own father—that wired-up sonofabitch, always working, forever on the go, his cup of coffee with him, smoking his Winston cigarettes, and the heavy black-rimmed glasses he wore strapped to his head, the flattop and the wind-burned back of his neck, one sky-blue eye squinted against the smoke. Whether at home or at work, he wore steel-toed, heavy-duty Red Wing work boots and cardboard-stiff jeans, folded back a good six inches at the cuffs, a red and black checkered mackinaw exactly like the one Kevin bought for me Christmases ago—a real woodsman, a *jack*.

My old man would make me do a job again and again, until it passed the muster of his inspection. I could've failed for a crumb that skipped under my broom or the mistake of stacking an entire cord of wood in the shed that he insisted was meant to go under the eaves, though to this day I'd still swear with my right hand down on a Bible that's not where he told me to put it. I had to tote and stack each piece again. He never listened. We never spoke. My mother left him when I was four. He cast out the hint that she'd gone west. Whether that meant Wyoming or California, I had no idea. Winters as a boy, I'd imagine her living on the sunny coast, walking barefoot on the sand with her white dress whipping about her, the sound of the surf crashing close. My father's "west" left a lot to the imagination, and I ran with it—seeing her stop and tuck her loose hair behind her ear, staring out into the blue ocean, wondering, always, about me.

The news about my dad was passed on to me a week after the fact, my platoon deep in the jungle on ambush. The original word had come from Susan, but it was Sergeant Haines who came and found me before I could even grab a shower. He led me away from the Quonset nearly out to the wire to tell me. "This is going to suck, Hazen," he said, hands on his hips, looking the other way. I remember feeling as if I were hovering in the air, not there, something like the out-of-body experience you get when you're in the field on half-rations for days on end and humping hard, spirited away, looking down at the two of us, as he went on to tell me how my father had died.

He'd been working alone logging in the woods when a spruce log had rolled and trapped him. No one could say how long he must have lain there in the woods by himself before the end came. While I was overseas, Susan had moved back in with her mother and so there was no one at home to notice he was missing. He could've been out there for days, and the longer nights. He was only fifty-three, and now that I'm two years older than that he seems to me to have died an awfully young man. For a moment, standing there in the visitor's parking at Kevin's school, I feel like an ass.

I take my hands off my hips then, positive now that I have to do something, when from behind there is an unearthly sound, a short screech, the squalling of rubber tires skidding fast on wet pavement. I turn crouched ready to leap for my life as a car comes careening at high speed through the lot, but what I see is even more terrifying. The blue tarp has risen, flapping frantically from underneath, and the noise, that goosed honking sound, is coming from one of the dead geese.

I jump off the curb and lean quickly into the bed to squash the rising goose down. It lurches to life again, knocking me good under my left eye, and I mash its head down hard, but it slides sideways, the tarp slips off, and it's out, free, and I see it's the feisty little gander who's not dead at all. He's very much still alive and real pissed off.

He squawks up and I grab him by the neck. He flutters at my face and feathers fly. I go tearing after him, leaning over the edge into the truck's bed with my feet in the air, one hand around his neck and the other grabbing around for something to knock him on the head with. I latch onto a handy shaft of a two-by-four to club him, marks or not, and I raise it over my head to bring it down hard, when close behind me, I hear a scream.

"Oh, God! No!"

I've got the gander's head squashed down with all my weight, bent over at the waist, leaning on the edge of the truck, my feet in the air, the club held high, and I look over my shoulder at the crowd of students who have gathered on the sidewalk to watch me murder the goose. The young woman who screamed is sobbing, her face turned to the chest of the young man who holds his arm around her.

"Call security!" I hear someone say. I look back at the goose pinned under my hand and I drop the shaft back on the tarp in the bed. Haul the goose out flapping like crazy and fold his flailing wings under my left arm the same way I'd seen Gromley do.

"It's okay," I call to the kids.

I fumble with the door but it's locked and I have to fish out my keys, and then get the door open, and slide onto the bench seat with the gander under my arm, hissing and squaloring, trying his damndest to nip me. I have to let go of his neck again to fit the key in the ignition, and he gets the meaty lobe of my ear, the flesh of my cheek. I throw him sideways in the cab, and get my hand on his neck, pinning him flat with my elbow. Start the engine. I raise my hand off the wheel, waving to the kids again that everything's really just fine. Then I back out as fast as I can holding onto the fighting goose. I start forward out of the lot, only to find I'm going one way down the wrong way, but it's too late now. In my rearview I see a security guard come racing into view, pulled along by a student who points after me. I think I'm far enough away that they can't read my license plate. I feel like I've robbed a bank as I turn out of the lot, hearing my own wheels squeal on the snow-slicked asphalt as I make my escape.

I MAKE IT THROUGH the lights of Lake Serene and halfway home before I find a comfortable way to get the little gander tucked under

164

the wing of my arm with my right hand clamped around his beak so that he can't sneak any more nips at me. He's crapped all over the seat, and it's on my pants and hands. He keeps retching, an even hoarser honk, from the gas or maybe from my choking him to calm him down. It is not a pretty sound. I ought to go and get my money back from that Gromley. I feel a dull ache starting at the back of my skull. I grimace in my rearview, seeing that the damn goose has given me a wallop that's going to deepen into a shiner under my left eye. My cheek and ear have been rasped red.

When I stop at the Agway in Upper Lake to go in and buy the paint, I have to hold down the goose and then jump away from him to get out of the cab before he can get another lick in. I leave him sitting in the driver's seat in front of the steering wheel looking out. Some old-timer gives me a toothless grin.

"Got you a nice pet goose there. What's the little fellow's name?"

I buy spray paint, little cans of matte black and brown, and masking tape. Brushes aren't cheap. I don't really have a plan.

The woman who rings up my order says sympathetically about my blackening eye, "I should see the other guy, right?"

The goose won't let me back in the cab. When I come up to the glass, he stands on the other side glaring, daring me to try it. A woman and her little girl go by hand in hand, staring.

They pass and before another crowd can gather I open the door and cover my ears and face with my elbows and arms and go plowing in, pushing the goose back against the opposite door. He gets in a couple of strikes before I get settled on the seat and hug him to me again, the bag with the paint and brushes knocked to the floorboard at our feet.

"Just sit still," I say, "would you, goddamnit, please?"

Gary David

"Don't ask," Dad said, fluttering the live goose loose in the yard. It flapped weakly on the snow, a little gander, I saw. When the gander caught sight of me standing by the chopping block with an axe in my hand, he whirled and hunched his wings, hissing with his head low, neck out. Then he hacked again, screeched, and waddled off poking around the yard for something to eat.

I stepped up to the truck, smelling the mess. He had crap on his clothes and the beginnings of a purpling black under his left eye, edged with a tint of yellow, the angry color of the sky left over Lost Lake in the wake of a storm.

Dad yanked back the tarp, and we stood looking down at the other two geese that were laying heavily lax, in attitudes of pure repose: undoubtedly dead. We each grabbed a goose by its neck and dragged them into the barn where we could work on them. Dad pulled the cord on the bulb light above the workbench, and we laid them out side by side.

"The paint's on the floorboard."

I brought the Agway bag back and set the cans and brushes beside the geese on the workbench. The gander stood at the doorway peeking in at us.

"I thought Mr. Pardoe said he wanted three geese." Dad always did exactly what he promised he'd do, no excuses.

"Two's what they get," he answered. "Six hundred's almost enough for a job like this."

The spine of our *Birds of America* book was frayed underneath three generations of tape, the hardcover thumbed the color of cardboard from years of hard use. I checked the index. Canada Bird, Goose I, 158. I smoothed back the pages to show a black-and-white grainy photograph of "Wild Geese on Crane Lake, Saskatchewan."

"Try the color plates."

I flipped back to Plate 22 before I found them. The Canada goose, "*Branta canadensis* (Linnaeus)," swam before a whistling swan, "*Olor columbianus* (Ord)." I weighted a wrench across the pages to hold them down flat. Dad and I looked from the painted pictures of the goose in the book to the muddied crud-covered white geese laid out specimen-like before us under the glare of the bulb light.

Dad sighed. "At least their tail ends are white."

Getting the neon-orange beak and feet toned down turned out to be the trickiest part. I shrugged. "We can always try a third coat."

While Dad continued to work on the first goose, I tried my hand on the second, detailing around the white notch on the throat. The rest of the neck I'd already blacked. The only problem with that aspect of the job was getting the black to stay black enough; the slightest breeze through the open door ruffled my work.

With hours of trial-and-error practice behind us, the second goose turned out better than the first, better, at any rate, than either of us had any right to expect, and I caught Dad eyeing the third bird, who'd taken up a front row seat on a bale of hay to watch. I could see him thinking how, now that we'd gotten the hang of it, we could do a really first-rate job on him.

Mom came out to inspect the geese, pinching her nose. She took a close look at Dad's face. She turned his cheek to the light. "Gromley didn't do that," she said.

"No," Dad answered. "It was my own fault."

"That sounds ominous."

She hugged herself against the freezer cold of the barn.

"They look good," she said. "But the size of them!" She laughed. "Monster Canadas! When do you turn them over to Mr. Pardoe?"

"I don't know," Dad answered, wiping at himself with a rag. "I'll call Blaze Farley before we eat."

We cleaned the brushes and capped the cans, using the rubber mallet to seal the lids tight. The gander had taken up residence in the barn, nesting on the bale of hay. Mom cast two handfuls of dried corn on the dirt floor and the gander leapt down and pecked them up as eagerly as a chicken, gulping each kernel back, his throat going, wriggling—alive as anything and none the worse for wear it seemed.

Suddenly, Dad laughed—the best I'd heard from him all week, a good sign. During a warm spring day, with the ease in the weather returning, he could joke and laugh, go so far as to clown around, tussling with me and Kevin to see who would get tossed off the dock into the lake for the season's first bracing swim.

"Lazarus," Dad grinned, proclaiming a name for him.

"Lazarus, huh? That really does sound ominous. Poor goose," Mom said. "Well, he's got a home now. At least until Thanksgiving."

ON THE PHONE Blaze Farley told Dad that Pierre Pardoe wanted us at the beach in front of the Lodge by 6:00 A.M. Billy Hirsch had signed on to fly the geese up, and she wanted to know if either Kevin or I would like to star as the hunter in the take. They needed someone to play an actor.

"Pierre will pay," she assured him—and I saw my chance. Dad was holding the receiver away from his ear. Blaze Farley projected when she spoke. The obvious follow-up question was "How much?" But Dad didn't dare ask, and I didn't dare ask him to. I still had $387.68 to pay to get her ring out of layaway at Elegant Emotions in Lake Serene.

"And there is one more thing," Blaze Farley said.

Dad nodded as if he'd answered back. No matter how many times Mom had told him, he couldn't get the hang of phone etiquette. "People can't hear a nod, Gary," she would say to him. But she had her back turned, listening, and for her part Blaze Farley hardly seemed to care whether Dad spoke up or not. She continued with her monologue.

"Pierre will need someone to go up with Billy Hirsch in the plane and drop the geese out. Could I ask you to do that, Mr. Hazen? I know you're the sort of man who could do that."

The same thought must have come to Mom, Dad, and me all at the same time: *What kind of man is that?* Mom turned around and Dad glanced up. The three of us looked around at one another, almost letting ourselves laugh, and then Dad asked the question I'd figured he'd come to sooner or later no matter what Blaze Farley said. "I'll tell you what, Miss Farley. If you let us keep the geese for meat when the shooting is through, I'll be happy to go up with Billy. Getting dropped out of a plane won't be the worst that's happened to them, I assure you."

That gave Blaze Farley pause. Then she said, "I'd have to ask Pierre, of course. But that sounds reasonable to me, Mr. Hazen. I can't imagine he's planning to eat them." She laughed.

Officer Roy

"I guess I'm going to become a movie star," Gary David said, yawning. We were lying naked under the comforter with the blinds pulled tight. The fire crackled behind the grate.

I knew all about the documentary. Voilà Films had had to secure certain permits, and I'd be on location the next day patrolling to make sure there weren't any violations. They'd hired Captain Tabert to direct crowd control.

"Oh, you'll need Trapper for sure!" old Paul Stauffer kidded him. If every winter inhabitant of Lost Lake turned out, there'd be a curious throng of all of about fifteen folks. That afternoon I'd helped Captain Tabert string out the yellow tape to keep anyone who might show up to watch off the beach. Billy Hirsch had been working his launch since the day before to keep a takeoff path cleared through the ice.

"You know," I said, "now that you're going to be in a film, Anne Marie Burke will set up camp in your front yard. You'll never get rid of her."

"Josephine," Gary David said. I knew what he meant—stop

being jealous, don't be petty, Anne Marie was nice enough, she didn't mean any harm, she had it tough living on her own with her son—but somehow I couldn't help myself, feeling ashamed as I warned him again: "And you watch out for that Blaze Farley. In the movies of hers I've seen, she's always having an affair with someone's husband."

"I'm not anyone's husband," he tried to joke back, but I wasn't about to take that.

"Not yet you're not," I said and wrestled to climb on top of him, kneeling on his chest to pin his arms, my hair hanging down around us, bringing us face-to-face. "Remember, mister, I'm an Academy-trained environmental conservation officer. You don't believe me? I'll show you, Gary David Hazen." I pushed the hair out of my eyes. "Now, where did I put those handcuffs?"

When the alarm went off at 5:30, I felt to find him, patting over the cold sheets on his side of the bed. Of course, he was gone. As many nights as we'd slept together since he'd first come to me out of the dark, we'd never woken up at dawn in each other's arms. He'd returned home to his father.

"Mr. Gary Hazen," I said in the most gruff, deep voice I could muster. "Scare me, scare me," I said. I flung back the comforter to have myself a steaming hot shower before donning the authority of my wool uniform to keep me warm through another cold day's work.

THE HAND-LETTERED SIGN over Billy Hirsch's weathered flight shack on the beach across the street from the Lodge proclaimed "OVER 50 YEARS FLYING THE ADIRONDACKS!"

Billy's father, Sam, who'd begun the business all those years ago, had been flying the North Country since the days before you had to have a license. He didn't see the reason to obtain one, and the rumor was that, at ninety, he still flew, using their plane to hop from

Bear Lake, a few straight miles over Teepee Mountain, to Saranac or Little Upper, the way most of us used an automobile to make a quick trip to the North Way or the Lake View, but they never let me catch him at it.

For twenty-five bucks a ticket, Billy took tourists up for a bird's-eye view of the North Country. But like most everyone who lived up here, he'd do just about anything he could to cobble together a living. Billy Hirsch carried cargo and chartered fly-in fishing, hunting, and camping trips to remote lakes. He was on call for medical emergencies and ran the mail year-round. Once the lake had frozen solid, he'd swap off his pontoons for skis.

Beside the flight shack, cordoned off from the street behind the yellow tape, sat parked two big white vans with the name Voilà Films! scripted in a pretty lilac color down the sides. There was no question about wearing my jacket today. A light snow was on the fly, floating about without a wind to drive it, and the sky hung low, quilted in a rowed patterning of dark blue and pale gray. At the end of the fifty-foot-long dock that stretched out into Lost Lake, Billy Hirsch's propeller whirred loud as the plane warmed up.

Members of the crew surrounded Pierre Pardoe, who stood looking down into the bed of Gary Hazen's red and white Ford, gesticulating over what I imagined were the geese Gary David told me he and his father had disguised. I was too far away to see Gary Hazen's black eye. Gary David stood well off to the side, tall behind them. Our eyes touched. Suddenly, I got that sixth-sense tingle that we were being watched. I glanced around, half-expecting to find Lamey Pierson, only to see it was Susan Hazen who had her eye on us. She stepped down the wide front stairs of the Lodge carrying two large, steaming Styrofoam cups of coffee.

"Feeling a little sleepy this morning, Officer Roy?"

She sipped her coffee, watching me, and then she cut her eyes at her son, who hadn't been able to keep himself from looking back at us, and who quickly became absorbed in checking the wristwatch that we both knew, knowing him, he'd forgotten to wear.

Susan offered me the second cup. "I thought you could use it."

I opened my mouth to politely protest, but no protest came out. I accepted the coffee with a nod. "Thank you, Susan."

Together we turned back to watch Gary David step forward to help his father cradle the two geese up out of the bed, handling them carefully as the two men walked across the beach and onto the dock.

Mr. Hazen climbed in through the sliding cargo door of the plane and Gary David waited until he'd gotten himself settled before he passed him the second goose. We could see Billy with his '70s Elvis sideburns and aviator sunglasses behind the controls in the cockpit. A cameraman sat in the plane; the harness to hold him was strapped in an X across his chest. Another cameraman had taken up position on the dock with all of his equipment. Pierre Pardoe was waving and pointing, directing everything and everyone all at once. He had a headset on and a battery-powered bullhorn in his right hand. Pardoe stepped close to the gaping door and pointed over the lake. He banked his hand in the imitation of how he wished for the plane to pass, and Gary Hazen yelled back to him over the roar.

While the plane was preparing to taxi out into the channel, the blond lion's pride of women who served as Pierre Pardoe's associates latched onto Gary David and paraded him toward the trailer marked WARDROBE.

Captain Tabert raced up and parked beside my Cherokee in the lot. He left Trapper in the back. "Never fear, crowd control is here!" he said and tipped his hat as he hustled past Susan and me to man the line.

Actually, more folks had shown up than we'd expected. Among those I knew were Anne Marie Burke, armed with a disposable Insta-matic, and Val, wearing her own red quilt coat. Rick Schoonmaker had left his morning post prepping in the kitchen of the Lodge to come out to talk with them.

Father Anthony, taking his morning constitutional, slowed his marathon walker's waddle as he came hustling off the slope past the North Way. He stopped when he saw us, smiling broadly. "Officer Roy," he said, "Susan," and greeted her with a hug. "So," he said, rising up on his toes to see. "Where is our budding Olivier? 'Nay, mother, I know not seems!'" Father Anthony beamed, rubbing his gloved hands together. "Art! We need more of this sort of thing in Lost Lake, don't you think? Lake Serene's got nothing on us."

The pitch of the propeller on the plane climbed higher, blurring up a few notes, as Billy Hirsch pressured the throttle and eased the pontoon plane through the slivering of ice. It floated free into the open channel. We stood quietly sipping our coffee as he aimed the nose of the plane at the other end of the lake and the pitch of the blades sang higher still, and then the plane surged forward against the dark water, picking up speed as it went. The hulk of it hurtled faster and faster, running heavily, the water splashing up a wake behind, and slowly began to rise. Lumbering goose-awkwardly itself, it lifted only a few feet above the water, and flew straight on down the length of the lake, laboring to rise. The floatplane became a speck at the far end and disappeared around the bend of dark pines, whining small as a mosquito, and then reappeared, climbing about in a wide arc to circle back around our way.

The plane made a low, strafing pass, and I could see Gary Hazen at the open doors. He wore the X of a harness across his chest just like the cameraman seated beside him. The cameraman on the dock followed them as they flew to the south end of the lake and banked over the Hazens' house. Pierre Pardoe continued to direct the rehearsal, yelling into the headset like a man with Tourette's.

Billy Hirsch circled the plane around again and again. They

seemed to be trying to find the right angle for the shot. The sun popped out. Finally they seemed ready to shoot, and as the plane hummed into view we saw Gary Hazen take the first goose in his arms.

"Isn't this exciting?" Susan laughed.

Blaze Farley roared up in her Range Rover just as Pardoe called loudly through the bullhorn, "CAMERA.

"ACTION!"

The plane descended so that the gusts of wind wouldn't play havoc with the goose as it fell. The angle of the camera position seemed to miss the fact of the plane and that we were shooting in town—a backdrop of pines and rough gray rock rose naturally on the opposite bank behind the scene. Before they reached the swimming area at the foot of the beach, Pierre Pardoe dropped his left arm. Gary Hazen leaned out of the door with the goose in his arms to clear the pontoons and Billy Hirsch banked steeply, slowing almost to a stall. The weight of the harness and the blast of the wind stretched Gary Hazen's mouth straight across his face and plastered his hair. Susan reached out and grabbed my arm. Gary Hazen threw the goose out of the plane.

For a second, we all looked up open-mouthed. The goose, left behind in the sky as the plane balanced straight and roared ahead to pull out of the dive, did look like a Canada. It arced gracefully out into the air, neck stretched, and paused, jerked short, as if it had been stopped by a shot; but then, that quick, with the loss of momentum, its clipped wings flapped straight up over its head, and the goose did an ungainly half-flip and plummeted, twirling butt first into the lake. It hit with a *smack* sharp enough to be heard from shore.

A stillness filled the trailing silence left by the plane, and then Val popped, burst out in laughter, and then we were all laughing and laughing, crying we were laughing so hard, grabbing onto each other's arms.

Pierre Pardoe glared at us purple-faced, and then he began to scream in French into his headset.

Billy Hirsch had to land the plane and Gary Hazen and the cameraman unhooked their harnesses to climb back out onto the dock. Pierre Pardoe began to flap his arms in front of Gary Hazen as if it were his fault. Gary Hazen was standing very still, his face turning a much more alarming shade of red than the hue of embarrassment that colored Pierre Pardoe's. I'd been faced with that look. Before I'd even realized the position I was putting myself in, I'd left Susan and Father Anthony fenced off behind the yellow tape, ducked under it, and stepped quickly out onto the dock, hurrying to put a stop to this before someone else got punched and charges filed. I caught sight of Blaze Farley double-timing toward them, too, her boot heels hurrying the wood behind me as I reached the far end.

"Mr. Pardoe," I said, "I'm Environmental Conservation Officer Roy."

He turned his wrath on me. "What!" he screamed. "*Who?* I am surrounded by *yo-kels!*"

Gary Hazen ground his jaw looking at Pierre Pardoe, and then he grabbed the other goose and barged off the dock.

"Time is money, you people! Let's film the other shot while we're waiting for them to fix this goose so it works right!"

His crew scrambled for the wardrobe trailer. Gary David appeared in a brand-new hunting outfit. He looked like an advertisement for Cabela's. When he saw me, he grinned sheepishly.

A picture-perfect, camouflaged duck blind had been constructed beside the reeds and cattails at the far end of the beach. Pierre Pardoe stood Gary David in place and posed him so that he was leaning out of the dark box, and a technician brought him an over and under shotgun and a box of shells. The shotgun shone brand-new. I stayed in listening range only long enough to hear Gary David shyly ask what it was he was supposed to be shooting at. Pierre Pardoe removed his hands from his hips and pointed over the lake. "At the sky! There!"

Susan stood by her husband. Gary Hazen had laid the goose out flat on the tailgate and taken a hand drill from his toolbox and was turning it to bore through the goose's beak.

"Some show, huh?" Captain Tabert winked. Val and the rest of that crowd had piled into Rick's Place after Rick to have a hot toddy or two while they waited for Act Two. Blaze Farley, the breezes ruffling the faux fur of her ankle-length coat, stood alone at the end of the dock, feet close together, hands in her pockets, looking off across the empty, gray expanse of the lake. It reminded me of a scene I believed I might have remembered her in, but I couldn't recall which one, or if, in fact, she was performing it for us for the first time right then.

Gary David took aim at the sky.

"ACTION!"

He pulled off two shots in quick succession.

"CUT! CUT!"

Gary David banged out twelve more takes before he ran out of shells.

Pierre Pardoe sent one of his assistants to ask for the second goose, and Gary Hazen strode back past us with it under his arm. He'd taken a mess of lead fishing weights from his tackle and wired them through the beak and tied clear fishing line around the wings to hold them down to its sides. He climbed back into the plane and began to buckle his harness without waiting for any further instructions from Pierre Pardoe.

When Gary David stepped off the beach, the little crowd now watching from the front porch of Rick's Place with drinks in hand cheered for him. "Our hero!" Anne Marie Burke flashed a picture, immortalizing his sweet embarrassment.

Billy Hirsch revved the plane and launched out of the cleared channel. The plane rose slowly and wheeled around. Everyone was in place. Blaze Farley stood beside Pierre Pardoe as he spoke into the headset. He rehearsed Billy Hirsch through two more passes. When the plane swung around again, he called for the camera.

"ACTION!"

The plane glided in as close as it had before and then slowed and banked. Gary Hazen leaned out with both hands and set the goose free. The Canada paused when the wind caught it—stalled like a ball caught at the height of its flight—and then it turned, and dove gracefully into the lake—a true swan's dive. The feeling the shot left me with was both beautiful and sad.

The cameraman stayed focused on the place where the goose lay, the water still rippling out and out. No one spoke until the water had gone perfectly still, and then Pierre Pardoe clapped his hands. "Voilà! That's a wrap!" And Blaze Farley and the rest of his crew and his assistants and even the local crowd on the porch applauded the director.

When Gary Hazen landed, he refused Pierre Pardoe's outstretched hand. Instead, the first thing he did was to jump down into the launch and yank the cord to catch the engine. Then, standing into the wind, he motored about, nudging through the thin ice, until he'd retrieved one goose and then circled for the other, hauling their wet carcasses into the boat with him. He motored straight back for the dock. Billy Hirsch reached for the rope to pull him close. Gary Hazen grabbed the geese, dripping in each hand as if they'd drowned, the paint blurred off, and their feathers beaten from the rip of the wind, and stepped up on the dock. Pierre Pardoe tried to match his stride, pleading something, but couldn't get him to slow down, and finally stopped, gave up, flapping both hands after him as if he didn't care.

Gary David followed. Susan sat waiting in the cab.

I found out later that Pierre Pardoe had wanted Gary Hazen to take the third goose he'd agreed to paint and go up again for another take, just in case. Blaze Farley cornered me by my Jeep, asking if I knew anyone else who might help them paint a third goose. "That Gary Hazen's a bullheaded man. He lives in his own little world. He doesn't understand how film works. He should see me work! Directors put me through hundreds of takes for every film I make. And Pierre's such a darling man, really he is. You can't take the things he says so personally."

I told her I didn't know anyone else up here who was capable of helping them the way Gary Hazen had, unless maybe it was Lamey Pierson.

"Lamey Pierson? I don't know him. Of course, we'd pay. Would he know where to get the geese and what to do with them?" she asked, calculating as she chewed the end of her sunglasses.

"I imagine he would" is what I told her, though as it turned out they didn't need to use him. The second shot took. They were only going to shoot a third dead goose to make sure.

Susan Hazen

After we'd plucked and prepared the two geese, I froze one breast and put the other straight into the oven. Outside we could hear Lazarus honking at any animal brave enough to dare the yard—from a possum picking over the compost to the occasional stray dog that happened to sniff past the house. Our "guard goose," as Gary David had taken to calling him, had already become more territorial about the stake of our place than any of the champion Labradors that Lucy Pfeiffer ever "gave" us for half price. When Gary and Gary David finished their lunch and suited up to go back out to split wood, Lazarus heeled closely after them, waddling heavily. He was growing plump on the kitchen scraps I was hand-feeding him. He lived in the barn, roommates with the owl, whom Lazarus had warned to keep his distance in the rafters, if he knew what was good for him.

Deep into my Wednesday of washing and hanging and folding laundry, Blaze Farley rang the front bell. I imagined I looked a fright, sleeves rolled up and my hair awry from the clip I used to keep it out of my eyes. I glimpsed her through the glass as I hurried to answer the door, unrolling my sleeves and patting my hair into place. She appeared as if she'd stepped right out of the pages of one of those ad-thick fashion magazines. She wore a blue suit without a blouse, a white silk scarf tied to the side so as not to block the plunging view of her cleavage, and her orange hair done up just so to show off the delicate nape of her neck. Her figure was so long and slender that I wouldn't have believed the dark beer she drank, the plates of chips and salsa she wolfed down at Rick's, if I hadn't witnessed it for myself. She said she couldn't come in. She had to be in New York City for a dinner engagement and was already running late. "As usual."

She held an envelope in her hands. "Mr. Hazen's not here? I wanted to bring this by myself and say thanks for all his help." She presented it to me.

"I'm sure he'll be sorry he missed you." I slipped the money into the pocket of my apron. It felt a little thin. The six hundred dollars I'd been dreaming of came to us bundled in a thick wad.

She waited, but I wasn't going to count it, at least not in front of her. "The nine hundred we agreed to pay Gary is in there."

"But," I said, "I understood from Gary that he'd agreed to do the job for three hundred a goose. He painted two geese. That's six hundred."

"Pierre insists. He's paying him for the job. He's extremely pleased with the footage, and he's very sorry he lost his temper. We don't want there to be any hard feelings."

I looked at her. I knew she was a famous actress, but she really did seem sincere. "I'll tell Gary."

Blaze Farley smiled. She had the most stunning smile. It was sort of shocking. Her teeth were so white, each tooth perfectly shaped.

"Thank you, Susan," she said, taking my right hand in both of hers. "I'm so glad we're neighbors.

"Ciao!" she chimed and started to click down the front steps, and then she stopped. "I almost forgot." She reached into her purse and pulled out a second envelope. "This one's for Gary David. I hope four hundred dollars is acceptable. You know, you have a very handsome son, and he played his role beautifully. Acting seems to come naturally to him. In fact, Pierre has an idea that so long as Voilà Films is in town, he might as well stick around until Saturday and take footage of opening day of buck season. I told him he couldn't imagine such a spectacle. And I was thinking that we might be able to use Gary David again in some way. Who knows! We could have a budding thespian on our hands." She smiled her smile.

I stood in the doorway and watched her go—giving a honk of her horn as she flew south—before taking out the envelope and peeking inside: nine newly minted one-hundred-dollar bills. I covered my mouth.

Gary David's envelope I left waiting for him propped against the salt and pepper shakers on the kitchen table. The empty cookie jar on the counter in the kitchen seemed like a good place to hide our cash. I deposited the money there and turned to get on with my day, but I couldn't help myself. I turned back and uncapped the cookie jar and pulled the envelope out again, thinking how much easier such a windfall was going to make the coming winter. I glanced out the kitchen window at the woodpile and then down the hall at the front door before licking my fingers and counting out each bill faceup on the counter. After I'd taken in the sum effect of all those rather self-satisfied-looking Benjamin Franklins staring back at me, I shuffled the bills together and tapped them straight.

"Really, Susan," I laughed. I took a deep breath. "Pickled beets."

WHEN MY HUSBAND arrived home that evening, I noticed with some satisfaction that he counted the money twice himself.

TOM BAILEY

"Well," he said, rubbing the back of his neck. "Feels nice, doesn't it, Susan?" he said. "But we can't keep it, of course."

I'd been sitting at the kitchen table over a cup of tea waiting to surprise him. But when my husband said that, I felt something go still inside me. "The extra three hundred?"

"Any of it," Gary answered.

"What do you mean?"

"Susan."

"Gary. Don't be ridiculous. We need a freezer, a new generator, a boiler, a new battery for Kevin's truck, quite possibly an alternator. We could use new curtains in our bedroom, in case you haven't noticed. I could make them myself—if I only had a little extra to buy the fabric. Why shouldn't we have new curtains?" I stopped. My heart was beating fast.

"That's not the point."

"Oh, Gary, spare me. The point is Pierre Pardoe asked you to do a difficult job that he couldn't find anyone else to do. You did that job, and he's paying you nine hundred dollars for doing it well. Blaze Farley insisted. They have the money to give, and we deserve it, Gary. It's more than a want. We need it. We do."

"Not that badly," he said, but less adamantly, I thought. Nearly resigned to the obvious was what I hoped. I pressed my point.

"The truth is we do need it that badly. You're making this complicated. As far as I'm concerned, Gary, this is a simple business transaction. Easy math."

Gary stood looking down at the floor and then he looked up at me. A single vein stood out zigzagged like a lightning strike down the center of his forehead.

"You're starting to sound to me suspiciously like Armound Pollon, Susan."

184

Gary turned and grabbed the envelope off the counter. He snatched the top off of the cookie jar and rammed the money in and rang down the lid. He turned back to face me with his arms crossed.

I stood as squarely before him.

The two of us stood faced off in the thickening silence of the kitchen before I dropped my hands from my hips and shrugged as if I didn't care anymore. "You may be through with work for the day, Gary Hazen, but I still have to finish making our dinner." I retied my apron strings. My husband still hadn't budged an inch, blocking the counter. As I reached past him, banging down a pot, I said what I knew even as I said it that I shouldn't say, but which he'd gotten me just riled enough to feel good about stinging him with.

"All I can say is you'd better fill those four tags this season. Winters are long up here in the North Country, Gary Hazen. And you're not doing anything else to make things one bit easier on us."

WE SLEPT ALL NIGHT with our backs turned to each other, and the next morning I waited to flap back the quilt until I heard him and Gary David leave the house.

First thing after I'd dressed and had my breakfast, I yanked the celery root and parsley root, hauled them up clinging with dirt, set five heads apiece into old sap buckets full of holes to let the air flow, and arranged the buckets side by side in the cellar. Celery can last up to two months. Cabbage can be kept good and fresh up to eight weeks. With a little more care I could keep my chicory greens growing through the winter, chives and parsley, too. Winter squash would keep in the cellar, though our dry, cool attic was the ideal spot for it, and so I risked the bowing of the ladder. I stored food all over the house to hold us through. There were times when I had to laugh at the recognition of such squirrelishness, but that morning I was having trouble seeing the humor in anything, though at the same time I'd begun to feel that maybe I, too, had acted a little unreasonably. I still felt we were entitled to that money, but it wasn't as if we were strangers to the cold. We'd make it through the winter without extra money. We always had. Maybe, I thought, I was getting Lucy Pfeiffer–soft in my middle age.

I grabbed onto the rail and hauled myself up from the cellar only to pause on the top step to the kitchen. There Kevin stood stuffing a cold biscuit in his mouth with both hands as fast as he could, both cheeks stuffed out, looking squirrelly himself. Clean clothes, which I'd carefully folded, bulged hastily packed out of the book bag slung over his shoulder.

"Kevin," I said, overjoyed to welcome our son home, but unable to keep the disappointment in the way he'd been behaving out of my voice.

My nineteen-year-old stopped, caught, and then, without look-ing at me, he busied himself, bustling to go.

"I can't stay, Mom. I have to be back in time for class. I just needed to pick up a few things . . ."

I waited for my son to turn, but he wouldn't face me.

"So you came by when you knew your father would be at work? That's awfully brave of you. What are you doing, Kevin? What's going on in your life?"

He looked at his watch. "I'm really running late, Mom. I have a test to take."

"Were you planning to call or maybe drop us a postcard some-day to let us know where you were? Where are you staying?"

"Jeanie's," he said, still not looking at me. "I'm with Jeanie now."

"Kevin," I said, changing my tone. "This is important. Why don't you stay and talk to him?"

His eyes sparked at me then. "What would I talk to him about? There's no talking to him, Mom. You know that."

"I'm not sure I do know that. But you could try. You could both try a little bit. Certainly that would be better than feeling forced to sneak in and out of your own home like a robber."

"I'm not sneaking," he said, shaking his head as if he were oh-so-misunderstood. "I'm in a hurry, Mom. That's all."

I followed him to the front door and held it open for him. He paused when he heard the hiccuped hum of our old generator that Gary and Gary David had been busy working on all morning in the barn.

"When will you be back?" I asked after him as he hurried down the steps. "Tomorrow's Friday. Can I tell your father that you'll be going on the hunt with them Saturday?"

Kevin glanced back at me one last time without answering before climbing into the cab of the beaten and battered old Dodge. Just then Lazarus came tearing around the side of the house to see what the fuss was about. When he saw the strange truck, he raised his wings and charged it, hissing, and nipped at the front tire. His warning duly delivered, he turned and strutted calmly away to shake and preen himself at the foot of the steps. Kevin looked blankly through the windshield at the gander. Then, without bothering to roll his window down and ask who Lazarus was or where he'd come from or how he'd come to live with us, he throttled the engine and threw his arm over the seat, craning over his shoulder, and backed all the way down the length of our long drive onto the road—I realized—so that he wouldn't have to turn around in the back yard by the barn.

Gary Hazen

From the center of Lost Lake it takes me a good half an hour to drive out to Blaze Farley's refurbished railroad baron's lodge—Forever Wild—deep in the woods. I sit idling beside her unmarked mailbox, the unlikely size of a bronze canary cage, set atop one of the two stone-wall pillars that mark her posted private road.

I draw the envelope that I swiped out of the cookie jar from the front pocket of my mackinaw and slowly unfold it. I peek open the flap and count the money again. I tuck it back and tap the envelope on the dash. Then I roll down the window and yank open the box and slide the envelope in on top of Blaze Farley's other mail, a bill from the Mohawk Power Company and a magazine called *In Style* with her face on the cover. I close the box.

"There," I say. I put the truck in gear. I almost make it to the end of Blaze Farley's road before I feel myself coasting and then I tap the brake. Something Susan said is eating at me, and it's not the cheap shot she took at me about filling our tags.

I put the truck in reverse and throw my arm over the seat.

Back at the mailbox, I grab the envelope, lick my fingertips, and count out six one-hundred-dollar bills. I stuff our take into the front pocket of my mackinaw. The three hundred dollars I still can't convince myself I earned, no matter what my wife says, I put back in the envelope and leave in the box.

THE FRIDAY BEFORE the Saturday opening of gun season we always take the day off. Susan serves on altar guild and leaves early to walk down the hill to Saint Pius's to help set up for that evening's Hunters' Mass. Gary David chooses to use his free time to sleep in. Later, he's volunteered to take the truck to the Agway in Lake Serene to pick up the part we need to put our old generator back together, and I told him that as long as he was there he might as well take the cash Blaze Farley gave him and deposit it in the bank before it burns a hole in his pocket. But if I know my older son, it'll be noon before he gets up and showers to go. With time until then, I decide to drive out to the shooting range and sight in my rifle.

I use the key chained to my belt to unlock our metal gun cabinet and heft the weight of my father's well-cared-for Remington .30-06, an old model 700. The oak stock with its checkered grip gleams, and the barrel and bolt shine steel blue—the time-tested trombone action sliding easily in and out, oiled good as new with a thin coating of WD-40. Another key from my ring clicks off the trigger lock and I set it on the shelf.

Hanging on a peg beside my sons' rifles and our shotguns is the shell bag that Gary David and Kevin pitched in to buy for me last Christmas. Though for my comfort it's a little too close to the size and shape of a woman's purse, and seems worse than useless to go to the trouble of carrying along with us on a one-day hunt, the least I can do to avoid the waste is to put the gift to work holding onto their bullets for them. My own .30-06 shells I'll continue to keep safe in looped elastic above my breast pocket, the way my father kept careful track of his.

I pocket the half-full box of 150 grain Remington Core-Lokt bullets and tuck the rifle underneath my arm, the barrel pointing at the ground, bolt out, safety on. I cradle the rifle out to the truck and set it in the rack against the glass.

Dues for the Lost Lake Gun Club run us three dollars a year. I leave the engine idling before the metal cow gate posted with NO TRESPASSING and PRIVATE signs and climb out to unchain and swing it open, its hinges squeaking, and climb back in and drive through. I pause again on the other side and step out and walk back and close the gate and click the padlock, yanking it to make sure it's locked behind me again.

The pavilion that houses the range stands constructed of an unfinished, weather-treated wood-planked two-by-four floor and a new, bright silver corrugated tin roof to shield the shooter from sun or rain or snow, with benches set up to clamp a rifle steady while zeroing in a scope. The range faces a steep bank that's been bulldozed sheer. From one hundred yards, I'd have to fire up at more than a forty-five-degree angle to shoot out of the hollow. The earth absorbs the impact of the shells. Here I don't have to fret over a bullet powerful enough to carry for over a mile and still kill.

Mine's the only truck in the lot. Most hunters wait all year to take a few days off from work once gun season begins and so can't spare a weekday morning to prepare. But the way I think about going on this hunt, getting ready is simply another part of our job, though of course the real work won't begin until tomorrow morning when we wake at 2:00 A.M. and won't end until we've finished filling our tags. I rummage in the bed for something to shoot at, find a squashed, empty Valvoline can. I take the rifle down off the rack, hang it over my shoulder on its leather sling, and walk around the pavilion and wedge the can waist high in the dirt in the middle of the range. I pace off one hundred giant steps and turn. From that distance the bull's-eye the can presents glints dully under the waxing of the morning sun.

I slide a shell out of the box and slip it into the chamber, bolt the bullet home with a satisfying click of the action. I shoulder the rifle and sight down the length of the barrel, line the can up in the notched V of the open sights that I prefer, flick off the safety. I catch my breath and pressure the trigger, hearing as I always do the quiet coaching of my father's voice, gently, saying: *Squeeze.* The can leaps into the air, dirt flies. *Crack!* I lower the rifle from my shoulder and unlock the bolt. The shell flips out, and I press the red dot to catch the safety. Cordite reeks in the air. I bend to retrieve the brass and bury it down in my pocket, stride back to recover the can. No need to waste another shell.

AS IT ALWAYS IS for this particular Friday evening's Hunters' Mass, Saint Pius's is packed. Only Good Friday, Easter, and Christmas Eve see this same sort of action around Lost Lake—standing room only around the sides, though, as always, there are seats up front. Susan genuflects and leads Gary David and me into the first pew.

The congregation joins together singing the processional: "Oh, Joyful, Joyful." The music ends with a final wheezing strain of the organ, and everyone shuffles about, racking the hymnals.

Father Anthony bows before the cross. He turns. "May the Lord be with you," he begins and the capacity crowd in the little church thunders back, "AND ALSO WITH YOU!"

Father Anthony looks out at us as if we've just woken him up. He grins.

"May the Lord be with you!" he tries again, cupping his right ear, and we shout back even louder than before, "AND ALSO WITH YOU!"

The echo of it rings in the bell in the tower above us.

Father Anthony looks up at the tone of it and then down at us, pleased. He raises a finger to add, "And may everyone who's come here this evening to pray for a buck bag one."

"Amen, Father!" someone from the back of the church calls out, and everyone laughs, craning around to see who it is.

Later, during the Passing of the Peace, Father Anthony does what he always does in an attempt to touch everyone in his congregation. He steps down off the altar to hug or take the hand of every single person in the church.

"Peace be with you!" he says as he wades out into the crowd, reaching all around, shaking hands, grabbing people by the arm to pull them close, hugging.

"Peace."

We take his cue and turn to touch each other. I lean down and say "Peace" to tiny, white-headed Mabel Dix from the courthouse who sells us our hunting licenses. Knowing how stingy she can be about doling out tags, I imagine she sits so close to keep an eye on the collection plates. Chet and Val Harrington from the Lake View are sitting behind us. "Chet," I say, "peace," shaking his hand. "Better enjoy it. Busy as you're going to be starting tomorrow morning, this'll be the last peace you'll get for the next couple of weeks."

"I sure as heck hope so," Chet says. "I got bills to pay."

"Talk about 'peace,'" Val says from under a red hat that squashes down her scrub of Brillo-colored hair. "I wish you'd give that joke a rest one year, Gary Hazen."

"Don't bet on it," Susan says and they hug.

"Peace," I say to Gary David and grip his hand with my right, holding onto the knot of his bicep with my left. And Susan and I look around at each other from either side of him to exchange our first direct look in two days.

"Peace?" she says, raising an eyebrow, and I nod. *"Peace."*

My wife tiptoes up to give me a hard hug.

Stantons and Steeles and O'Briens and LeFevres pack the pews. Father Anthony knows us all. Even Armound Pollon is there, standing in the very back, surrounded by his clan, Dirk and his wife and girls, too. Our eyes meet. We may not be exactly at peace, but we're not at war. We exchange nods. Father Anthony doesn't miss a soul. The church grows quiet with the occasional cough, the snuffling of colds. A baby wails while Father Anthony works his way from the rear of the church back up to the front on our side of the aisle toward us. Everyone remains standing, waiting on him.

"Peace, Gary David," he says, leaning in to give my older son a hug. "Peace be with you, Susan. Peace, Gary." He slaps my back.

After the blessing of the Body and Blood, we file up front to receive the Host. I step out of the pew and stand waiting for Susan and then Gary David and Mabel Dix to step out into the aisle before me. We file up to the altar in turn and Father Anthony presses the wafer into my palm.

I receive the wafer into my mouth, letting it melt on the back of my tongue, and then I take the cup. The Blood burns a bit going down the way it always does. I walk back around to my seat. I sit between Susan and Gary David in silence, our heads bowed.

Out in the parking lot, still humming the refrain of "Lord of Our Fathers," Susan takes my hand in hers. The sudden cold makes her words go white in the air.

"Just look at the stars!"

We stop and lean our heads back to gawk up; a trillion lights glitter the sky, twinkling close enough to touch. It seems that all we have to do is reach up and take hold of them. A faint green band pulses beyond the moon, a faint glowing show by the Northern Lights. Orion poses, ready with his bow. The Big Dipper sits bucket big on our horizon. The long tail of the North Star shines down. It seems to point out our house.

I hold the truck's door for my wife and son. I shut it behind them and glance up the hill at our house as I walk around the bed to the driver's side. I left the kitchen light on for Kevin in case he happened to come home while we were gone.

Lamey Pierson

 He costed me.

part three

Brad Pfeiffer

They just missed their turn. It was about as simple as that. Two couples from out of town. Tourists, sure. They ate at the Lodge and then bundled up cozy in their down snowsuits. They were going to race their snowmobiles to the other end of the lake, back to the cabin they were renting. But it was snowing pretty good. They went flying down the length of Lost Lake through the driving snow in that squalled-white dark. There's a fork in the lake and you do not want to go any farther south. That thin ice has been the end of a few folks, not to mention deer and dogs. And it was for them, too.

They missed their turn. Of course it's posted, THIN ICE! But the guy was whirring along. He'd had some to drink, I guess. Anyway. When the first fellow saw what he'd done, his wife on the backseat, the shore at that end of the lake rising black before him—no cabin warmth of lights left on to welcome them—he realized his mistake. He began to carve an arc to turn around and then disappeared. That's what the only one of the four of them who lived said, the woman. She was on the second snowmobile hugging onto her husband's waist. They were on the tail of the first snowmobile and when they dove under she was bumped off backward, let go, and fell clear of the hole they left. No warning, she said. Like being rushed under by the sheer of an avalanche. They were all on the same ice. The same floe. And when the lights of the first one submarined under you think her husband would have tried to swerve. But it was only a matter of a split second or so.

And so they were gone. It happens that way. In my thirty-seven years of being a ranger up there it seemed to me I saw more than my fair share of accidents. The sorts of bizarre happenings that simply don't make sense logically. Though that's not to say they don't mean anything. These were not the sort of things my wife, Lucy, wanted to hear, one more minus besides the below-zero cold about living in the North Country. Afterward at Rick's Place after five or six beers, I might try to say something to Rick maybe or Gary, though sometimes I just couldn't say anything to them either, you know. The sorts of things that happen that just leave you staring into your draft. I don't mean to be sentimental. But I knew Gary Hazen his whole life, he was my best friend, and there wasn't a finer or more safety-conscious hunter in these woods, which is a case in point.

That particular night Gary and his sons came down to give a hand. Three blasts had sounded on the whistle at the fire station. Foghorn blasts that you could hear within a radius of ten miles. I'd gotten a call on my radio, and on my way I stopped and pounded on their door. It was late to wake them, and I knew they had to be up early, but I knew I could rely on Gary. I'd already radioed Billy Hirsch to meet us at the baseball field with his copter. I didn't know exactly what we'd find when we answered the call, but I had a hunch, a creeping along the spine, which I'd learned to trust.

When we arrived with my blue lights flashing the shore, the first thing we saw was the solid beam from the light of the second sunk snowmobile that Father Anthony had caught sight of from his bedroom in the rectory shining into the night sky and called in to report. Me and Gary immediately tied ropes about our waists before we risked walking out across that ice, his boys on the bank holding onto our tethers. By then other volunteers were screeching up to weigh in.

We found the woman sitting on the ice with her knees hugged up against her chest. She'd gone completely stiff, as if rigor mortis had set in, and when we picked her up, she did not bend. She was in shock. We tended to her first, yelling for blankets. Tend to the living first, I always preached in the Red Cross classes I taught; the dead will wait if they have to.

I was glad then that I'd called Billy Hirsch to meet us at the ball field. Even a minute, which we don't pay enough attention to going through the motions of spooning out coffee to get us going in the morning, can make the difference between life and death. Gary and I carried the woman back to shore between us with her arms and legs stuck out like we were moving a chair. The EMTs took over from there. The rotors went thumping over us in the night, the light from the snowmobile shooting up to flash over the numbers on the belly as Billy flew over us in the snow. They loaded her into the back of the ambulance and raced her to the ball field to meet him. The rest of us got busy fishing for the bodies with the big hooks, but there was a real danger of the crack spreading. In that water you've got about maybe five minutes before hypothermia sets in. People who haven't had much experience with freezing temperatures find this fact hard to believe. Your brain doesn't work right in that kind of cold. And the grip in your fingers goes. You've got zero coordination. It was only a matter of time, and they never had much to start.

You remember certain details: her husband's helmet was laid neatly on the ice beside her feet where she'd been sitting. He'd bobbed up, and removed it and set it there carefully, and they'd talked, she told me later for my report, but he was a big man, more than 240 pounds, and he couldn't pull himself up on the ice. Every time he tried, she said, the edge of ice broke off and he slid back in, and she wasn't big enough to help. She said she'd screamed and screamed. Her fingers were bleeding from scrabbling after him over the ice. She held his hands. He stayed up as long as he could. Finally he just sank under while she sat with her knees hugged up and watched him go. His snowsuit worked keeping him warm for a while, but then it filled with water and helped to take him down, gone heavy as if he'd been encased in Sakrete. What he didn't know was that his snowmobile had landed on the bottom just on the other side of the hole, not ten feet away, within easy reach of his feet if he could have gotten himself over there. The water isn't that deep at that end of the lake. If he'd have known it, he could have stood on the handlebars and kept himself above the ice. Maybe even've gotten his belly folded over the edge and made like a walrus and saved his own life. But he never knew.

As I said, her husband had been a fairly big man, and though we got the other two bodies out that night, easy to find trapped under the weight of the snowmobile that had flipped over on them, he had floated back somewhere underneath the floe, and so we had to sleep on that one—with the sort of dreams that brings—and wait until first light. The next morning there were fifteen volunteers gathered on shore to help do whatever they could. The temperature had dropped to eighteen below, with a windchill of something like minus forty-five, and the ice had healed itself overnight. We broke through again and finally got a hook in him. Then we pulled, strung out tugging across the ice. His gloves had waterlogged huge. It took Gary and his two boys and me and two other fellows, grunting and huffing for all we were worth, to skid the zippered body bag back to the bank. The whole gang of us had to pitch in to heft it into the bed of my truck for the long, winding ride up to the hospital in Lake Serene so that the county coroner, Dr. Beale, in the morgue up there could officially proclaim the three of them dead from drowning.

We gathered at Rick's after that one, I'll tell you. It was just 9:00 A.M., but he opened for us special and started pouring pints. For some reason that morning I couldn't stop talking about the woman's husband bobbing up and setting his helmet neatly on the ice at her feet. Both of them there talking to each other, trying to think of a way out. And those handlebars right there, nearly underneath him. A giant step away. I reached for my cold, sweating glass. If he'd have only known to step on them.

Father Anthony

I sat smoking in my threadbare easy chair at home in the rectory Friday night, resting after the evening's Hunters' Mass, feet in slippers up on the ottoman, chin in my left hand, flipping through the Bible spread open in my lap when almost as if by coincidence the onionskin-thin pages parted at the story of the Prodigal Son. I was beginning to mull over my homily for the Sunday after I returned from Albany. I decided to revisit the old story.

The message in the text came to me in a flash: Forgiveness reads so damn easily! Though the hard truth is that for most of us it takes a lifetime of living and dying to get to that peaceful place where we are able to open our arms and take someone back in our life who seems to have so selfishly squandered the offer of our love.

I reached for my Marlboros and the lighter.

That was why I'd said to him what I'd said to him. *They're good boys, Gary. Both of them.* It wasn't a feeling that I could explain to him; he had to experience it for himself. Forgiveness was like that; that's simply how it worked. It didn't arrive as a thought. You could think about the idea of forgiveness, of course, talk it out, reason with yourself, but that wasn't the mystery of forgiveness. Forgiveness was something else entirely. An emotion first, it happened in the heart, not the head. And you had to be prepared to receive it—there were no shortcuts to the felt knowledge of it. I smiled to myself remembering that investment ad on TV, thinking how my older parishioners would laugh when I drew out the sermon's motto of meaning for them in my deepest voice: "Forgiveness: You have to *eaaaarn* it."

Of course I'd noticed that Kevin wasn't with his family that night at church, and I knew how disappointed my friend must be in his younger son for not showing up. I offered up a last prayer for the Hazens that night before the hunt. *Father, bless and watch over them. Keep and protect them. Amen.*

The prayer triggered a second synaptic spark: *Forgive us, Father, for we know not what we do.*

I stubbed out the cigarette in the ashtray and stood stiffly to make myself a cup of decaffeinated green tea before I sat again to let myself be comforted to sleep by a lullaby of language: "The Song of Songs" or a selection from Psalms most always did the trick. Deep into the night I started awake at the blare of a horn. The lights in the rectory were on, the Bible left on my lap. My weathered Timex read 2:37 A.M. I leaned forward and cupped both hands against the frosted glass to see the Hazens' red and white Ford pulled up across the street. Gary had seen my lamp.

I looked and then I looked again. I rubbed the sleep from my eyes to make sure that they weren't deceiving me. In the greenish glow of the cab, I saw Kevin sitting sandwiched between Gary and Gary David on the front bench seat. *Well, well,* I thought, *what do you know?* He'd come home. This put a new twist on my sermon. With all this movie business going on in town lately, I thought I could tout this turn of events as *The* Return *of the Prodigal Son.* "Good luck!" I mouthed and flashed them two big thumbs-ups. Gary sounded the horn once more before facing forward and hastening out of Lost Lake.

Having gone hunting with them on opening day so many years in a row, I knew it would take over an hour to drive back into their spot, and then they'd have the long hike to get set in their separate stands before first light. I rubbed my palms together. Myself, I could still manage a few hours sleep before I set out for Albany. I had to admit, the thought of climbing into a warm bed instead of the cold and dark of the woods felt delightfully sinful. As much as I would have enjoyed the boys' company, I couldn't say I'd miss the freezing journey through the snowy woods trooping after Gary Hazen's wide back that morning.

Officer Roy

On the TV high in the corner above the counter at the Lake View, a weather guy wearing a tan summer-weight suit, ideal attire in San Diego, a long, warm way from Lost Lake, swept his pointer significantly down from Canada toward us, mapping out a sudden shift in the jet stream. The National Weather Service had begun to scroll advisories for the North Country across the bottom of the screen warning against the possibility of serious snow.

"Here you go, Officer Roy," Val said, landing my plate in front of me. "You need anything else?" she asked over the general melee, the low hubbub of men's voices and the ringing of spoons stirring creamers into coffee, sudden barks of laughter, and the clank of dirty cups and plates as she hustled to make room for the next wave of customers now crowding into the place.

I cut my eyes at the clock, which read just after 5:30 A.M. "Looks like a storm, Val. You'll be busy all day."

"That's what we're here for, Officer Roy! Anne Marie, let's put on another pot of coffee! Chet, are my other orders up yet?"

Val backed through the kitchen doors lugging a full bus tub. The parking lot across the street from the Lake View resembled an armed camp. Hunters carrying their rifles in plain view marched about their trucks, stomping off the cold. Inside, the tables and booths had overflowed, and every stool at the counter was taken. Of course, at the sight of me, a few of the men whispered and nudged each other, leaning forward or back to sneak a peek my way, breaking out in sudden suggestive laughter that I would never have been subjected to by the regulars I ate here with every day. It seemed to me that I most often encountered such harassment in clubby places where men ritually congregated. Over the past year, I'd come to understand that the looks and prods—the "honey" comments—were really their own fears. Gary David said his father didn't hate me, it was *change* Gary Hazen was scared of, but these men were terrified of a woman in uniform who wasn't playing the traditionally defined and acceptable role of a waitress or a nurse. Such men didn't know what to make of my sex encased in a green wool ECO's uniform, given authority over them by virtue of the badge shielding my breast, the enforcing power of the pistol holstered to my hip. They needed to make my gender recognizable in some easy way they knew how to control—and what could make me more vulnerable to their will than sexual subjugation? Understanding that, I'd been able to free myself from their desires to sit and calmly sip my coffee despite the elbowing and the nods. Even so, I thought to myself: They'd better be wary. I'd be out checking tags for the next few weeks, and there wasn't another ECO in our barracks who was better at that job than me.

Only a handful of these hunters were men I recognized; 90 percent of them were in from out of town. The majority of the jackets and caps and boots they wore appeared brand-new—Sorels without years of experience worked into the leather and fluorescent orange caps that looked worn right off the rack. At best, most of these hunters were weekend warriors. Once a year they found themselves in the deep woods, and they were too inexperienced to heed the dangers posed by snow. Most had no inkling of how quickly they could get hypothermia or become disoriented and lost in the woods when every recognizable tree and trail blaze vanished, blanketed white. I thought how the only folks who would be busier on this particular opening day than Chet and Val serving hot coffee, or maybe Rick Schoonmaker at Rick's Place tapping pints of cold beer, would be me and Captain Tabert and the rest of our barracks of ECOs and the rangers in this part of the park searching for hunters gone missing in a million-acre wood.

Val had ordered Anne Marie Burke behind the counter. She couldn't avoid me as she made her way down the line.

"Can I get you anything else . . . ?" Anne Marie Burke had almost let herself say "sir."

I wasn't in any rush. Lamey Pierson had been only too happy to help my investigation along by divulging the Hazens' secret spot, the location of the place where they parked to begin their hunt. I'd be there waiting on Gary Hazen when he came out.

I nudged my cup forward, anticipating the wait. "Just a touch. Please."

Anne Marie reached for the pot. I looked past her in the mirror facing us to see an alien flash glowing against the outside glass, as if extraterrestrials had docked their spaceship up to the Lake View. And then I saw that it was Pierre Pardoe and his film crew set up outside to film the hunters coming in and out of the diner. Beside him, bathed in the unnaturally bright, eerie white movie lights, stood Blaze Farley. She wore that big furry coat and one of those fuzzy faux-fur trapper hats with the earflaps down, her red hair spilling out from underneath in a flaming cascade down her back, as if she were on a shoot for *Vogue*. Prowling the nether dark behind her lurked Lamey Pierson.

Lamey saw me watching. Unfazed, he stepped up and cupped his hands against the glass as if he were using binoculars to spy on me, panting that happy-dog grin of his. We were in this together; he wanted me to know. He was checking up to make sure I did my sworn duty as an environmental conservation officer by pursuing Gary Hazen, even though I was sleeping with his son. It didn't matter that I knew I was being used. For once, Lamey Pierson had the law on his side.

I picked up my check to pay as Pierre Pardoe and Blaze Farley pushed in loudly jarring the bell, making way for the cameraman. It seemed they were attempting to take candid footage, but, of course, everyone in the place had stopped eating and talking to turn and stare.

Pierre Pardoe waved to the crowd. "Hello!" he said. "Don't mind us. Please! Act natural!"

The men at the counter and at the tables looked at him and then up and down at Blaze Farley. They cut glances at one another over their shoulders before going back to their breakfasts. Within a few moments, the clinking and careful murmuring built back to a nearly normal roar.

Pierre Pardoe directed the cameraman around the room, focusing in on individual hunters.

"Look at that face!

"Be sure to film that one.

"Him! He's perfect," he said, touching the shoulder of the cameraman, aiming him.

Then, scanning the room, he saw me and strode forward with both of his hands out before him.

"Ah, the policewoman who tried to save me from Mr. Hazen at the shoot!"

"Mr. Pardoe."

Out of the corner of my eye, I glimpsed Anne Marie Burke

standing behind the counter smiling and fluffing the back of her hair like a beauty queen as the camera came zooming in on me.

"This is true, no? Now that the geese they have gone I may make another documentary about this deer killing. What a phenomenon! It is so *primitive*. Let us have a shot of you sipping your coffee on the morning of the big hunt, may we?"

The men at the counter were grinning openly now, leaning forward on their elbows to see or standing up on the rungs of their stools to watch. I felt my freckles disappear.

"Please," he said.

Playing along would get this over with more quickly than protesting, which would simply prolong the attention. I picked up my cup and held it in front of me as if I were going to make a toast. My fiancé would see he wasn't the only thespian in the family. He'd have to share the billing on the marquee with me.

"Ready?"

"Action!" Pierre Pardoe said, and I took a sip and set the cup down on its saucer. "Cut! Perfect!" he said. Anne Marie Burke had followed my every move.

They turned away to set up their next shot, but I stopped him. "Mr. Pardoe," I said. "You know you really ought to film Anne Marie Burke. A waitress like her would be perfect for your film. She's the real thing, I can vouch for that."

He put his finger to his chin, appraising her. "Ah, yes," he said. "I see what you mean."

He waved for the cameraman, and the crew pushed past me to focus the spotlight on her.

"You really want to film *me*?" Anne Marie Burke said dramatically, splaying her hand across both breasts.

I put down enough money to cover the tip and picked up my

hat. I glanced back at the window, but Lamey was no longer there. He seemed to have disappeared, though I thought it more likely that he was crouching out there in the dark where he could keep a close eye on things.

I set my hat and snugged the chin strap tight, tilted the brim low to see my way past the movie lights, and ducked underneath the camera moving in for a close-up of Anne Marie Burke. She'd turned, tiptoeing to snatch the coffeepot off the top burner, her uniform skirt inching up higher and higher, and had the full attention of every man in the diner—in her glory. Good for her. If that's what she wanted. I meant it, too.

Gary Hazen

I'd been fully prepared to welcome my younger son home again, accepting his excuses in exchange for this, his timely return to go on our hunt, but the surge of pride I first felt when he slid in the mudroom door nose-dived into disappointment and disapproval again. Kevin stood, hands pocketed, casting around the kitchen, glancing at the sink, the clock, the floor, the beamed ceiling, the smoking Upland. If I'd taught him anything as his father, if he'd learned one thing at all from being my son, then he had to know better than to drink and ever handle a gun. I waited for Kevin's eyes to finally shift around to meeting mine and then, using a firm gaze, I gave him a spank-hard look. He glanced away, ashamed I hoped, and I made myself turn back to pouring out our pancakes. I reached for the boiling coffee.

Hearing a low scuff-kick at the door, Kevin had to unstick his hands from his Carhartt jacket to open it for Gary David, loaded up past his chin with split wood.

Gary David sniffed strong over Kevin. "Who was it over? Not

that Jeanie Prescott again?" By not answering Kevin convicted himself. "Aw, Kev . . . ," Gary David started and gently set down the wood like you wouldn't expect a boy to, being mindful of his mother still sleeping upstairs.

"Sit," I said and pointed to Kevin's seat at the table. I sloshed steaming black coffee into his cup to sober him up. "Drink that." I set down a stack of pancakes. "Eat those."

While Kevin dutifully sat, and drank, and ate, I scribbled a note to my wife:

> *Dear Susan,*
> *Let's call this $600 a compromise we can both live with.*
>
> *Your loving husband,*
> *Gary*
>
> *P.S. Kevin showed up to go on the hunt so no need to worry about him. He's with me.*

As we lugged our gear across the crust of snow to the truck, I inspected the low scudding sky, carrying the unmistakable smell of crystallized cold that almost always guaranteed a fresh snow—and maybe, just maybe, the first "real" one. If I did happen to win the pot at the Lake View, I pledged to use every cent of it to buy my wife a pair of pearl earrings or a pretty, hand-painted silk shawl—anything that my Susan might simply *want* that we as a family didn't absolutely *need*.

OUR SPOT IS marked by a dead-end, half-oval of log road, bordered to the east by a sheer, ice-flowing brook. Having wound and humped to be here early enough to get safely set in our stands long before dawn, we sit silently in the truck and stare through the glare of our headlights. A teal-colored Chevy and a brown Impala squat parked in our space. A neon-pink bumper sticker on the truck shouts: THIS BUCK HUNTS! We pop the doors and climb out into the shadow dark. It doesn't take a flashlight to show us by the heavy frosted glass that these fellows came in last night, trying to get a jump on a buck.

I know there are some who would call me a hypocrite. Yes, I admit, I have Susan's tag in my pocket ready to fill if the opportunity presents itself, but what I know about the difference between us is that if these men have broken one rule to try to shoot their deer before gun season officially begins, they won't hesitate to break another or another after that. Like Lamey Pierson, they are the sort of men who will do *whatever it takes* to tag their buck. They park their ATVs by the shores of a pond or lake at night and wait for a deer to bend to take a drink, then hit the brights to blind it stock-still as a cardboard target, and blast away.

Gary David clears his throat, breaking off the cold snap of silence. "What do you think, Dad?"

I try to put the best face on this that I can. The past week has been a trial, but Kevin showed up, even if he was about half in the bag, and Gary David's here, too, standing by me. We're here to hunt; we need to fill our tags. I tell myself: *There are one million acres of unbroken wilderness surrounding us.* We'll leave these men our ready stands, perfectly spaced, comfortable and safe, the shooting lanes cleared of brush. I think how I'd go to almost any extreme to avoid such men and the threat of some stupid accident. We'll turn our backs on their tracks and head the other way.

"Let's get the rifles, boys," I say.

I LEAD and Gary David and Kevin follow. We start down a gentle dip, following one of the many game trails—already scouting for sign—before starting up the slope. Underneath my feet I can feel the easy grade that the deer would take, going along the side of this slope to the lowest gap in the ridge. Deer won't fight terrain unless they're forced to. They flow with the lay of the land, giving in to gravity the way water will. Once they get through the gap they'll go from one lookout point to the next, wending their way between the humps. Of course, in our North Country they can't avoid steep terrain entirely, and so neither can we. The hill goes steep, mountains suddenly steeper. Bulked up warm, the silly shell bag tugging awkwardly across my chest, I feel heavy and robotic, old. I glance behind me at my boys. Gary David is walking easily, his breath lightly silvering. Kevin lags back at the first serious switchback. He's dragging fifteen steps behind Gary David. The second time I look behind me he's at the bottom of the path doubled over just off the side of the trail, giving up the beer.

Heart-shaped tracks crowd the trail before us, but the edges have crumbled. It's plain to see they're not fresh. Still, they prove we've taken the right route. A few of the bushes alongside the path have been recently browsed. I find droppings on top of the crust of old snow. It's early yet for scrapes.

I hold up my hand to Gary David and we wait for Kevin to catch up. "Feeling better now?" I ask. He's sweating and swipes a string of spit from his scabbed-over lip without answering. I turn and start to climb again.

We come to an opening in the evergreens, the trail ending abruptly in a narrow ravine. I stand at the top, peering into what seems to be a bottomless pit. And it's then, from behind us, a half-mile or so to the east, that we hear shots ring out into the night. They slap, *bang bang bang bang bang bang,* and then echo booming between the rows of hills. Then there are two guns, three, *bang bang bang bang bang bang.* All of them rage away. There are a few more distinct cracks. A pop. Then there is silence, a harder and stiller silence now it seems for having been disturbed so violently. Waiting crouched in the aftermath of such an ambush I realize my body has tensed tight, reminded of war. It's strictly against the law to shoot until first light, but from our right, from the east, we hear a thin but distinct "Ya-*hooooo!*" Weekend blasters, sons of goddamn bitches, crazy men. Where's Officer Roy when we need her?

We have to shoulder our rifles and use our hands to scale the roots and rocks. On the other side of the ravine, I choose a faint fork that angles us even more sharply northwest away from them. Taking the high road, we lift our knees for the difficult hike into the peaks where such men—the yahoos—rarely care to tread. We continue to push on, marching farther, faster, up and up, in deeper, and then on, up higher, and in deeper still.

On the downside of a saddle-humped mountain, in a circled clearing, we stop for a coffee break, pause to eat the sugared pancakes I pocketed along. I pour the steaming coffee from the Stanley and we pass the cup around.

Above us the close, cold-colored sky is going grainy with the hint of first light. From up here we have a better view of the low ceiling of clouds. No doubt about it now, it's *really* going to snow. I'm certainly concerned about this sudden change in weather, but I'm not worried. We're not greenhorns.

Gary David sits on his haunches, sipping from the cup. "How about those shots, huh? How could they miss?"

Even Kevin has to shake his head at that one. Purged of the beer, he takes a huge bite of the sugared pancake I handed him, talking around it. "Next time they might as well just bring a machine gun. I mean if they really want to get the job done."

Gary David shrugs. "Sounds to me like they already have one."

I allow myself a smile.

And as suddenly as that, sitting in the dark, under the good, bare, brightening sky, the morning cold surrounding us hard and crisp and clear as a shield, breathing in the smell of the coming snow, warm deep down inside our pulsing Carhartts, our week is transformed. This hunt becomes like all the others my sons and I have gone on since they were boys. And I can't help but think how it's times like these, moments like this pure still moment, that make me glad of who I am and that I've got my sons to remind me of it, to line the path and keep me on it, sons whom I trust to carry on the care for this life and the respect for it long after I'm gone. And it's in this simple flash of living that I can see the war and the killing I did clearly—the good it's done for me, perhaps the only good it can do for anyone: It helped me to recognize mornings and moments like this one, to note and appreciate them in a way and feel them with a white-flared intensity I would never have known if I hadn't ever truly cared and feared so for life, and not just my own.

Gary David passes me the cup, and I take another sip and glance at my sons. In this sudden second I very nearly manage to tell them how much I love them—*both* of them—different as they are and always will be for me, and how glad I am that they're here with me now. But even thinking to blurt out *I love you* shrinks my throat tight to strangling. I think, *This is what it means to be out here more than anything, deeper even than the professed and hammered-home responsibility.* And I suddenly realize the obvious untold reason I snapped at Kevin for not wanting to come hunting with us this season. The truth I know deep down is I couldn't bear to live without either one of them. I cast back the dregs of the coffee and snuff my sleeve, manage to croak a harsh "If you boys don't quit lollygagging, we'll never get a deer."

They shuffle to their feet and then we start again up the path through the brush, continuing our march. The snow lets loose and goes on the fly, whiting out the sky, covering us.

Val

"October eighteenth," I said to anyone who cared to listen. "Who but Gary Hazen would've thought to think of that?" That's always the way it is living up here in our North Country, a crapshoot. Mr. October posed in his flaming bikini suit. I patted his little round bottom as I walked past. The giant pickle jar perched big as a barn owl beside the calendar full with the pick-a-day swirl of five-dollar bills.

The movie people had cleared out and left us in peace, finally. *Good riddance* was what I said. Though I'd traveled all the way to the Forum Theater up in Lake Serene to see every one of her movies, I'd never been a big fan of that Blaze Farley's. Hell, I could act better than her—I did every day, day in and day out, smiling and nodding pleasantries to customers over the stage of my own counter with a migraine splitting my head that would register 6.8 on the Richter scale. If you asked me, I was the one who deserved a goddamn Oscar.

Out the front windows the snow was dumping down so fast and heavy now it looked as if Chet was up on the roof shoveling it down the way we sometimes had to do in the middle of winter so that the sheer weight of it wouldn't collapse the roof. Right away I'd had an inkling it was going to be our first big one. Even with the state plows running back and forth up and down the road, they couldn't keep 28N clear. And the TV told us that due to conditions the troopers were shutting down stretches of I-87, a precaution they took only two or three times a year. Since I'd arrived at 3:30 the barometer had been taking one of those stock-market-like crashing dives. That night the temperature would plummet after it as if it had jumped out the window at the news.

"How many we do this morning, Val?" Chet called through his little window. Blaze Farley had autographed an eight-by-twelve glossy black-and-white publicity shot of herself for him for letting them in to film, and he'd taken it straight back and thumbtacked it to the wall over the stove where he could stare at her all day—revenge for my Hot Buns calendar was what I accused him of, though he just winked and smarted off, "If you say so, gorgeous." But I knew my Chet. I wasn't worried about him. What chance did he have at Blaze Farley anyway? Let him look! Who I'd already caught gazing glassy-eyed at it more than him was Anne Marie—comparing herself would be my guess—her look, her lips, her hair.

"One eighty-eight so far," I called, thumbing through to count the last receipt. A fair number, though thirteen shy of last year's all-time high 201 record breaker. A few who'd heard the weather must've decided to stay home in bed. By first light most of the men had up and gone, but four or five who'd been huddled up against the counter watching the weather with me had decided to stay put. We'd gone through forty-eight pots of coffee. I put on a forty-ninth to pour fresh for them.

It was an unlikely snowstorm sweeping down from Canada. The Weather Bureau forecast the temperature was going to stay warm enough to hold it off and they were wrong. The real trouble, though, was hunters got their blood up, hot to go on opening day, and became as impossible to hold back as the coming cold front itself. Tourists would've tucked their tails and canceled on Rick Schoonmaker at the Lodge in a second without a qualm about losing their deposit. But hunters, they'd been dreaming all year of this, their one chance to tag a buck, and were not so easily turned back. You only had to live a little while up here, though, to know when to listen to the warnings on the weather, no matter what the lie of this kaleidoscope sky seemed to promise us one minute to the next, and me and Chet, we'd lived here our whole lives.

After the movie people had cleared out and the crowd of hunters who'd decided to risk it had headed for the woods and we'd bused the mess of tables and wiped them down and reset every one of them with new place mats and silverware for lunch, we huddled around the TV, smoking as we watched the weather maps.

Anne Marie was standing there. She'd had little twinkles in her eyes all morning since they'd filmed her, but now she had her arms hugged across her chest, flat against her pride boobs, her right hand clawing at her throat.

I blew smoke. "Just be glad you don't have a husband or boyfriend out there." Then I saw the bruise of hurt. There I went again. "I didn't mean it like that, honey," I said and patted the back of her hand. "Hey, did I tell you how great you were this morning?" How could it be so hard to find a good man? I got lucky with Chet, I guess. We raised five kids ourselves, though not a one of them lived anywhere near Lost Lake now, deposited over the country like dandelion seeds on the wind, which was a sore spot. Not one of them cared to take over the diner. We'd sell when the time came. Though I can tell you, I wasn't in any great big rush to be old and out of a job no matter how much I might complain. Sure, we worked nonstop, but I didn't look forward to waking in the morning without any more purpose in the world than to sit around twiddling my thumbs waiting for my Social Security check to come in the mail. Still, I meant it about being caught out there. To tell the truth, I'd never minded it that we'd always been too busy minding this business on opening morning for my husband to go hunting himself.

In the back I told Chet he'd better take a break and get rested up in case of another rush, the hunters regrouping back here after retreating from the woods.

On my way out, I stopped before the shiny photo of Blaze Farley. She was attractive enough, I guessed, but I really couldn't see what all the fuss was about. I'd seen her up close, and I'd stake the diner that the close-up photo she'd been so happy to pass out with her scrawl had been airbrushed younger than she was. That's Hollywood.

But this was Lost Lake.

I pushed back through the swinging doors. I surveyed the room. With the help of this unexpected snow, we had a shot at breaking the record for lunch. "Well." I shrugged. *Happy hunting.* After all, it was our season, too.

Susan Hazen

I found the note he'd left for me on the counter. I picked it up and read it. Then I read it again, more slowly. I fanned out the bills. Six hundred dollars. I felt the sting in my eyes. "Darn you, Gary Hazen."

I did not feel the thrill of victory. What I felt outside of the relief and then gratitude for a certain ease the money would afford us through the coming winter and a sudden flood of love for my husband was amazement that Gary still had the capacity in his character to so utterly surprise me with a gesture.

I made coffee and carried a cup to the kitchen table, where I allowed myself to sit and marvel over the idea of it before I dressed and began my day.

MY WORK ALL WEEK had been geared toward finishing all the seasonal jobs still to be done in preparation for the concentrated effort of cleaning and butchering the carcasses and packaging and packing away the meat as soon as my husband and sons began to bring their bucks home. I'd already sharpened all the knives, honed the cleaver, and sterilized the grinder and each of the cutting boards, taken out my black permanent marker and various sizes of Glad bags to package the different cuts of meat in—venison steaks and rib backs, burgers.

In the stockroom we kept a whole salted salmon and trout and bass fillets, and the bacon I'd traded my produce for, the crocks of pickles I'd made. We ran two big lie-down freezers in the cellar, including the one that we could now start shopping for to replace. Both were nearly empty by this time of year. I would spend the entire day defrosting, scraping, and picking out clumped ice. My goal was to get one of them cleaned and scrubbed out with scalding hot water and running cold again before transferring the fillets and chops from the other. I'd start on the second one that afternoon.

It was the sort of demanding job I purposely put off until opening morning to keep me busy not worrying about Gary and the boys until they returned home from the hunt. When the phone rang suddenly, jumping me out of my skin, I took the stairs up to the kitchen two at a time and snatched the receiver off the wall.

"Hello?" I said, out of breath.

"Susan Hazen?" I heard, and my heart caught at the deep voice of authority, until I recognized it.

"Brad Pfeiffer, what are you doing up so early? You're retired. You ought to be sleeping in."

"Are you kidding?" he said. "Sleep in on opening morning? The boys get off all right? Damn, I wish I was up there with them! What? Susan? Hold on a second. Lucy wants to say something to you."

"Don't you dare tell me how warm it is down there," I said before she could even get started.

"Eighty-three in the shade! Please, dear, *do* tell me how cold it is up there."

I stretched the cord close to the window, where I could see the thermometer fastened to the sill. "It's twenty-four degrees. No, wait. Make that twenty-three."

"I knew it!" Lucy said.

And that's when I looked up into the sky growing light over the lake. It was snowing, a regular blizzard. I'd been holed up in the cellar and hadn't noticed. "And it's snowing."

"Brad, it's twenty-three degrees and snowing!" she crowed back into the room. "Brad doesn't know what to do with himself. He's been itching to call. Yesterday at the supermarket I found him sulking over the hunting magazines again, and I bought him *Golf Digest.* I promised him a new bag of clubs for his birthday. You can't imagine the deals we can get at our Sam's Club, and there are courses everywhere down here. But he says he won't play. 'Me, a grown man chasing after a little white ball to knock it in a hole?' he says. You know how stubborn that man can be. He insists on wearing those camo T-shirts, even when we go to the beach!"

"You could come back."

"Susan. That's sweet of you, but I am *not* coming back. No way, no how. It'll take me the rest of my life to thaw out before I'm ready to die. He's holding his hand out for the phone. We love you. We'll call again soon."

"Sue," Brad says. "Have Gary call me when he gets in. Damn, I wish I were up there with him and the boys! I've been watching the Weather Channel. I hope they dressed warm. Susan," he whispered, "you should see these shorts Lucy's got me wearing. Gary would laugh to bust a gut. I'm a sight. I look like a polar bear in tights."

I smiled. "I'll have him call as soon as they get home."

I hung up the phone and turned to the window again and crossed my arms, watching the sky fall down on us, and that's when I felt the grab in my chest. The pain and surprise in my heart staggered me so that I had to turn from the window and rest my hand on the kitchen table. Then I pulled out a chair and I sat there, stunned. People will tell you they don't believe in such things, but then again they've never felt anything like it before, have they?

Gary Hazen

The country we find ourselves in has changed from fat hemlock and maple. Now it's rock rugged, spruce filled, and shale scaled. A tremendous valley opens out to our left, and in the speck bottom of it there's an iced-blue mountain lake. Chances are we'll never hound down a buck and, ready or not, it's time for me to plan a strategy and split us up.

I pick the first suitable tree for Kevin, a curiously forked, crooked wood pine. If possible, it may be snowing even heavier than before. Even so, he'll have a wide view of the expanse, the natural path ridgeline coming up, and the new day. We leave him there, looking sleepyheaded but with the hard march having sweated the last of the alcohol out of him, and then Gary David and I push on up and over the long slope. I place him at the top of the next piney ridge. Then I push on up and down and around along the same ridge for another half mile before following a well-used game trail downhill into the mess of thickets and tangling scrub below.

The single beech I find has a great sky-reaching spread of limbs.

It's a perfect spot, completely surrounded by taller spruce—so my sil-houette won't stand out against the sky. I climb up and squirm a com-fortable way to wedge myself in between the limbs. I level my rifle and slowly sweep the aimed V over the intersection of game trails that bur-row under the brush and bare briar thickets, the crosshatch confusion of hardwood whips, sighting out my shooting lanes. If I can't manage a perfectly clear view of a buck, I hope to be able to see enough of him—antlers or hocks—to piece together a clean shot.

I settle back into the warmth of my coat to wait. It's impossible to predict what will happen next. We could be out here all day. The driven snow quickly covers my shoulders and arms and the orange safety vest I'm wearing, erasing me, and I brush it off as best I can before I'm whited out again. It's grown significantly colder since we left the truck, but I'm sweating from the work of our walk. I unzip my jacket and my glasses steam. I slip them off and circle the lenses clear with the collar of the T-shirt I wear underneath my mackinaw. I slip them back on so that I can see clearly. Give a sigh of relief. As inauspi-ciously as this day began, everything's worked out all right, I guess. We made it in the nick of time. It's winter's dawn and we're ready and waiting, the opening daylit hour of the first day of gun season each year when the most bucks are shot, before they've been alerted to the fact they're in season again, and we're far enough out in these woods that I'm sure we won't have any trouble with the yahoos and their carelessness.

Then I hear the shaking of the brush, a racked buck stumbling toward me through the thick-tangling scrub. *Impossible,* I think, but know, too, from all the stories I've ever heard or even told, the statis-tics I know to quote, that it's exactly this unexpected moment that I should expect and for which I should be ever vigilant. I finger a car-tridge out from the elastic above my chest pocket, feed it in and gently lock home the bolt, flick off my safety and snug my cheek, seat the sights, pointing the aimed V upwind. The buck is sixty yards off. He stops and sneeze-snorts a warning, and I feel the hollow hurry in my chest, the fevered, hot-to-cold itching sweat that he's somehow caught my scent or simply *sensed* me in this tree, but then he starts crashing and crunching carelessly forward toward me again—the new morning's icy light catching the clacking flash of his huge brushlike rack.

There's an impact thump like kicking a plump pumpkin, the shot echoing crisply, and then a rush as the buck tumbles heavily into a white-staticked silence. And I'm breathing hard, raspily recovering from a full dose of buck fever as I shimmy fast down the beech. My rifle seared empty, the bolt thrown open, I jump from five feet, climb to my feet, dust the snow quickly off, and quickly chamber another round.

The buck's fallen just behind a tall drift, inside a mess of thickets and wrecked snow. Just last year my sons and I sat around the kitchen table beside the cast warmth of the Upland reading aloud the unbelievable newspaper account of an experienced hunter who'd been gored nearly to death by a big buck he'd wounded crazy, how he'd had to crawl himself out of the woods holding onto his own spilled entrails. I start forward. From where I am I can see the flecked red shining brilliantly. There's a flailed path back where he sprinted, then fell.

I tiptoe in, safety off again, finger on the trigger, use the barrel to press aside the buck-colored brush, and peek carefully in.

Kevin

The first shot slapped Kevin straight up out of an uneasy sleep. He'd been dreaming Jeanie had him pinched by the nose and was fussing and fussing at him like a crow. He staggered, grabbed the branch in front of his face, feeling the uncomfortable ache of having wedged himself by the crotch into the crotch of the oddly grown, crooked wood pine, and touched the cold hurt of his exposed nose, ran the drip of it onto his sleeve.

He heard Jeanie's cawing again and then he looked straight up to see the crow alone on the top branch laughing at him from behind the curtain of falling snow. He pointed his levered .30-30 at it and watched it flap slowly up and wheel away within easy reach of his sights. Rings of sound continued to ripple by him, smoothing out and out until the snow cushioned the woods silent and peaceful again. Kevin wondered who had taken the shot, his father or Gary David. If either of them had taken a shot, he knew neither had missed. He himself hadn't even bothered to load his rifle. Then he heard a second flat slap. It shocked sharply past, the echoed ripples touching lightly by

235

him again. *Good,* he thought, *because if we get two, we can leave. We'd
have to leave, or we wouldn't be able to pack out all the meat.* Though
if he knew his father, *Mr. Gary Hazen,* they would carry out every
single slab and scrap of venison and usable hoof and horn, regardless
if they *could* or not. His father made a special carpenter's glue from
the hooves, rigged gun racks with the wired forelegs. He even took the
incredible time necessary to hand-buff indestructible knife handles
from the horns. So Kevin sat cramped and cold in the tree, hoping
they had gotten two, but hoping just as hard that they wouldn't get
three.

The thing was, leaving Jeanie's dorm room the night before, he
had promised again—more, this time he'd gone so far as to *swear* to
her—that he would tell his father that morning *before* they went
hunting. But, of course, he hadn't. He *had* meant to. On the way
home he had stopped in at the Lantern and had eight beers to pump
himself up for it and, sitting at the bar glowing gold, he had felt cock-
sure, strong as he had the Friday afternoon before, thinking again that
what he really ought to do was just kick his goddamn father's ass—
but when he'd climbed out of his beaten Dodge in front of the house,
he'd felt the cold. He'd felt suddenly too tired to hash or duke it out.
Somehow he'd scratched at the door and had stepped into the warmth
of the kitchen without saying anything. Then they were in the truck
and, head down, he was paying for the beers and no sleep with every
uphill step, he'd hiked way the hell out here, and now he was in this
tree, hoping his father and brother both had gotten their precious
bucks so he could go the hell home and get some sleep.

Kevin glanced at his watch. By now an hour and a half had
passed since his father and brother had left him. Since then it had
begun to snow in earnest, half-dollar-sized flakes silently filling up the
woods. Such an early snow was unusual, though not unheard of. More
unusual still was how amazingly cold it had grown for that time of

year, but after three winters of hardly any snow or any serious North Country cold, his father had predicted an October blizzard far back in the strangest wet, chilly August any of them had ever seen or even heard tell about. Kevin himself had to admit he loved the snow. There was something blanket-comfortable about it. And in the snow he didn't mind the cold so much. Jeanie didn't much like the cold either, but she loved the snow as much as he did.

Snow.

Kevin closed his eyes against the four-walled whiteness, but felt her setting up on an elbow again, watching him for his reaction. She was touching a single hair on his chest, slowly curling it around her perfect red fingernail, queuing up the question mark of it. He'd wondered to himself then if she wanted him to yell at her or just scream or maybe whoop for some sort of joy. But the proof that Jeanie was pregnant had knocked him out. TKOed, his dream-self stood up out of his floored body and walked out the door and down the hall and down and around the steps, out onto the perfect, snow-covered campus lawn. Then, as if he were a kid again, he was angeled out in the snow, on his back waving his arms—his wings—his legs, the sweep of his robe, and the snow was falling softly down, down and down, blanketing him, his whole body down to his tingling toes, his chest icing ice-solid, blueing his lips, sticking white to his eyelashes, softly white, padding white, and the growing weight of it white-pressing his eyelids past zigzagging reds into a deep, dark-sliding blackness: avalanched alive. That's when he'd opened his eyes to find Jeanie still staring down at him. In this snow dream his planned life died, school and a degree, his newfound discovery that he'd been born to teach, froze and then melted that easily away and he saw himself getting up out of the bed of some house that his smiling father and his happy goddamned brother would help him build, getting up every single morning at 5 A.M. to go to work to afford to be able to pump gallons of gas into yet another used, rusty, worn-out old truck, working every available odd overtime job just as his father had always done, frugal with every spare second of his whole life, just to keep the baby (then babies) in diapers, in bonnets, in pureed pears. He saw a gray lunch-box lunch, his own Stanley thermos (bought on sale), sawdust in his boots, the always-aching shoulders, earning his father's calluses, wearing his father's chosen life as if it were his own.

Then, though, he'd felt Jeanie's lips burn straight down to kiss his naked chest, reawakening him, his desire rising through the cold to hard-aching reality again. He'd rolled up from underneath it all slowly then, and their lips had met, and he'd tasted her tears, arched up to her as she gripped him, and they'd made love again and then again before he went to face him, his sworn word, their bond, sealing it, sealed: their future lives.

"Just goddamnit," Kevin said to himself. He scraped away from the tree and peeled back his sleeve to check his watch. It had been nearly three hours now since they'd split up. There hadn't been any more shots, but neither had his father sent Gary David back to fetch him so that he could help with the carcasses. He glanced around his assigned clearing. His eyes stung, felt sandpapered bald from lack of sleep. He circled them wet and then, with the unloaded rifle slung over his shoulder, he worked himself loose from his set stand, and started down the tree. He'd use the shots as an excuse to go see.

THE TWO SETS of boots tracked a sunken path through the new-fallen snow, his father's footsteps bigger, pressed deeper, and then Gary David's smaller and lighter, pressed just inside the trail breaking bigger tracks, his older brother trying—or so it seemed to Kevin, it had always seemed this way to Kevin—to fill them. He trudged on after them, purposefully stepping just off their beaten path, making himself do the harder work of breaking new snow.

Inside a stand of wind-strafed pine, Kevin stopped where he could see his father had set Gary David. He saw where the tracks stopped to go up, but Gary David wasn't there. He circled the tree. On the other side, his father's bigger boots trudged off, and then he saw where Gary David had jumped down into them, sinking into his tracks again. Kevin's first panged thought was that his father had come back for his older brother but not for him. Then he noticed that both sets of tracks headed out. Neither set pointed back. And then standing under the pine puzzling down, Kevin grinned, and then standing alone under the tree in the snow patting over his pockets to confirm it, he laughed out loud: His *father* had been carrying the shell bag!

In their marched hurry, and because it was not the way the Hazens had *always done things*—not the way his *father's father* had done it—not a fixture in the way his dad had orchestrated, ordered, and directed every hunt for the past eight years that Gary David and he had been traipsing through these woods after him—he'd simply and ridiculously forgotten to dole out their ammo to them.

But Kevin saw at once his own caught dilemma: It was as obvious as it could be that for the past three hours he hadn't even tried to load his rifle. He'd been sitting in his stand, sound asleep, dreaming. *Unforgivable.* And his father wouldn't forgive or let him forget about it either—not ever. Kevin could hear the told story of it over and over again during their clinking breakfasts at the diner, the head shaking and chuckles it would always get.

Gary David must have realized the mistake as soon as he'd gotten himself good and safely situated and, of course, it had been his older brother who had climbed all the way back down and who had fallen in behind their father and who was probably trudging back toward

Kevin right now, sacrificing his own precious hunting time for his younger brother who hadn't even tried to load his rifle and who didn't even give a damn. Kevin felt pretty shitty about that. But he still couldn't help but smile—no matter what the consequences. The whole forgetful episode reminded him of a mistake he himself might easily have made any hour of any day of any week, but it delighted him to no end that his father had done such a typical, stupid thing. *He* is *human,* Kevin thought, pleased and amazed. It was a good feeling, and he stored the warmth of it away, thinking how he might very well need it sometime later that day.

He started off after them then, feeling almost happy, feeling better, at least, than he had felt all day. He followed the two sets of tracks for a long while, slanting along the ridge and then downhill, bounding through drifts. The first thing Kevin caught sight of was a caution of safety orange. He stopped, seeing, but through the veil of snow unable to imagine or make out at all what it was exactly he saw. It looked to him as if he'd caught his father scraping and groveling. He was on his knees, bowing low, inchwormed up as if he were praying in the snow, from behind the brand-new shell bag still strapped on his back. Then, from ten yards, Kevin saw his brother, Gary David, sprawled flat, the snow red-mapped telltale around him. He heard his own howl. Shocked still, he saw the rifle barrel choked off in his father's mouth.

Father Anthony

Black ice. I wasn't even going the speed limit. I was halfway across the bridge when I felt the little Saturn begin to spin, and then, that quick, I was turned around looking the other way. "Oh, Lord!" I called out and meant it. I had plenty of time to think. I fully realized every instant of the moment, not that my life "passed before my eyes" exactly, but I was completely aware of going backward down I-87 toward Albany at fifty-three miles an hour. A pickup truck was facing me and I saw the man's face clearly. He was about thirty-five. He had pleasant features, dark eyes, a brown beard, and his mouth was ohed round at me going the wrong way. And then I hit the end of the bridge and spun back around and sailed over the embankment pumping the brake to no effect as I swooped into the snow-covered median. The steering wheel was shaking in my hands, the whole car buffeting about like I was in a spaceship coming through reentry. I dipped down the one side and began to rise into the oncoming lanes, and then my heart leapt. This was it! I glimpsed my end. And my death seemed so—I could not help this thought—*stupid.* And that's when I hit the drainage grate.

I woke to the man's concerned features I'd seen so clearly in the pickup truck behind me as I'd faced backward down the interstate. Snow was falling fast all around us, his back and shoulders covered as if he were wearing a white cape.

"Father, are you okay?"

I was being held back by the balloon of bags, bubble-wrapped safe, though I'd burst my nose. The blood was shockingly bright against the white of the snow.

I touched his arm. "Bless you for stopping."

"Can you move?"

"I think so."

He helped me out of the car. Someone must have called in on their cell phone when they saw me go over the embankment, because ten minutes later a fire truck and an ambulance arrived. A bright yellow truck pulled up with its orange lights flashing, Miller and Sam's Towing. The highway patrolman was the last to arrive. I'd had the good fortune to crash close to an exit. The EMTs wrapped a wool blanket around my shoulders. I took the cup of coffee they offered but could hardly hold it, my hands were trembling so badly. The patrolman walked over to take a good look at the car before he strode back through the snow to take down my version of what happened.

They sat me in the ambulance facing the front of the Saturn that had crunched up like an accordion against the concrete-and-steel drainage grate sticking up in the snow, the obstruction that had saved my life and the lives of others. Dumb luck that I hit it. Call it mystery! I certainly wasn't aiming.

On the opposite side of the interstate, traffic had backed up to see what the flashing lights were all about, rubbernecking at the scene.

I looked at them looking with such raw curiosity at me, and I shuddered again.

The EMTs insisted that I go to the hospital since I'd been knocked unconscious for a time, but I was not going. I would not hear of it. My own experience had awakened me to something. I couldn't have said exactly what it was at the time. I only knew that I had to get back home. I was needed there. I rode to the garage in the warmth of the tow truck with Mr. Miller, who had introduced himself to me.

"Where were you headed, Father?" he asked. He had an unlit pipe in his mouth.

"Albany," I said. "But it's just as well I didn't make it. Don't not smoke on my account," I told him, but I didn't reach for my cigarettes. I'd left them in the Saturn. I vowed to quit right then and there.

"Can you drop me by a rental place?" I asked him.

"I'd be happy to, Father," he said. "But you've had quite a shake-up, and if you can believe what the weather service is saying now, these roads are only going to get worse. It might be best if you didn't drive. Why don't you let me ride you back up to Lost Lake."

"That's very kind of you," I said.

I'd vowed to quit, but I wasn't above inhaling. "That smells nice," I said.

"It's cherry," he said. "Sir Walter Raleigh."

I turned to look out the window in the good-smelling, close warmth of the cab, the wool blanket pulled close around my shoulders. Even the gray sky seemed to glow with a certain brightness. And I knew one thing: I was happy to be alive. I inhaled deeply again and held it. Maybe, I thought, I'd take up a pipe.

Lamey Pierson

Walked right by and stopped and turned his head. Looked me straight in the eyes he did, a dog-big coyote as I ever seed. Our North Country wolf. Tiptoed through the clearing, stopped by the back tire of her truck, and pissed a stream. Calm as could be. Twenty feet from the blind I made the day before. Bunkered over now with snow. My front-row seat to look-see firsthand my getting back at him I waited all these years for. Coyotes got balls! And if I'd had my rifle he'd of lost them. 'Course that coyote knew all along I didn't. Which is why he let me get a good look at him in the first place. He bent and sniffed in the direction she gone running after them three boys. Still looking at me the whole while he padded away through the trees. Going the other way with his nose to the ground, taking the same trail as them Hazens had. Onto them like she should've been. Like I told her to be. Like I was onto her and Hazen's older boy. The truth don't lie! No sir, it don't. Whooie! Sex-y! Better even than some of them kinda movies I seed. A live show. And a whole lot more woman than she looked to be at first in that green uniform of hers.

My stomach was grumbling, past lunch when Officer Roy towed the second one back wearing cuffs. THIS BUCK HUNTS! Sure he does. More than twice her size, a big, pink, fat boy he was with curly hair on his chin. I never seed him before. She opened the back door and shoved him in. No door handles. Good as any jail cell is what he'd find out. She shut that door and climbed in the front to use the radio, calling in loud for backup out of breath. It was Tabert who answered, the one with the dog, the captain now. They gone and butchered a little doe right there in the bed. You talk about dumb. It fell into her lap; she just happened to ride up. I seed them drag it out, all three of them huffing at it. The car and truck they come in sat parked along that creek bend before the Hazens' red and white Ford. Weren't none of my affair, though the snow was coming down, and she was bent on nailing them. What she needed, she needed to keep her eyes peeled. No matter what else he was, Hazen was a hunter. He'd bring down a buck. And if no one was waiting in the clearing when he got here he'd fix his deer with his wife's tag. Then he'd be legal the rest of the season. We'd miss our chance! Course O'cer Roy wouldn't thought to think of that. She didn't know Gary Hazen the way I did. She started back into the woods after the third one. Her pistol out.

I rubbed my palms together, warming to the thought of getting him caught. For that girl to do her bounden duty like I told her the spot right where to. If she'd just listen to ole Lamey. I'd watch all day. Long as I had to after waiting all these years for him to finally fuck up. I smacked my lips, tasting my revenge. A flavor like bacon fat and Yukon Jack. Sweet.

He costed me.

Officer Roy

It was the most blatant case I'd seen since I'd taken my vow as an ECO, and I understood what Captain Tabert tried to convince me of about my stakeout in the clearing, watching for Gary Hazen: "No need to jump the gun." It was only the first day of the season. If Gary Hazen was lucky enough to get away with falsifying a tag today, then so be it. Lamey could make a complaint that I'd let Gary Hazen go because I was sleeping with his older son. No one would take Lamey Pierson's version of the truth seriously: The proof that I was doing my job sat handcuffed in the back of the Cherokee with the doe's blood all over them. And that was how I made my decision to let Gary Hazen off the hook.

I pulled into the clearing behind the Hazens' red and white Ford F250 at dawn to catch the three out-of-towners in the act, frozen in the flash of my headlights. It was immediately apparent that they must have shot the deer in the dark before gun season officially began, but that wasn't the only crime I was arresting them for. I had the evidence of the half-skinned doe in a black Hefty bag in the back of the

Cherokee. Worse, her coat still showed a fawn's fading spots. She didn't weigh eighty pounds.

As I put the handcuffs on, I read them their rights. After that, I had to ask why they'd done it. At best, it seemed a waste. The second one I caught, the big one, shrugged, acting tough and bored now, though he'd actually squealed as I chased close on his heels with my pistol drawn and he'd been easy to bring down.

"What's the big fucking deal?" is what he answered, seeing his friend caged in the backseat as we came in sight of the Jeep. "It's only a baby bitch deer."

I had to wonder what tough-guy flick he thought he was starring in. His fear was the only thing about him that made him remotely real to me. I'd been trained to remain professional in such instances, uninvolved on a personal level when making an arrest, but I'll admit I felt good about getting them out of the woods.

The third one, who'd gotten away while I was busy arresting the other two, met Captain Tabert and I on the trail he'd left for the shepherd Trapper to track, stumbling back toward us through the knee-deep snow, holding his rifle over his head to give himself up. He'd managed to stay hidden until late afternoon, but I'd been confident he wasn't going to escape. It was already starting to grow dark, the temperature dropping, and there wasn't a plowed, paved road for miles; no way he was going to make it out of this million-acre wood alive. He was soaking wet, nearly hypothermic, shivering so that he could hardly talk. His lips were as blue as if he'd been sipping on a grape soda. "P-p-p-please," he pleaded for us to take him in.

BACK AT THE barracks early that evening after I'd booked the three of them and filed my report, I had to admit I felt a little amazed at myself at what I'd done. I felt I'd finally accomplished something as an

ECO besides issuing a ticket or checking tags that earned me a place higher in the ranks.

"Good job, Jo!" Paul Stauffer slapped me on the back.

And Captain Tabert said, "I've been telling her she'll get a commendation for this one, no doubt about it."

"For sure you'll get your picture on the front page of the *Gazette*." Ellie inflated the scenario. "Why, soon you'll be as famous around here as Billy Hirsch got to be for flying that girl to the hospital in that storm!"

The radio squawked and then crackled loud. Ellie rolled her chair sideways to answer it, and the barracks fell hushed at the call for possible assistance. What we heard was what Susan Hazen had kept to herself waiting worried for as long as she could. It had been dark for two hours already by the time she finally let herself pick up the phone and dial the forest rangers at the Five Ponds Wilderness Station. We heard for ourselves who it was the rangers were going after. And since it was no secret that I'd been investigating Gary Hazen, everyone looked from Captain Tabert to me.

"Jo," Captain Tabert said—volunteering us. We scrambled back into action, grabbing the emergency gear, the first-aid kit and blankets, flashlights. Ellie was already on the horn letting the rangers know where we'd be. She reported that we'd already located their hunting spot. We knew right where to start our search. Thanks to Lamey, I thought.

Kevin

It was past 6:00 P.M.: fourteen hours since they'd stepped out of the truck in the clearing beside the frozen stream at 4:00 A.M. The temperature had risen a bit during the day, but now, with the long winter's night around them, the cold was closing in. Kevin stoked the fire, and the flames jumped wild, hissing. His father lay close beside the heat of it, covered as warmly as Kevin could manage.

When Kevin had first realized what had happened, he'd felt his world physically tilt, heave, then slither from beneath his feet. He'd landed, clutching snow, felt his stomach lurch and roll—he couldn't help this and it wouldn't stop—then, still stringing spit, he'd crawled quickly forward toward them, patting blindly over the crushed and blinding snow. Kevin had let go of his brother's pipe-cold arm and had reached out and touched his father's wrist to feel a thin pulse hiding just below the skin. With the realization that his father was still alive, he'd forced himself to shove his brother's death aside and had pulled himself up through the horror of it with one single-minded but saving thought: *fire.*

He used the butt of his rifle like a shovel to dig a pit beside his father and made a teepee of twigs and browned pine needles and hunched over to shield the match as he lit it. The needles glowed orange, connecting like wires in a bulb, and then suddenly blacked, curling smoke, out cold.

Kevin flung away the dead match and tried again, telling himself over and over to take his time. He squeezed his hands to try to make them work correctly. That's when he remembered the worn passage from *The Odyssey* still folded up in his back pocket. He ripped the paper in half and crumpled it, giving himself two chances. He folded over the cover of the pack and flicked the match out, burning. He held it down low, cupping the tiny flame round with the palms of both hands against the wind, ignoring the frying of his own cold-numbed skin. The paper caught and the pine glowed again and then burst into flame. Soon the sticks that lay on the layer above the needles began to crackle. With that first real dry burning snap, Kevin's heart rose. He added another twig. And then another. He built the fire as quickly as he dared.

As he fed the fire, Kevin glanced over at his big brother sprawled in the snow—his gentle big brother, his kind big brother, his good big brother, his quiet big brother, silenced now. His face looked as cold and impassive as if it had been sculpted out of marble. He lay perfectly still, looking straight up into the snow coming down. Gary David was dead.

Kevin stepped quickly forward and grabbed his father's .30-06 and flung it into the woods. He began to struggle frantically out of his coat, flapping about like a scarecrow in the wind. He covered his father with his jacket. Finally, Kevin tucked in the sleeves about his father's arms and chest, and pulled up the hood to keep the snow off of his face. He did not think about being cold himself. He was not cold, glancing again at his brother slowly being buried under the falling snow.

Kevin turned back to his father. He was afraid to touch his wound. But he had to touch it—there was no one else to touch it. His dad was no longer able to tell him what to do—if only he could tell Kevin what to do now. Kevin thought again of all those years of helping Brad Pfeiffer with every sort of emergency. Kevin ought to know what to do, too; his dad had taught him. He knew a lot. But he didn't want to have to know. Kevin knelt beside his father. Half of his father's face was gone, the left side of his jaw and cheekbone hallowed cadaverous. Kevin could see his tongue. His hat had been knocked off and his hair had turned completely white. Once carefully combed, it now stuck up as if frozen in fear of what he'd seen. His glasses had been blown apart and his eyes rolled uncontrolled beneath the lids. His father's body sagged into his skin, his strength sapped out of him. But his father wasn't dead. The miracle was that Gary Hazen had missed from such close range. It looked as if he'd fumbled the long barrel of the .30-06 around on himself, shoving the butt of the rifle down through the snow, and jammed his thumb through the guard to shove at the trigger, jarring his aim. It had only taken a twitch to nudge the bullet from simply blowing out his brains.

"Dad?" Kevin said, the only thing he could think to say, said it as if it were a question he was asking of his father, afraid to speak too loudly for fear of what else his voice might trigger. "Dad," Kevin said again. He ran the sleeve of his jacket across his nose and cheeks, roughing either side of his own face.

What had his father done? Kevin knew. He could never forgive himself the carelessness of killing his own son: his father had assumed full responsibility for what he'd done. No excuses. But his father had not been thinking clearly; he'd not been himself. In that eternal second he'd lost control. He'd given in to the *feeling* of what to do. He'd chosen the quick consolation of trying to take his own life, of leaving Kevin alone out in the woods, of abandoning their mother. How could he abandon his wife?

Grief overwhelmed him. Kevin felt scared, like a little boy again—the boy who used to listen so carefully after this man, the boy who'd looked up to his father without question, without reservation, who never let him out of his sight—who had modeled his life after his father's. He'd wanted to *be* his father. When had that changed? The shaking he felt turned him from the inside out—quaking him—he was that afraid now to be left alone with his brother's death, the sole responsibility for saving his father's life. He knew he wasn't that boy anymore—he would never be a boy again—and now his father was no longer that father. His father had made an awful mistake, he'd allowed himself an *inexcusable* choice, he wasn't infallible, he was all too human, merely a man, *no excuses!* His father blurred, already ghosting away beside him.

Kevin unzipped his sweatshirt and yanked it off. In one motion he pulled his T-shirt over his head. He zipped the hooded sweatshirt back on. Then he tore the T-shirt with his teeth and ripped it into strips to make bandages. Kevin applied the compress to his father's face. He pressed the cloth against the wound and held it and then he peeled back the soaked bandages to look. The blast was puckered ugly, a deep dark ragged red, seared pink at the edges. White shards of bone needled his skin. Kevin could have stuck his fist into the gaping wound. He laid strips of cloth across the hole, dressing his father's face as best he could. He could pack the snow in the wound, but he had to keep his father's core temperature up—that was the vital thing.

Kevin climbed to his feet, trying to shake off the rubbery lethargy that had taken hold of him. He tried to focus on what he had to do next. The question he had to concentrate on was whether he could manage to get his father down off the mountain. He was afraid to try to move him. Dragging out a buck was one thing, but he couldn't fix his father to a tumpline. He'd already lost a lot of blood. They were steep miles from the truck and the snow was deep. He could make a litter. Sled him down somehow. Or pick his father up in a fireman's carry. But his father outweighed him by fifty pounds. He wouldn't get far in this snow. He could build up the fire and leave him and go for help on his own. But by now their tracks would be covered by snow. He wasn't entirely sure he'd be able to find his way out to the spot where they'd left the truck. *What if he got lost?* What if his father froze or bled to death while he was gone?

He could not help his big brother. He could not let himself think of Gary David now.

Kevin made the decision to stay with his father by the fire. His mother would send the rangers after dark, he reassured himself. The rangers would find them in time. They'd enlist Captain Tabert's shepherd. That was his father's only chance of making it out of the woods alive. All Kevin had to do was to keep his father warm until help arrived. That's all.

Kevin knew he had to build some sort of a shelter to shield them from the wind and snow. His father's pulse remained faint but steady. "I'll be right back, Dad." He set out in search of two long sticks with pronged tops. He speared them into the snow on either side of his father. He searched through the woods until he kicked up a skinny, downed sapling long enough to set between the sticks. After he'd done that he cut more fanned branches from the surrounding spruce. He shook them free of snow and shingled them on top of each other at an angle against the sapling. The most difficult part was finding a way to mat the limbs together so they wouldn't blow off. When he'd finally finished, his father lay inside the shelter of the squat, rough-looking lean-to that he'd built to cover him. The back blocked the wind. And it would keep the snow off of them. It left his father facing the fire, banked before the heat.

Kevin swiped his forearm across his face, sweating. He realized he was soaked. Without his even being aware of it, he'd begun to chill, to chatter dangerously himself. He startled at the fact that he was freezing—that he himself could freeze.

He had to be more careful.

"Come on, Kevin," he said, goading himself, "*think,*" and heard the thickness in his speech. One of the first things his father had taught him and Gary David about surviving in the cold was how dangerous it was to be caught wet in the snow. They'd helped plenty of people who had hypothermia, like that woman his father and Brad Pfeiffer had found sitting on the ice after that freak snowmobile accident that killed her husband and that other couple. She could have walked straight to the lights on shore, but she hadn't. Paralyzed by grief, she hadn't thought to.

Kevin tried to make himself think. By then, the day's light had already begun to fade. He felt light-headed. Kevin had the distinct impression that none of what was happening was real.

He looked to his brother again, rubbing hard up and down his own arms trying to warm himself—and the idea of it was suddenly there in the air as if Gary David had whispered to him what to do to keep warm—and then he knew.

He tried his best to remove his big brother's coat gently, but it was no use. His brother's arms had already gone stiff and heavy, skinny as he'd always looked to be, and Kevin grunted trying to bend them, wrestling him out of the full nelson that was the hold of his bloody coat. He'd forgotten to take off his gloves first and the sleeves rolled inside out.

Something dropped out of Gary David's coat pocket into the snow. Kevin picked up the black velvet box, the pink receipt from Elegant Emotions, the jewelry store up in Lake Serene. He opened the box to find a little diamond ring. He stared down at it, mystified.

Kevin left Gary David nearly naked on top of the snow with the question of the ring posed on his chest. He used his big brother's coat to cover their father and layered on his brother's quilted shirt and thermal top over his own sweatshirt. He'd found the thermos and he concentrated on that now that he had the fire blazing and the shelter built. He cast out the dregs and packed it with snow before setting the old metal Stanley at the edge of the coals. When the thermos filled with melt, he poured some into the cup and drained it off. He knew not to force liquids on someone who was unconscious. Kevin's fingers were black with soot and stained with dried blood. He bent again to check his father's pulse before lifting back the coat to change the dressing. His father's eyes snapped suddenly open as if Kevin's touching the wound had pressed a button, flicking them on. They rolled around unfocused, and then winked out, twitching underneath the lids. The wind squalled about the shelter. He couldn't see three feet in front of them. He huddled deep into his hood and pulled his brother's wool socks on over his hands. The sips of hot water traced a line of warmth to his stomach. The snow continued to pile up.

The only thing left to do now was to wait. Kevin sat beside the fire with his legs hugged up, his chin on his knees. He let himself chatter, his body shivering to heat itself, sipped water from the thermos, and occasionally used a stick to stoke the fire. Brad Pfeiffer taught the signs of possible hypothermia as the "umbles"—*stumbles, mumbles, fumbles, grumbles.* Kevin fixed his father's covers again and scooted closer to the fire. He tried to think of anything else but how cold he was. He watched as the trees grayed and the white fled the sky. The flames leapt brilliantly against the blackness. Sparks popped and arced sharp as shooting stars.

Kevin had never in his life seriously considered dying, but he felt the quickening at the idea of his own death pulse through him then. It was awfully dark and the snow had tapered off, the blizzard ending as quickly as it had begun, but now the night cold had descended fully upon them. Kevin stoked the flames and was lost for a time staring into the white heat at its heart. He blinked back up to see a coyote standing at the edge of the circle of light. The coyote's eyes blazed red. He stood there, watching them, that close.

Kevin yelled, "Hey!" as he would have at a dog, and then he tried to stumble up, his legs gone clumsy beneath him from sitting beside his father for so long in the freezing cold. "Go on! Beat it!" The coyote stood looking calmly at him. "All right," Kevin said and grabbed for his .30-30. On his knees, he clawed open the shell bag. He levered a shell into the chamber and pulled the rifle to his shoulder. The coyote backed out of the light and disappeared. It could as easily have been the spirit of a coyote. All that remained was the white of the snow gone gray, and the deep blue-black beyond the firelight, the velvety curtain of the night.

Kevin stood with the rifle in his hands. He could feel the boom of blood in his ears.

He carried the loaded rifle on its sling over his shoulder as he gathered yet another armload of wood and piled it in the shelter where he could reach it effortlessly. He sat cross-legged beside his father with the rifle across his lap. His father had told him how coyotes could sense death from miles away. He kept his finger on the trigger, ready to fire.

Of course, Kevin had no idea just how truly cold it would get that night. If his father had ever allowed them to pack along a radio, he would have heard the steady broadcast of warnings being issued by the weather service, and if he had heard them, he might well have tried for the truck, realizing that if there was no chance of making it, there was also little other hope than to try. The coming cold, sweeping down out of Canada behind the snow left by the blizzard in the mountains that night, chilled by an arctic wind, would dip close to seventeen below.

Even without a weather advisory on the radio, though, what Kevin could sense, sitting deeper and deeper into the night, past 6:00 P.M., then 7:00, 8:00, 9:00, 10:00, 11:00, 12:00 midnight beside his father, was the increasingly still and silent razor-edge of the air. Around one o'clock in the morning the clouds rolled out as swiftly as they'd swept in the morning before. The stars above them blazed, banked close and white-hot looking, cold and bright against the sky. With the air gone so curiously still, even the fire seemed to be having more and more trouble breathing, the flames going thickish and slow, glowing blue, low and close over the orange-red embers.

In that flickering light, Kevin allowed himself another look at the hump of snow that covered his brother's body. Beside him, his father's eyes were still rolling uncontrolled between snapping suddenly open to out-cold closed. Kevin wished he could talk to his older brother, who could help him make sense of what had happened, what was happening to them.

From just beyond the edge of trees he heard the yip and curling cue of the coyote's calling. He sat and listened to that keening. Suddenly, he had a staggeringly clear image of his mother standing before their kitchen sink looking past her own reflection in the glass with her arms hugged close, watching out for their safe return. He let himself imagine Jeanie's pretty face. He tried to picture their child—a boy blond as him maybe or a dark-haired, curly-headed baby girl. He tried to fathom the deep pain of growing up without a father—of not knowing what a father was, as he had always known who his father was, who his father had to be, whether he, Kevin, always liked it or not: the act of fathering, the acts of a father, the *actions* that were the nature and gift and pain and pleasure of true fatherhood. The caring—the *carefulness*—which was the belief in holding onto something worth preserving and passing on. *Love.* Kevin felt the tide of emotion that had been at its lowest ebb flowing back into him again. He looked to his dad.

Since he'd found his father and his brother, Kevin had had no choice himself but to act, and he had acted. There had been no one else to do it, and he had done what he had to do. But now, left alone in the dark, trapped by the snow, feeling what he could not yet know in the coming cold, Kevin felt a sudden futile flaring. No matter what happened to them then, he wished his father could know that what had happened to Gary David that morning had not been his fault. It had obviously been an *accident* and accidents happened, no matter how carefully you planned or dreamed or wished for something else. *Didn't he know something about that?* Kevin wished then with all his heart that he'd made good on his sworn word and had told his father that he and Jeanie were going to marry, about the baby they were going to have. He'd planned to stand up and say to him: *I will live my own life, make decisions as my own man, but I will respect you and the way you raised me always.* And that's when he heard himself say out loud: "I love you, too, Dad." Kevin felt rushed through blue space. He trailed his father back to find himself seated beside him before the fire again, overwhelmed by the aftershot shocked understanding of what, all along, his father had really been trying to teach Gary David and him about surviving in the cold. Then, without his having to think further about it or even plan, Kevin angeled his own stored warmth down over his father. He closed his eyes and dreamt that the rangers stumbled upon them just before dawn.

Captain Tabert

By the time we made it to the spot where they'd parked to start their hunt, their trail had been buried for hours under more than a foot of new snow. Trapper tried his best, he really did—he pulled hard to get away from their rusted, red and white Ford—but after that straining start, he lost the scent. Me and Jo circled back with him. Then Trapper stopped stock-still. He growled low, and then a snarl rippled back his lips, showing his pink gums, his teeth bared. And lo and behold Lamey Pierson stood up out of a sheltered drift.

"You're just lucky you come back," he said to Jo. He spat the snow. "That Hazen's a tricky cuss. He's outfoxing us. It's too cold and dark for anyone with sense to still be out here. He must be up to something. This a way," he said.

I raised an eyebrow at Jo. No matter what else he was, Lamey was a top-notch woodsman, and I was inclined to follow. I didn't have a better idea. So we fell in after him.

The night had gone perfectly silent, muffled by the deep cushion

of snow, except for the sudden pops, like gunshots, tree limbs shatter-
ing down in the cold.

It was slow going. It took hours. We came to a ravine we couldn't
cross, though that's where their path led, and we had to hike out of
our way to get around it and then traipse back to pick up their trail
again. Lamey did the tracking. He hunched along, mumbling to himself, looking up at the sky or touching the limbs that lined either side
of the trail. I couldn't see a thing even with a flashlight, but Lamey's
camp of shacks was close by and he had a sense for the terrain, and he
seemed sure he was onto something. They'd pushed a long, steep way
out. But then that was just the sort of thing Gary Hazen would do,
the kind of thing folks had always admired him for. There were times
we had to wade through waist-deep drifts. I didn't even want to know
how cold it was. I could no longer feel my toes. I worried about Trapper's paws.

The rest of the evening fled past and then we put midnight
behind us. We pushed on.

It was six in the morning, nearly dawn though it was still dark,
when we first heard the coyote. Sometimes you just got to go with
your gut. We started plunging down off the ridge toward that yipping,
his howling leading us on. With nothing but cold to smell, Trapper
started pulling for him, ears perked. I gave him all the lead I could and
still keep up. Then through the slatted dark of the black trunks and
blue night and the glow of white we finally caught sight of the coyote
sitting on a mound of snow with his head thrown back. Trapper
hurled himself against the leash.

The coyote flickered off through the trees, and we were dragged
fast onto the scene captured in the beams of our flashlights with too
much to think about and see all at once. The little lean-to domed over
with snow and the first body that Trapper started pawing after under
the mound where the coyote had been sitting turned out to be Gary

David, naked and looking past us. When Jo saw his blue face with the ice in his lashes, she cried, "Oh, my God!" and staggered back and dropped onto her knees in the snow as if she were the one who'd been shot. While I held Trapper back from Gary David's body, Lamey strode straight up to the other two, Gary Hazen and his son Kevin. The coals of the fire beside them were still glowing, but the last of the available wood had ashed gray. He bent to check for their pulses and stood up in my spotlight, shaking his head.

The first gray light of day was just beginning to hint at things. I turned and shined my light around the clearing, and slowly the story of what had happened unfolded before me. The facts would be confirmed once the state troopers finished their investigation—the shell bag Gary was carrying, bullets and angles, distances, the factor of snow and the uncanny cold. I made myself take a good look. Though it wasn't something I wanted to see, it was a sight I never want to forget.

I turned back to Jo cradling Gary David's head in her lap, weeping openly now, an opened black jewelry box in her hand.

Then Lamey began to laugh, a sound bad as a hyena's cackle. This insane sort of laughter at Kevin's lying on top of his father, looking to have laid down his life to try to save his father's as his father looked to have laid down his life for his other son, turning the gun on himself at the mistake of shooting one of his own boys. And Lamey laughing and laughing at Gary Hazen's carefulness gone so horribly wrong. I have two daughters of my own. I whirled on Lamey and snapped his chin back, shutting his damn mouth. He smiled with the blood smeared on his yellow teeth and a new black gap, tongue out, yellow eyes still laughing bright, and Trapper went after him to protect me, snarling and snapping, but I grabbed the dog back. I still had a grip. I would've forfeited my damn job and wouldn't have cared at all if I had at the time, already beginning to try to imagine how in the world I would ever tell Susan Hazen what had happened to her husband

and both of her boys. But Lamey let it go. "I just can't win," he said with a last shake of his head and shut up, too, except to shrug at what he'd been laughing at, mumbling as he turned away, "You might want to check for yourself, but I believe Gary Hazen and that youngest boy of his might still be left the tiniest little bit alive there yet." Startling me into action, already turning, grabbing at the walkie-talkie on my belt to call in Billy Hirsch in his copter, and bringing Jo to her feet like an exclamation point, sending us scrambling after the blankets to get them down off that mountain and save them if we could.

Brad Pfeiffer

That morning when we got Father Anthony's call, Lucy and I threw a few things in a suitcase and drove all the rest of that day and through the night, too, without sleep to make it back to Lost Lake. Lucy kept yammering the whole while. She blamed the snow and cold. "Thank god we moved to Florida! We made it out in the nick of time! It could have been you that Gary Hazen shot in cold blood!" I'd heard about as much as I could; I'd done what she'd made me feel guilty enough to do, but I was through. I pulled over onto the berm of the interstate and rolled to a stop, reached across, and opened her door. We must've been in Georgia. I remember red dirt, rusted cans in a ditch, glittering glass, a yellow McDonald's cheeseburger wrapper.

"One more word," I said as evenly as I could, "and I'll leave you right here on the side of the road."

She didn't say anything else the rest of the drive, scooted way over against her door with her purse hugged close, though I felt her peeking over at me every once in a while like I was some dangerous stranger she'd climbed into the car with. And well, I thought, seeing the end of my own life playing out before me, stuck sucking in air-conditioning before a TV that merely portrayed a sorry imitation of a life I used to actually love to live, and about half-wishing it had been me out there to take that bullet for my friend, maybe I was.

Susan Hazen

Father Anthony knows; I have confessed. Left bereft trying to survive with a frozen heart that winter after Gary David's death was as close as I've ever come to truly understanding Lucy Pfeiffer's wish to sell out and move far away from here, to get shut of the place for good. Every quiet, considerate step of Gary David's that I woke not hearing in the morning halls filled me with the same aching echo of dread, and there are nights still when I turn to my husband in bed, and we grope the darkness between us, feeling all over again from the outset our despair at the absence of our son, our loss—holding onto each other for dear life. We lost our older son—our dark-haired, curly-headed boy! And there's no getting him back, not on this earth, in this life, pray as we might.

Stepping out of Saint Pius's, the light white-blinds me. Gary takes my right arm; Father Anthony guides my left. Together, we take the stairs, Father Anthony's white-robed arms winging over us, his purple stole flapping. "Susan," he comforts, "Gary," as the bell tolls. We crunch across the gravel lot and down the hill to stand beneath the crooked wood pines that rise bowing low over Gary David's grave.

267

Officer Roy

Outside it had begun to snow; a squall of flakes hid Lost Lake. Spring had gone by, another gun season past, winter upon us again before I ran into Gary Hazen face-to-face in line at the North Way.

I'd stopped in after a morning shift to pick up bread and eggs, pausing in the narrow aisles as I shopped to say good morning to the other customers. I was next in line to pay when I felt someone's eyes on me. I turned. Gary Hazen was standing behind me, still gaunt with grief.

We airlifted Gary Hazen and Kevin straight to Mercy. After he'd stabilized, Gary Hazen had had to remain in the hospital in Syracuse for almost a month, recovering from the series of surgeries he went through to give him some semblance of his old face again. At Gary David's funeral, I sat with Val and Anne Marie Burke squashed together into the little church with the rest of the mourners who'd come to pay their respects, the crowd that packed the pews and overflowed out the open double doors into the snow-trampled parking lot.

I watched as Susan and Kevin trailed the casket that Kevin had built
for him down the aisle outside, my eyes blurring as unseeing as Susan's
were when she passed me by. For their part, the local men—Rick
Schoonmaker, Billy Hirsch, Captain Tabert, Chet Harrington, and
Brad Pfeiffer—served as pallbearers. Armound Pollon donated the
hardwood planks for the coffin from his own mill, bringing the lum-
ber by the house himself on one of his company's red, white, and blue
trucks, and stayed to help Kevin make the cuts. I was in uniform,
ready to go on duty. Captain Tabert, who'd witnessed me accepting
Gary David's ring, had offered to give me time off to go back to Guilford for a while and be with my family. But I'd refused. Lost Lake was
where I wished to be; the place was my home. I wouldn't leave Gary
David now. Instead of taking time off, I'd asked Captain Tabert for
more hours, every second of overtime that he could spare. Dead on
my feet, I zombied through days and then weeks, and months passed
by. Complete exhaustion seemed to be the only way I could bring
myself to sleep.

We're all doing the best we can. Of course, the Hazens didn't
carry medical insurance. The six hundred dollars Gary Hazen earned
from the filming together with the pot at the Lake View didn't begin to
cover their hospital costs. To pay their soaring expenses, Voilà Films,
with the backing of Blaze Farley, came to the rescue by establishing a
generous foundation under the name of the documentary, *As the Geese
Go*. The film was dedicated to the memory of Gary David Hazen, and
a carload from Lost Lake—Val and Anne Marie Burke and Father
Anthony among them—accepted the formal invitation to attend the
premiere at the Forum Theater in Lake Serene. Val said they rolled out
the red carpet, and Blaze Farley met them under the marquee lights in
all her shimmering glory to pay homage to the event. They sat with her
and Pierre Pardoe. She told me how the entire house shushed with the
cries of the geese flying over. Gary David popped up out of his blind

and eyed down the barrel and fired, twice. Together, holding hands, everyone watched the goose dive into the lake. In its wake, the ring of ripples at its death touched out in all directions.

By then I'd heard that Kevin and the young woman Gary David had told me he'd been seeing had married and that she was pregnant. The word about town was that Jeanie's parents had been adamantly against her having the baby at all, but she would not take her parents' no for an answer. After months of grieving in that big house alone, Gary Hazen and Susan asked Jeanie and Kevin to move in with them when their daughter, whom they named Lily, was born in July. Working together, Gary Hazen and Kevin built a fruit and vegetable stand fronting the road before the house. HAZEN'S GARDEN-FRESH PRODUCE proclaims the newly painted sign over the booth. All summer I felt the throb every time I chanced to drive by and see Susan and Jeanie sitting together with Lily, sharing the shade. People said that when he got out of the hospital and was able to go back to work in the woods it was Gary Hazen who insisted Kevin return to school. Now when Kevin isn't in class studying to be a teacher he works part-time with his father. In his spare time, Gary Hazen has become a familiar sight pushing his granddaughter in the stroller along the road from the Lake View Diner past Saint Pius's and the Lost Lake Apartments to the Lodge. Lazarus, the pet goose they keep, likes to trail along, close behind as if he were on a leash. Tourists that pass occasionally slow their SUVs, beep and wave, laughing or smiling at such a curious sight. Lazarus goes low or rises up, flapping, hissing at the vehicles until they're safely past.

I'd anticipated running into Gary Hazen face-to-face again sooner or later—perhaps out in the woods making a routine check on his tag. That fall Brad Pfeiffer returned to town again for the week it had taken him and Gary Hazen to fill their two tags. He said that he and his wife, Lucy, have come to a new "agreement." Kevin didn't go with them; neither he nor Susan is on record as purchasing a license. But meeting up with Gary Hazen so unexpectedly in line at the North Way still came as a shock. Since the funeral I'd been left considering all that I might say. But seeing him and his damaged face, not one of those sentences I had imagined between us materialized. I shook my head, trying to shake it off, feeling shaken up again from the start— the end result of what my investigation of Gary Hazen had finally revealed rushing back all at once as if I'd just that moment stumbled upon my fiancé staring up with ice in his lashes. My eyes swam up to meet his, and the binding power of our shared grief passed between us: *understood.* The two of us came together then, colliding as suddenly as that, standing before the cash register in the North Way surrounded by a blur of characters from Lost Lake who looked on as we held on awkwardly to each other.

epilogue

Gary Hazen

I turn to take a last reading on Lost Lake. It's nearly dark and the naked woods stand stark against a clean dusting of snow. The orange of the sunset black-backs the body of water, mirroring deep purples across lake and sky. Low clouds are scudding in from the west. More snow perhaps, but the cold is coming for sure. We can bet on it. From the ball field I hear the consenting clamor of geese. The arms of the crooked wood pines that border the lake seem to wave in the still evening air as if they're trying to flag me down. They're telling me something; they have something left to say. The rise of pride I feel in the husband and father that my younger son, Kevin, has become exacts the price of a fierce hurt. Beyond the balm of forgiveness that Father Anthony continues to bestow upon me each time I go to confess, I've had to come to terms that my penance is to *live* with the knowledge that I killed my son.

The pines have reawakened me to something that as a forester I've long known by heart: *The work we live to do is work we'll never see completed.* The snow will continue to fall. The geese will come back, just as they will continue to go. I have my faith. The strength of belief. But this is the truth in our story the pines need to relate. *This,* they whisper, *this is the grace that keeps this world.* Honor it.

I glance once more around the yard to see if there's anything that still needs to be done before we eat and turn in for the night. My Susan is framed in the light of the kitchen window, her hair swept up off her neck. She catches me looking. Our eyes meet and she offers me her gentle smile. I raise my hand to let her know I'll be right in.

The last thing I do before I call it a day is to leave my gloves on the truck's dash against the glass where I find Kevin has left his.

About the Author

TOM BAILEY is the author of *Crow Man*, a collection of short stories, and *A Short Story Writer's Companion*, a book on writing short fiction. He is also the editor of *On Writing Short Stories*. He has received a Pushcart Prize, a National Endowment for the Arts Fellowship in Fiction, and a Newhouse Award from the John Gardner Foundation. He lives with his wife and three children in Selinsgrove, Pennsylvania, where he teaches in the creative writing program at Susquehanna University. *The Grace That Keeps This World* is his first novel.